"What 

"Us?"

"Yes, us." Lucas chuckled softly as he extended his hand toward her, seeking her hair. He could smell her—vanilla. Vanilla and spice and something else, something Rachel. Her own scent.

I want her.

One hand was in her hair then, tipping her face toward him. He bent lower, so that his lips brushed her cheek. "You smell so good, Rachel, you feel so right...." And she did. Absolutely perfect. His arms stole around her, pulling her against him, leaving no room for doubt. She fit him. Perfectly.

"Damn you, Lucas! I told you no!"

"Rachel, it's okay. This is us, sweetheart."

She wrenched herself away from him. "No, Lucas! It's not okay. Maybe it never will be." Her arms were wrapped around herself, sobs wracking her body.

That was the truth she could not hide from.

Dear Reader,

This year may be winding down, but the excitement's as high as ever here at Silhouette Intimate Moments. National bestselling author Merline Lovelace starts the month off with a bang with *A Question of Intent,* the first of a wonderful new miniseries called TO PROTECT AND DEFEND. Look for the next book, *Full Throttle,* in Silhouette Desire in January 2004.

Because you've told us you like miniseries, we've got three more for you this month. Marie Ferrarella continues her family-based CAVANAUGH JUSTICE miniseries with *Crime and Passion.* Then we have two military options: *Strategic Engagement* features another of Catherine Mann's WINGMEN WARRIORS, while Ingrid Weaver shows she can *Aim for the Heart* with her newest EAGLE SQUADRON tale. We've got a couple of superb stand-alone novels for you, too: *Midnight Run,* in which a wrongly accused cop has only one option—the heroine!—to save his freedom, by reader favorite Linda Castillo, and Laura Gale's deeply moving debut, *The Tie That Binds,* about a reunited couple's fight to save their daughter's life.

Enjoy them all—and we'll see you again next month, for six more of the best and most exciting romances around.

Yours,

Leslie J. Wainger
Executive Editor

The Tie That Binds

LAURA GALE

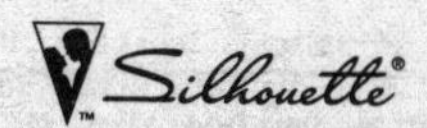

INTIMATE MOMENTS™

Published by Silhouette Books

America's Publisher of Contemporary Romance

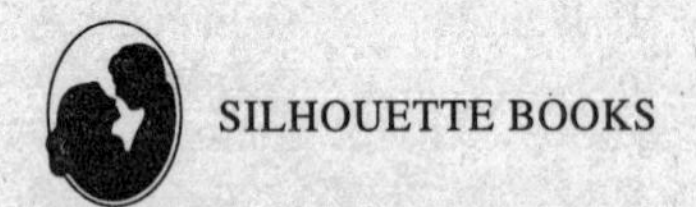

ISBN 0-373-27330-4

THE TIE THAT BINDS

This edition published by arrangement with Harlequin Books S.A.

Visit Silhouette at www.eHarlequin.com

Printed in U.S.A.

LAURA GALE

is an Arizonan, born and bred, always interested in language, reading and writing. Moving to Australia allowed her to try something different careerwise, and the fiction writer that had been concealed behind her academic facade finally emerged. After moving to Australia, Laura discovered that—for the first time in her life—she had time to try her hand at writing a book, something she'd always claimed she would do…if she had the time. Having picked up her first Harlequin novel when she was twelve, romance was the obvious place to start. In 2001, her first effort at a romance novel won the Emma Darcy Award, and suddenly it seemed that writing might become more than a hobby. The EDA brought her to the attention of Silhouette editors, and *The Tie That Binds* is that first novel.

Laura believes in romance in real life. She has every reason to: she has been married to her high school sweetheart for over twenty years. Together they have embarked on a variety of adventures, including raising four sons. Moving to a new country is nothing compared to that!

This book is dedicated first to my mother, who was able to read an early version of the manuscript, but whose battle ended before she could see it published. It is she who taught me to color outside the lines, and to revel in the joy to be found there. She knew this was possible.

Also, to my dad,
who taught me the value of the word *Why*.

To my sisters, Rebecca, Melissa and especially Amy, who has hit the ground running as my PR rep. To all the other readers (Geri!) who helped me believe that I had written a book. To Monica, for the Spanish—any mistakes were made by me.

And, of course, to Bill who supports me and believes in me, who knows how to cast me in my best light. And, finally, to our boys, who accept what Mom is doing as if every mother does this sort of thing. I love you all!

Author's Note

Our family came to know about the miracle of bone marrow transplants via City of Hope, in Phoenix. I can't adequately express our gratitude for their work. Any errors in describing the treatment are entirely mine.

Chapter 1

Armor. Armor is good, Rachel Neuman decided, as she stepped into the elevator at the main office of Neuman Industries. Even if it was of the tomato-red, short-skirt, long-jacket variety of armor. It had a certain protective allure to it.

They don't call it a power suit for nothing, she reflected.

Today, she needed all the support she could get, from all possible sources. Including her clothes. She meant business and she needed to *look* like she meant business.

If not, she wouldn't have come anywhere near Lucas's office, a place she'd avoided for the past five years.

Y todos vivieron muy felices. Rachel would do what she could to see that it came to pass that way, that everyone would live happily ever after.

I will do what I must, mija, she vowed silently. Indeed, she would.

Why would she come here now? What the hell can she possibly want?

Lucas Neuman passed a hand over his face, his initial grimace chased away by a cynical smile. He slammed shut his laptop, shoving it away, drumming agitated fingers on the shiny oak desk.

What reason could she possibly have for seeing me five years after she walked out?

Reaching toward the telephone on his desk, Lucas stabbed the button that would call his secretary. "Jennifer," he said, "what can you tell me about the ten-thirty appointment you've penciled in this morning? I know it wasn't there yesterday."

"Yes, that's right, Mr. Neuman. She called fairly late, when you were out of the office."

"And?" he prompted, attempting to suppress his mounting irritation—or at least keep it out of his voice. He didn't have a lot of patience these days, but he didn't need to shoot the messenger. In this case Jennifer. "Any idea what it's about?"

"Well, not exactly," Jennifer responded, sounding uncommonly flustered. "She was…well, she was evasive when I asked." Lucas heard her take a deep breath before rushing on. "Actually, Mr. Neuman, she *said* she was your wife," her disbelief conveyed itself in her voice, "and that it was family business. I didn't…well, you know, I didn't push her after that. Do you want me to call and cancel, or do you want me to bring in security, not let her come in?"

"No, no, that isn't necessary," Lucas reassured her. "I'm sure it doesn't merit that. I was just curious." Nonchalant would be a good way to sound, even though *curious* was an understatement. "Thanks, Jennifer."

Lucas listened for the click that would signal the disconnection from Jennifer's phone and leaned back in his chair, alone with his thoughts. *So Rachel is coming here today. God, I hope she isn't going to be difficult. I hope she doesn't make a scene.*

Reaching toward the humidor on his desk, Lucas selected and lit a cigar, watching as the smoke drifted toward the ceiling.

"Now there's something Rachel wouldn't appreciate," he murmured, thinking of cigars and Rachel's utter revulsion at the act of smoking. She hadn't been a health nut herself, not exactly. He shook his head, shaking off the memory.

Rachel had been to his office only once before. That day, five years ago. The day she'd brought him an agreement to separate. He'd been shocked, he recalled. Unable to comprehend what was happening.

Rachel had walked out on him. Quite decently, quite civilly, but she'd walked out nevertheless. He'd have been perfectly content to let things go on as they were.

He had loved her so much then. So completely. But he'd grown up. He no longer believed in love, not like that, not ever again.

He leaned back in his chair again, watching the smoke float to the ceiling, still pondering.

And then it hit him. Knocked the wind right out of him. It was so obvious.

Maybe she finally wants a divorce.

Stepping off the elevator at the seventh floor, Rachel approached the reception desk and introduced herself. Upon the icy instructions from the woman seated at that desk, she found a place to wait. Until her appointment.

Rachel couldn't help thinking that the woman's demeanor complemented the decor perfectly.

Neuman Industries—where Lucas was employed and where she was sitting—had been the family business since the 1930s, when Lucas's great-grandfather had started the company as nothing more than a provider of cement during the WPA projects of the Depression era. His son, Lucas's grandfather, had expanded the business to encompass large development projects: apartment complexes, office buildings, shopping centers. With Arnold Neuman leading the company, Neuman Industries now designed such projects, as well as constructing them. Lucas himself had been not-so-subtly encouraged to join the company, heavily encouraged to obtain his M.B.A. Lucas had thrown himself into the business with gusto.

As far as Rachel knew, he still did. That would be his style.

"Ma'am," the overly bleached-blond receptionist intoned in Rachel's direction, "Mr. Neuman is ready to see you now."

"Thank you," Rachel responded, rising from the couch, marveling at how clearly the receptionist had conveyed her contempt for Rachel without ever saying anything precisely negative. The receptionist had made an effort to avoid calling her Mrs. Neuman. Or even Ms. Neuman. Furthermore, she was refusing to escort Rachel to Lucas's office.

Rachel approached Lucas's closed office door, rapping on it smartly and entering the room without awaiting a specific invitation. She saw Lucas at his desk, sitting on the other side of a haze of cigar smoke. He leaped to his feet, apparently not prepared for her entrance, the receptionist's statement notwithstanding.

Lucas felt as if he'd been punched. Air simply wasn't moving in and out of his lungs the way it should have been. Mechanically he touched the cigar to his lips one last time before blindly plopping it into his ashtray. He stood, knowing he was surely gawking like a teenager. And not very happy about it.

God, she is beautiful. The words seemed to ring inside his head.

He stared at her, knowing he was staring, unable to stop. It felt good to see her, which Lucas didn't consider to be a good thing at all. He shouldn't respond to her in a positive way. Still—seeing her, having her there in front of him—it stunned him. It had been so long. He had stopped thinking about her…and about the lack of her. Now, though, Lucas found himself stuck on the thought. *She's beautiful, simply beautiful.*

Of course, Rachel had always been lovely—not that she'd ever seemed aware of it. But she'd grown up in the past five years, too, so that the woman before him now was exactly the culmination of the potential she'd shown before. She still wore her rich, dark hair long, the mahogany highlights glinting even in the artificial light of Lucas's office. Her amber eyes still shimmered, still seemed to look into his soul. Her skin still glowed apricot. Her mouth, always rose-petal soft and tipped up at the corners as if just ready to smile—none of it had changed.

And yet all of it was different. She seemed pale beneath the apricot; gray smudges vaguely visible below her eyes. Those eyes brimmed with shadows Lucas had never seen before, her mouth held tension in the corners along with the ready smile. Despite her very evident curves, she seemed thinner than he might have expected. She seemed tired—weary, even.

Something isn't right, he realized suddenly, startled that he could detect such signals from Rachel after all this time. He wasn't especially glad to know he was in tune with her that way. He needed to maintain some distance, even some animosity, he thought, if he was going to leave her with the desired image of himself—that of a man in control, self-assured, unshaken by the arrival of his estranged wife. Even though that image was the complete opposite of how he felt. Still, he was skilled at presenting a front that hid his feelings.

He did it in business all the time, when necessary. Like now.

"Hello, Lucas." Rachel smiled tentatively, sitting down on the couch without reaching to shake his hand. "A bit smoggy in here," she commented, eyeing the cigar smoke hovering over their heads, momentarily desperate for small talk.

Lucas continued to stare, annoyance at his inability to control the situation—and his reaction to Rachel's presence—threatening to dwarf whatever other emotions he felt.

"Never mind, Lucas," she said, rattled by the glare he directed her way, seeking to defuse his reaction to her observation. Attempting to ignore also the erratic beat of her heart. "I'm just surprised to see you smoking." She followed him with her eyes as he returned to his chair, somewhat relieved that he had broken his unblinking perusal of her, knowing it didn't mean his mood was improved. "But then—" She shrugged, affecting a calm she did not feel. After all, she had well-developed internal armor by now. "—I suppose it suits your playboy executive image."

"Is that what you think I am?" he fairly snarled, having decided to go on the offensive, given that he had blundered his way through her arrival. He knew a brusque attack could set the enemy back, and he *was* thinking of Rachel as the enemy at this point. Aggression would be his weapon of choice in this case. He certainly had no intention of trying to charm Rachel. This was not the time to question his reasoning, either.

"Actually," Rachel was answering him, "it's not something I think about. But I imagine you might see yourself that way. More or less."

They stared at each other for a few minutes. "Do you want

anything to drink?'' he inquired grudgingly, professional good manners instinctively forming the words. Maybe there was comfort in small talk.

''Just some water, please. I won't be here all that long.''

Lucas stabbed a button on his phone. ''Jennifer, please bring a glass of ice water and some coffee.'' He leaned back in his chair, his eyes narrowing as he zeroed in on Rachel again. He needed to shake her composure the way she had shaken his. ''Why are you here? Jennifer told me you claimed family business.'' He folded his arms across his chest, affecting a bored yet confrontational stance. ''Does that mean you're ready for a divorce?''

She started slightly. ''I hadn't even thought of that, Lucas,'' she answered, her eyes momentarily wide with surprise. ''We could do that now, I suppose. But I'm actually here because...well, it really is family business. I'm hoping we can...put aside our differences and do what needs to be done.''

She broke off as a knock came at the door. Jennifer entered, pushing a cart holding a coffeepot, a mug and assorted condiments, as well as a pitcher of water and a glass of ice. She wheeled the cart to the side of Lucas's desk, where she made a great show of pouring a cup of coffee, adding one teaspoon of sugar and handing it to Lucas—demonstrating for Rachel's benefit her thorough knowledge of Lucas's preferences. At least where coffee was concerned. Rachel wondered briefly if this woman knew Lucas's preferences in other ways, too, then forced herself to ignore the question.

Meanwhile, the woman pushed the cart closer to Rachel and left the room with a flourish.

Rachel suppressed a smile, privately noting the receptionist's continuing silent protest at Rachel's presence. Rachel knew Lucas would never understand if she tried to explain what had occurred. He had always been oblivious to certain things. Jennifer's performance had been utterly wasted on him. Silently Rachel poured herself a glass of water and settled back into the couch, openly examining the man who was still her husband.

So there he is, she thought, *looking incredibly like Pierce Brosnan at his James Bond best. Only better. Unfortunately.*

Seeing him warmed her, she acknowledged, although that, too, was unfortunate. She'd wanted to be immune to him in every way. She needed to be immune. She just needed his help. She didn't need *him.* There was a difference.

Still, she could hardly avoid noticing that Lucas was now a full-grown, highly potent man, no longer the boy teetering on manhood he'd been when they had married. That fact was having an impact on her heartbeat, she knew. But there he was. He stood over six feet tall and was still lean and fit, despite having filled out some in the years since she'd seen him. Little lines had etched themselves around his eyes, lines that might be laugh lines or something else. He certainly wasn't smiling now, so Rachel couldn't draw any conclusions on that score. He still wore his black hair short, undoubtedly still disgusted at its tendency to curl if allowed to have any length. She didn't detect any gray in its blackness.

His charcoal-gray eyes were the eyes she remembered—she saw those eyes every day. Dark and yet clear, having always reminded Rachel of Apache Tears, the clear black gemstone found throughout Arizona. She'd always been able to see what he was feeling in those clear gray eyes. But not anymore.

Everything about him was so familiar to her, yet she was not comfortable with this man. She couldn't be sure she knew him at all. Five years changed a person. They had certainly changed her.

Lucas watched her link her hands around her glass of water. He took in the details: short, well-maintained fingernails—maybe some kind of clear polish. Competent hands, he thought, nothing frivolous there. No rings. Not even the ones he'd given her all those years ago. That change bothered him. He couldn't't—or wouldn't—consider why.

"So," he began, trying to steer the conversation back where he thought it was supposed to be heading, attempting to draw in a deep breath, "you were about to mention family business of some kind."

She sighed and looked away, lending credence to his suspicion that something was wrong. She took another sip from her glass before setting it down.

"Yes, Lucas," she began. "Well, there's no easy way to say this, so I guess I'll just...say it." She shrugged again, completely unaware of the habit.

"That's a good way to start," he responded.

Looking him square in the face, she stated, "I need your help, Lucas."

"My help?" His eyebrows shot up. "You need money?"

"No, Lucas," she answered patiently, as if catering to a child's limited attention span. "I'm not interested in your money. I've never asked you for money, and I'm certainly not about to start now. What I need is more...personal, I guess." She paused, catching her bottom lip between her teeth. Taking a deep breath, she rushed on.

"We have a daughter, Lucas. She's four. She'll be five in December. She's ill. She has leukemia. She needs a bone marrow transplant." She paused in what was clearly a prepared, carefully rehearsed speech, a speech she was nevertheless having difficulty delivering. "The chemotherapy has done what it can. She can't really do that anymore. And while bone marrow transplants used to be a 'last resort' thing, they're a lot more common now, especially once a patient has gone into remission. They're effective with children and used fairly often with the kind of leukemia she has. But—" she swallowed "—a compatible donor must be identified. Usually, the best matches are blood relatives. I'm not that match. No one in my family is. We've even done a donor drive at the hospital, and while it did a lot to improve the donor registry we have in this state, especially among Hispanics, it didn't identify a compatible donor for her. That means we need to explore other options."

She started to run her hand through her hair, then resorted to patting it when she remembered she had it clipped into a ponytail. "There are options, alternative means for obtaining bone marrow—but we need to exhaust the obvious routes before we turn to less traditional means. Those ways...would not be the first choice left to us at this point." She took a deep breath. "Siblings are usually the most likely source, but with no siblings...'' She shrugged again, letting that serve as an answer. ''The best choice now is to test you, Lucas. As her father, as a blood relative, it's logical that you may be the match she needs. I know she has your blood type, not that that guarantees anything. So,'' she drew out the word, heard the quaver in her voice, ''I'm hoping you'll agree to be a donor for her. Or, more precisely, I'm asking you to be typed so we can see if you're a suitable match for her.''

Lucas sat transfixed in his chair, too overwhelmed to move.

So here it is, he thought vaguely, *Rachel's second visit to my office and I'm having my second out-of-body experience.*

Chapter 2

"What the *hell* are you talking about? Have you lost your mind? Do you think I'm stupid?"

Rachel paled at Lucas's tone and, no doubt, at his volume, but gave no other outward sign of her trembling nerves. "What part are you having trouble with?"

"The part where you claim I have a daughter! That *we* have a daughter!" He laughed without humor. "And everything else that comes after that!"

Lucas stood, his agitation so deep he simply could not hold still. He began pacing behind his desk. "I don't believe any of this, do you understand? If you want money for some reason, fine. Admit it. We'll talk about it. I'm not sure I'd contribute to the upkeep of some kid that can't possibly be mine—if you actually have a kid of your own, if you've been that irresponsible—but trying to convince me that the child would be *mine?* If that's what you're trying to do here, Rachel, you might as well leave now. I don't have time for lies." He quit pacing and whirled to face her. "Are you listening? Forget it! Don't expect me to buy a story like that! Do you hear me?"

He was yelling and he knew it, but he was powerless to stop. It occurred to him that if a scene was erupting, he was to blame.

But what other reaction could he have to Rachel's ridiculous claim?

"Of course I hear you, Lucas," she responded quietly, with dignity, although she was shaken. She'd be damned if she'd let it show.

"Where should I start?" Mentally enumerating, she began quietly, unruffled only on the outside. She had to make him understand—it was too important. "Okay, Lucas, I repeat: I do not want your money. I want your bone marrow. Or, rather, Michaela does."

"Mee-kay-la?" he sneered.

"Yes, Michaela. I named her after my parents—Michaela Juanita. *Papá,* of course, is Michael and *Mamá*'s middle name is Juanita, as is mine." She sounded tired but proud. "She's beautiful, too. Smart. Sweet. *La niñita más linda del mundo.*" Rachel gave a start, alarmed that she had accidentally said aloud her private motto that her daughter was the most beautiful little girl in the world. "Anyway," she rushed on, "she is indeed your child—"

"Oh, give it a rest, Rachel! She can't be mine and we both know it! Our sex life was practically nonexistent when you decided to walk out."

"Practically nonexistent, yes. But not entirely." She refused to rise to the bait. This was not the time to argue over who had done the abandoning. "Think about it, Lucas. We weren't celibate with each other, even at the lowest point in our marriage. Our sex life was irregular, yes. Inconsistent, yes. But not nonexistent. And before you start suggesting I was sleeping around, let's just recall which one of us sought external...companionship. That was you and you know it." She clamped her lips together, regretting her outburst. Bringing all that into it would not help her cause.

"Maybe you just hid it better than I did."

Her eyes shot daggers at him, but she didn't say anything. Instead, she just opened her briefcase and pulled out an envelope. "Didn't you ever wonder why I wanted a one-year separation before we talked divorce?"

"That's a good question. Since you started the whole legal thing, why didn't you finish it? Why didn't you file for divorce?"

"Why didn't you?" she snapped, her breathing rapid. "Oh, yeah, I forgot, Lucas." She mockingly tapped her forehead. "You didn't need to. Everything suited you just fine the way it was. You had a wife if you needed her, and other more interesting playmates for the rest of the time."

Dios mio, *but I hate to lose control.* Rachel took a deep breath, willing some calm to enter her spirit. "I did what I had to do to deal with the situation. So I went to the trouble of making it legal. I think I never filed for divorce because once we were separated, as far as I was concerned, we were divorced. It was over. Our lives were completely separate from that day on. Anyway—" she paused, trying to stick to the matter at hand "—Lucas, back to the question. Given that our marriage was finished in the day-to-day way, why do you suppose I wanted it to officially, legally continue for another year?"

"Maybe so you could foist some other man's child off on me," he suggested coldly. "Get me to pay for the kid's upbringing. Maybe you already knew you were pregnant, knew that you had to cover yourself somehow. Maybe you thought your other man would claim you and then he backed out. How would I know what happened? I sure wouldn't have bought this story then, if you'd brought it to me. Just like I'm not buying it now."

At least he wasn't yelling anymore.

"Fine, Lucas, we'll play it your way. I wanted some other man's child to have your name. Of course I did. How clever of you to figure it out."

Her voice fairly dripped with sarcasm. Lucas squirmed in spite of himself.

"Is that how it's done in the world you live in? Do people you know do such things? If so, you need to find some new friends, Lucas." She tapped the envelope on her lap. "Now give my question a little thought. Why do you suppose I wanted an official year of separation?"

Lucas considered the question again, thankful he could continue in the icy vein. "Well, at first I couldn't believe you were serious about leaving, let alone that you were thinking about doing anything legal about it. I couldn't believe you'd gone to a lawyer. I was amazed and maybe even amused by what you were doing. Later—'' he cocked his eyebrow ''—later, I just figured you thought I'd come back to you—you know, that I'd come to my senses eventually—and that you thought a separation would be easier to undo than a divorce.''

He'd never thought any such thing, but he was still on the attack and the words emerged all by themselves. They sounded good to him—and they kept rolling. ''Nowadays, Rachel, from my perspective, it's convenient to be married. I mean, I'm not at risk around other women since I already have a marriage in place. I'm not the type for bigamy.''

''Apparently, you weren't the type for monogamy, either, Lucas,'' she responded sourly, her eyes flashing.

Ouch, Lucas thought, mentally cataloguing Rachel's first flares of anger over the whole business. He would have expected anger before this, had always wondered at her composure. *Maybe she has claws after all.*

''So,'' Rachel said, ''to return to the topic, how long before you realized that I intended to go on living without you?'' Her sarcasm was back.

''Several months, I guess.''

''Did I really seem that pathetic to you? That I would cling to you that way?'' The words were ripped from her. ''You thought I'd take you on any terms you dished out?'' She eyed him incredulously, stunned to the core.

''Okay.'' She started afresh, one deep breath later. ''For the record, I asked for the separation because I wanted our child to be born legitimately. I didn't want there to be any question about it—''

''I'd say there are all kinds of questions about it, Rachel.''

''Not if you agree to be tested. If you're a match…well, it's unusual for nonblood related individuals to match. Of course it happens, or there'd be no need for a donor registry. But I'm sure we can dig up the statistics on the likelihood, something that would at least partially satisfy you. Secondly, if you agree to be tested, you can request a DNA-based test. DNA work is what you'd really be interested in, right?'' He nodded, and she continued. ''Well, as I said, you can pursue that.''

Looking down in her lap, she commented, ''I brought some things for you, Lucas.''

She began sorting the enclosures she'd dumped out of the

envelope. "She is your daughter. Legally she is yours. We were still married at her birth. I named you on her birth certificate." She placed a page on his desk in front of him. "Check the dates, Lucas. We were still together when she was conceived." Watching him carefully, she plopped a stack of papers on his desk. "There are a lot of medical test results. *Dios mio,* but she's had enough of them. But what I told you before, that she has your blood type, not mine and not a combination, is here on this report." He opened his mouth, but she waved him off. "Sure, I could have run blood type IDs on potential lovers, choosing one who shared B-negative with you, then managed to get pregnant by him exactly during the dying moments of our marriage. But I didn't."

Handing him something else, she said, "Of course, there's also the fact that she looks like you. Her eyes are just the same as yours. Her hair—it's not only the same color as yours, it even curls the way yours does. Mine is completely straight...." She paused, waving the photo in the air, emphasizing her point. "Her bone structure, her nose and mouth, that's more like me. That's her on her fourth birthday," she was pointing at the snapshot she'd placed before Lucas. "She was diagnosed several weeks after that. She'd had symptoms for a while and I was just starting to face things. But that day, she was feeling good."

She smiled briefly, remembering, then sat back in her seat to wait. She knew Michaela was a lovely little girl. She had definitely inherited her father's black hair, not her mother's brown. She also shared his smoky-gray eyes, eyes that were nearly black at times yet had a translucent quality that Rachel had never seen on anyone else. Rachel knew that Lucas would not be able to block out the obvious resemblance.

Michaela was a spunky, active little girl. She was curious and direct. She was quick to smile and laugh. Or at least, she had been, before her illness had begun to wear her down. Yes, in Rachel's view, she was the most beautiful little girl in the world, but it wasn't just her physical appearance that made her that way.

Lucas knew the color had drained from his face, felt his breathing halt. He recognized himself in the child. How could he not see it? Still, he couldn't accept it, couldn't believe that he'd been a father for over four years and hadn't had a clue. He felt humbled, although he wasn't capable of identifying the emotion at the time. "You said we can check DNA?"

"One of the tests used for donor type is based on DNA, so yes, you'll be able to obtain significant information that way. I'm not sure on the details. You'll need to talk to the doctors about it."

A brief silence ensued.

"If I don't do this, what happens to her?"

Rachel took a shuddering breath and her gaze dropped to her lap. Her voice came in a whisper. "Well, you are not absolutely the last resort for a donor. There are some other techniques. I don't think she can take much more chemo—"

"But you already said that wasn't working."

"Well—" she took a deep breath "—it did what it could. Technically, she's in remission, but it took longer to get her there than we expected. She's weak. She needs continuing therapy to keep her well. In her case, the bone marrow transplant is the best—"

"People die of leukemia," Lucas stated flatly.

"Yes," Rachel whispered. "They do. Technically, it's a kind of cancer."

Lucas released a long breath, contemplating the cigar resting in its ashtray, deciding not to pick it up. There was a chance his hands were too shaky to manage the task.

"We might still have some success through the donor registry, too. It happens. But if you don't do it... She needs this, Lucas. Frankly, her long-term chances aren't very good. They never are. Without this kind of care, it will come back. Or spread."

"But this treatment can cure it?"

"Well..." she hesitated "...they're always cautious about throwing around the word *cure.* But, yes, this treatment is a ical step in helping patients maintain remission and live life leukemia free." Finally she looked up at Lucas again, her golden eyes dark and shadowy. Whatever emotions caused those shadows were off-limits to him and he knew it. That was as it should be. Right?

It hit him then that he didn't know what those emotions

might be. Not anymore. How he felt about that...well, he didn't know that, either.

Rachel's control, which had been eroding since she entered Lucas's office, was in danger of snapping. "Look, Lucas, if I had a lot of reasonable options, I wouldn't be here. I wouldn't have involved you. I've raised Michaela on my own, as my daughter. It didn't occur to me to involve you until things got...bad, because I've never involved you in anything where she's concerned. I knew you'd have accusations, I knew it would be ugly. Why would I set myself up for that? There was no reason to force that until now. Until now—" she sighed, her breath catching on emotions that she kept in check "—I had no reason to try to involve you."

For better or for worse, she added silently. *Keeping your daughter from you seemed like my only option at the time. That's just how it was.* Suddenly Rachel was angry—angry at what life had dealt her daughter, angry at what she needed from Lucas. "If you understand nothing else, understand this—I will do whatever I can to help my daughter, including come to you. If you won't help voluntarily, well—" she faltered, but flared again "—I'll see if you can be legally forced to do it. At least to find out if you're compatible."

She knew that would get his attention. Lucas would go a long way to avoid confrontation of that kind. She was pretty sure he wouldn't want this dragged into the public arena of the courts. His parents certainly wouldn't. At least, not on her terms.

"Right now," she continued, "I'm talking about hope. That's the best weapon I have—that and continuing medical care." She took a deep breath and pressed on. "You are her father and I just can't ignore that when her life may be at stake. In good conscience I need to give you the chance to know your child. To deprive you of that wouldn't be fair to either of you. You've gone long enough without knowing each other. I never would have planned for you to meet this way, of course, but..." Again, her voice trailed away. "I probably should have found a way to tell you about her before now, but there wasn't an obvious good time or way to do it. Or at least I didn't think there was, knowing what our reunion would be like. I had to protect her from—" Rachel caught herself before she finished the thought, before she said, I had to protect her from you. She couldn't be sure if Lucas realized what she'd been about to say.

Lucas understood what she was saying. He didn't want to, because it made him uncomfortable. Still, he did understand that this might be his only chance to meet the little girl, a child Rachel swore was his daughter. If he truly might hold the key to her cure—to her *remission,* he corrected—how could he withhold that? How could he walk away without finding out?

Lucas James Neuman, who had steadfastly avoided personal involvement and responsibility as well as emotional entanglements for the past five years, who went out of his way to avoid conflict of any kind, was being slammed in the gut by something he didn't want to recognize but was afraid he did. He thought it had something to do with doing the right thing.

It was then that he knew he would do what Rachel asked, even though he wasn't sure what it involved exactly. He was human, after all, and this was the humane thing to do. Had there been no possibility it was his own child, he would have chosen to do it, to see if he could help. So if there was a chance that it *was* his kid, he didn't really have any other option.

"I'll do it, Rachel," he stated. "What's next?"

Rachel's shoulders slumped, her eyes closed, the sting of unshed tears causing her to blink. She jumped to her feet and looked for a private corner where she could compose herself, where she could hide. She found herself standing in front of the bar, hugging herself, swallowing over the lump in her throat that seemed to be connected to her tear mechanism. Otherwise, why would her eyes suddenly water and sting—and surely those same eyes shouldn't struggle so to focus on a bottle of Jack Daniels, be so unable to read the fine print on the label.

"Are you okay?"

His voice behind her startled Rachel. His hand on her shoulder caused her to jump and recoil in one motion. Her effort to gain composure had been so complete that she had not sensed his approach.

His presence, so close to her that she could breathe his oh-so-familiar scent, was doing nothing to help her in her quest for calm. His touch—or rather, the place on her shoulder where he had touched her—still burned. He had caused that quivering inside her with just that simple touch. Rachel hadn't felt such sensations in years. In fact, she hadn't felt it since the last time Lucas had caused it. Certainly, no one else had inspired it in the past five years. But she couldn't reflect on that. Not right now.

"No...yes, I mean, I will be. I just need to...collect myself. Just give me a minute." She glanced up at Lucas, caught the flicker of something liquid and black in his eyes, felt herself melt somewhere deep inside. He seemed so like the Lucas of old—and she was responding to it.

Biting her lip, she broke their eye contact, looking somewhere, anywhere, for a route that would put distance between them. Between the counter of the bar and Lucas's solid body, she didn't have much room to move. But she had to. She had to get away from him.

She turned abruptly, finally freeing herself of his presence, and drifted back to the couch. Dios mio, *I need some space.*

And she needed him—there was no way to get around that. But she couldn't need him for herself. Only for Michaela. She couldn't trust him, no matter how much he might seem like the Lucas she used to know, however briefly he might seem that way. No, she couldn't let those kinds of thoughts cloud what was happening. She couldn't afford to. She was better off keeping certain emotions, and the paths to those feelings, well and truly buried. It had worked for her so far. It was the only way.

"Okay," she said on a deep breath. "You'll need to talk to Dr. Campbell." Normalcy, that's what she needed to project. But it wasn't terribly convincing. Her careful facade had cracked, and they both knew it.

"Dr. Campbell," she continued steadfastly, "will explain the typing procedure as well as the donor procedure. Typing has to be done first, of course, then if you're compatible, they'll set you up for the donation procedure. He'll be able to tell you about DNA, too. He's at Phoenix Children's Hospital, in the Samaritan Medical Center."

"Is that where...Michaela is?"

"Yes," came her prompt answer. "Lucas, you have to understand. Michaela's a very sick little girl. Her leukemia came on fairly quickly and it just sapped her energy, her strength.

The chemo took whatever was left. She doesn't...she doesn't look much like that picture anymore.''

''But she can again, right?''

''Yes. In time. But it will get worse before it gets better.''

She met his eyes again, this time wondering if her eyes reflected as many silent messages as his. And wondering what those messages were. There had been a time when she had understood them. Now she couldn't be sure. Now she wondered how much Lucas had seen in her eyes this afternoon.

''I can make time today to see this doctor.''

''*Bueno.* That would be great. Let me see what I can do.'' She pulled out a cell phone, quickly punching in numbers.

''Hi, Linda. It's Rachel. Is Evan available? I need to schedule an appointment with him today.''

Within a few minutes, Rachel had set the appointment and ended the call. ''Three o'clock it is then, Lucas.'' She slipped the phone back in her briefcase and gathered her things.

''Lucas, you know there is nothing I can do to repay or thank you adequately for doing this. If there were, I'd do it. Please know how grateful I am.'' She started toward the door, knowing he was just a few steps behind her. Her personal radar, the one that sensed him, was working again.

''Rachel.'' His voice stopped her. ''Why didn't you tell me before? I mean, that you were pregnant?''

She looked at him carefully before responding. ''Deep down, Lucas, I think you already know the answer.''

''But five years, Rachel. That's a long time to hide such a big secret.''

''It was never a secret, Lucas. We were separated, remember? It was part of the new life I started for myself and, well, I just lived my life. There was no reason to think we'd ever run into each other. We don't exactly move in the same circles. That was part of the problem in our marriage. Not seeing each other, moving in different circles.''

She smiled sadly. ''It's funny, you know. You were always going on about how you needed me to support you. But I had needs, too, Lucas. I needed a *husband.* I thought I had one, but you...vanished somehow.

''I wanted to tell you about the baby so badly, Lucas. I was excited.'' Rachel looked down at her hands, the ones gripping her briefcase strap so tightly that her knuckles showed white. "I found out I was pregnant when you were in Las Vegas, that last trip. But I wanted to see your face when I told you, so I didn't call you." She lifted her head, seeking his face this time, too. "Of course, you didn't call me, either. And once you got home, well—" she shrugged "—a different kind of conversation was forced then, wasn't it? Telling you about the baby didn't seem to be a priority anymore. I knew you'd make accusations, that you would make it ugly. I didn't need that."

And, her words conveyed, *I don't need it today, either.*

"I figured if I was going to end up on my own, at least I was going to do it on my own terms."

Lucas studied her face but said nothing.

She tossed her head, trying to look beyond Lucas as she focused on something in the past. "I tried to live with the way things were, Lucas, I really did. I tried hard to be reasonable. I even believed, for a while, the things your parents said—that my inability to cope was the problem. It took time before I decided I had the right to expect more than you were giving, that you weren't being fair." She reached for the doorknob, knowing she needed to make her escape. Emotions were coming too fast to handle; *those* emotions were trying to surface. "Do you have any idea what I do for a living, Lucas?"

He shook his head, indicating he didn't know.

"That's what I thought. You weren't in touch with what I was doing." She sighed again, her words empty of criticism, full of resignation.

"Aside from everything else that happened between us, Lucas, I didn't tell you I was pregnant because I couldn't. You wouldn't have listened to me. Listening to me simply was not on your agenda then. Maybe I could have forced you to listen, but...how? I never figured out a way. Anyway," she said, seeking a positive note, "I appreciate that you listened today. This was important, too."

Opening the door, Rachel was nearly flattened by the huffing figure of her father-in-law as he stormed into Lucas's office. "Damn you, Rachel! What the hell do you think you're doing here?! You left my boy—you're out of his life! There's nothing for you here!"

Rachel couldn't help it. She stared at this vile individual, this repulsive creature—this man who had been instrumental in causing her so much grief, his features distorted by hatred—and by something else she didn't want to contemplate but which she recognized anyway. She owed this man nothing. She thought of being polite, then dismissed the idea. In spite of herself, Rachel burst out laughing.

"Oh, Arnold," she said, shaking her head, "you haven't changed a bit! And you know what, Arnold? I'm not happy to see you, either. But I'm not the least bit interested in anything you have to say, so—save it."

"Dad," Lucas cajoled in hushed tones, "don't speak to Rachel that way. You're in the corridor, for God's sake. Everyone's listening." He was embarrassed, for all three of them.

"Oh, Lucas," Rachel cut in, tsk-tsking at his foolishness. "Give it up, will you? Your father has *always* spoken to me like that, sometimes even worse. Everyone has always listened. Except for you." She sobered suddenly. "Somehow you never noticed."

She looked again at Arnold Neuman, then back at his son. Her husband. The father of her child. "This is your father, Lucas. This is what he is."

With that, she turned on the high heel of her black pump and headed toward the elevator. She stepped inside and the doors closed promptly. Not quickly enough, however, to drown out her father-in-law's parting words: "Yes, get out of here! And don't come back! We don't need your kind in here!"

Rachel leaned back against the cool stainless steel wall of the elevator. Only then did she notice she was trembling.

Lucas grabbed his father's arm, propelling him inside his office, out of the corridor and away from prying eyes. And ears.

"Are you out of your mind, Dad?" He glared into his father's flushed face, noticing how flat his black eyes looked. "How could you talk to Rachel, or anyone else for that matter, in front of the entire staff that way? This is a place of business, isn't it?"

His father chuckled smugly, slapping Lucas on the shoulder in good-ol'-boy camaraderie. "Oh, don't work yourself into a lather, boy. There's no reason for you to defend Rachel, you know. It's nothing but the truth.'' He made to leave the room. ''Like she said, it's nothing I haven't said to her before.''

With that, Arnold Neuman left Lucas's office.

No, she doesn't belong here, Lucas acknowledged silently. *But not the way you mean it, Dad.*

Lucas didn't quite know what he meant by that thought.

There it was again. Lucas couldn't draw a breath. He wasn't sure what it was, but knew he had first felt it when he'd seen Rachel's name on his appointment calendar. He'd felt it when she'd walked into his office. And he'd certainly felt it when she announced that they had a daughter.

He walked over to his desk, grabbing his lighter and reaching for the cigar he'd discarded earlier. He put it in his mouth, watched as the lighter's flame flared. Somehow, it just wasn't what he wanted, even if his gripping ability had returned. He dropped the lighter on his desk and tossed the cigar back into the ashtray.

Instead, he walked over to the window, gazing out at the expanse of Scottsdale that spread before him, eyeing the mountains visible in the distance. He raked his hands through his springy black hair, ultimately linking them on the top of his head. Seeing Rachel again had thrown him, no doubt about it.

''God, she is beautiful.''

There…it was said. The words had not left his head since Rachel had walked into his office. He'd been utterly unprepared for it. Maybe saying the words would chase the thought away.

It didn't.

She was always beautiful, he thought, *but now…*

He shook his head and took a deep, ragged breath. He tried to shake off his unsettling thoughts, tried to calm the stirring of his body that seeing her again had caused, was still causing, if he was honest about it. He knew she'd felt it, too.

When he'd touched her, just for that instant, he'd felt a shaft of heat knife through his arm, electrifying something inside him. Utterly brief physical contact had done that. Desire, instantaneous and fierce, had fired through him, body and soul. He'd felt her respond, felt that flash of awareness, he was sure he had, especially when she'd finally looked up at him. Her eyes had hinted at her deeper feelings then, the only moment in their entire meeting when her guard had been down. He was sure of that, too.

Maybe there's hope, he reasoned, *if a little touch like that draws that kind of response.*

Damn, where did that thought come from? Hope for what? Seducing her? No, Lucas, don't go there. Hell, he decided, *you'd better find yourself a woman. It's obviously been too long.*

He rested his forehead against the cool glass of the window and closed his eyes, willing his thoughts in a less dangerous direction.

He'd never seen Rachel dressed like that—so professional, he decided. So composed and serene, although she'd always had those qualities. He contemplated her outfit: bright red, a color that suited her. Fitted, not hiding her curves but not emphasizing them, either.

What would her job be? He wondered, startled that he really didn't know. She'd asked if he knew, but she hadn't told him.

He shook his head, shoving his fists into the pockets of his custom-tailored pants, rocking back on the heels of his Italian-made shoes.

"At least now I know why she looked tired," he spoke aloud. "God, she has a right to be." The words hit him hard.

Guilt gnawed at him. He pushed it away. He didn't want to think about what Rachel had gone through, facing their daughter's illness. If he did, he had to justify to himself the fact that she'd been alone—as if he had no role in her unofficially single status. As if he had in no way contributed to her circumstances. That felt like an acknowledgment of responsibility toward someone else, and he didn't like to think about that. After all, she'd been the one to leave. She'd brought her single status upon herself. As for him, well, his first responsibility was to himself. Wasn't it? The mantra his parents had always fed to him didn't work this time.

He knew helping this child was his responsibility. Even as he fought the knowledge, even as he had made his demand for medical proof, in his heart he knew the child was his. He knew it was *their* daughter, not Rachel's daughter with some other man.

He knew Rachel well enough to know that she had too much

honor, too much integrity, to have resorted to the sort of schemes he'd accused her of.

Yes, he had loved her. She was the only woman he'd ever met who had captured his attention, his mind, his spirit. She'd come from a different mold than any other woman he'd ever met. And he'd married her.

But he should have married someone who understood what his wife needed to be. Someone who had been prepared for the role. A woman who, unlike Rachel, was the right *type.* A woman who didn't grab his heart the way Rachel had, the way she had from the very first moment he'd spotted her at the University Health Clinic, filling out forms for the required measles shots. Not that that was the most romantic way to meet a woman, Lucas conceded, but it was how he'd met Rachel.

Rachel, he had adored. Rachel had had depth, vitality. She was interested in *everything.* So curious, so smart, so *real.*

So unbelievably beautiful. Tall enough with full, gentle curves that had always taken his breath away. The amber eyes, the apricot skin. The miles and miles of thick brown hair that Lucas had always thought of as chocolate silk. How he had loved to bury his face in it, combing his fingers through its softness.

And her scent: she'd always smelled of vanilla. Vanilla and a little spice. Natural and sweet and warm. It stirred him to remember, to think of what had drawn him to her in the first place.

She'd been a bad choice for a wife, though. For him, anyway. His parents had warned him, over and over, but he hadn't listened to them. He had fallen for her so hard, nothing else had mattered. But she hadn't understood the requirements of society life. She hadn't found them important or interesting. She hadn't supported her husband as she should have.

Lucas's parents had simply said she wasn't capable of it. They had always pointed to her "background" as being the cause. Sometimes, when they felt bold, they actually mentioned her "ethnicity." What they really meant was that she was Mexican-American, not "pure" American. That was simply unforgivable where they were concerned.

Privately Lucas had always found their prejudice ironic. After all, his family was only a couple of generations away from being working-class immigrants themselves. Lucas's own colorings—his charcoal-gray eyes and inky black hair—looked more Hispanic than did Rachel's.

Lucas had viewed his parents' attitude as something he couldn't change even if he didn't agree with them. His parents belonged to a certain segment of society that stroked itself, reassured itself, with ethnic prejudice. That was not Lucas's way. Still, what they had said about Rachel not fitting in with his family had had a certain ring of truth to it.

Several years later, reeling from his wife's departure, Lucas had finally agreed with his parents.

His reverie was interrupted by a sudden *whoosh* of air, announcing the uninvited arrival of Alana Winston.

Gorgeous, glamorous Alana, with her silvery blond hair, her sky-blue eyes and the statuesque body she kept perfectly sculpted with the help of a personal trainer and, Lucas suspected, a plastic surgeon. He didn't know for sure. Didn't care that much.

And it didn't matter anyway. Alana simply understood the value of her appearance, particularly when she was a man's companion. She'd started working for Neuman Industries shortly before Lucas, just after she'd finished school. She still worked for Neuman Industries, although Lucas had asked himself more than once what it was, exactly, she did. His father always assured him that she "knew how to take care of people," but had never been more specific than that.

Lucas glanced toward Alana again when he heard the unmistakable sound of her clicking the lock on the door.

"Oh, Luke, darling," she gushed, approaching, wrapping her arms around his waist. "I just *heard.*"

"Heard what, Alana?"

She pressed her hips against him, linking her fingers through his belt loops. "Why, Luke, about *her,* of course! Trashy little Rachel showed up here today! Forced her way in to see you, until Arnold tossed her out!"

Impossibly long red acrylic fingernails locked around his waist, keeping his body tight against hers.

Grabbing her wrists, disconnecting her fingers from his pants, Lucas said, "Watch what you say, Alana. Watch your mouth."

"Are you watching my mouth, Lucas?" she said, smiling suggestively, licking her lips. "I'm sure my mouth could provide you with some...distraction." She pushed her body against him again, tipping her head back to look into his face, exposing her exquisite bare neck.

"Stop, Alana." Lucas pulled away, wondering at some level if this was part of Alana's official job description. She reached for him again, believing she knew exactly how to seduce him, how to change his reluctant mind and resistant body. She did, of course. That was Alana.

He extricated himself from her grasp again. "I said stop, Alana. I'm not interested."

"Of course you are, darling," she purred. "You've always been interested. You already know there is nothing I won't do to soothe you. Let me help take your mind off all that unpleasantness." She removed her blazer, tossing it carelessly onto the chair behind her. Her ivory silk blouse did nothing to conceal the black lacy bra she wore underneath—a fact of which she was perfectly aware. She stretched her arms over her head, arching her back, ruffling her cloud of ash-blond hair, knowing that the silk of her blouse would outline the hardened state of her nipples. Licking her lips again, she said, "Well, Luke? What's it going to be?"

"Stop it, Alana, and get the hell out of my office." He turned away, disgust rocketing through him.

His body apparently had other ideas—physically, a response was possible. She left nothing to the imagination, and he was feeling ragged after Rachel's visit.

"You know, Lucas, you've been mad at the world for what seems like years now. Why is that, do you suppose?" From behind him, her arms curled around his waist, stroking slowly downward. She pressed her breasts into his back, the purr returning to her voice. "I bet I could make a guess, Lucas. You've been without a woman for too long, haven't you? Quite a while, if the gossip is true. I could help you." She whipped around him then, to stand in front of him, her arms still locked around his waist, her body pressed tight against his. "You'd like it, Lucas. What do you say?"

Hadn't he just decided that he needed to be with a woman?

What was there to stop him accepting Alana's offer? The release might help.

Sex with Alana would be hot, and...a little dirty. That was part of the appeal, he knew.

And suddenly this moment lost all of its attraction for him. It was cheap and meaningless, and he didn't need that. That was the reason he'd not been with a woman in so long. Sex, as an animal act or as a means of release, had no appeal for him. A mere physical coupling wasn't the answer to his perpetual bad mood. While he wouldn't contemplate what the answer might be, he knew it wasn't tawdry sex.

Pushing Alana away from him, he straightened his clothes. "Dammit, Alana. Get away from me." He glared at her, hoping he looked as repulsed as he felt. More calmly he continued, "Rachel had an appointment, Alana. She didn't barge in. She left. Dad didn't throw her out."

He picked up the envelope Rachel had brought him, scooping the contents back inside.

"Do you want me to wait for you, Luke? Or go with you someplace else?"

"No, Alana, I do not. I don't want you at all, in any way."

"You could if you tried." She stood with her breasts thrust forward, her hands on her hips, sure she could change his mind.

Lucas looked at her, taking in her undeniably sexy presentation, her blatant invitation. "No, I don't want you, Alana. It has been a long time since I've had sex, but I certainly don't want to be reinitiated by you."

She laughed. "Right, Luke. Like I said, I'll be ready when you are." She was purring again. "Just keep thinking about it, Lucas. You're a virile man. You can't deny your physical needs forever. I'll be ready whenever you are."

"You'll have a long wait." His decision made, Lucas knew he spoke the truth. "I've had enough of you, Alana."

So saying, he slipped into his jacket and left his office.

"Jennifer," he said, stopping at the reception desk, "I'll be out of the office for the rest of the day. I don't have any other appointments for today, but I'll be out tomorrow as well, so please reschedule whatever is listed then."

He left the building, getting in his Lexus with no particular idea where he was going. Eventually, he found himself near

Indian Bend Park, a man-made flood control area that cut through the city of Scottsdale. He parked the car, left his jacket behind and began strolling along the winding sidewalk. Suddenly he realized he was facing a playground. He listened to the squeals and shrieks of the children, punctuated by occasional bursts of laughter or bouts of crying. It was May, and the weather had been mild so far; the brutal sun of summer had not yet rendered the playground equipment too hot to touch. Lucas watched the children interact among themselves and with their parents. On this weekday, mothers were the primary parents in attendance.

Finding a bench, he sat down. He opened Rachel's envelope, pulling the photo from it. He stared and stared, trying to come to terms with the face he saw reflected there. His eyes, his unruly hair. The hair he hated on himself, he found endearing on his daughter.

Rachel's apricot skin, her delicate nose and mouth, the curve of her eyebrows—all were reflected in Michaela. But her dark eyes and hair, they came from her daddy.

Our daughter, he acknowledged silently. There was no other possibility and he knew it. He pulled out the birth certificate, seeking the date of birth. He did the quick calculations, counting back nine months, already knowing what he would discover, but needing to confirm it anyway.

Quickly he realized that Michaela would have been conceived in March or maybe even February—long before his ill-advised trip to Las Vegas. Long before May 18, the day the agreement to separate had gone into effect. The separation might have come anyway, of course, but he knew it had been a direct response to his time in Las Vegas the week before.

His mind whirled back to that murky time, five years ago, to what he had privately labeled "the end of the marriage"—the end even if they weren't actually divorced, a time he rarely reflected upon. In fact, he rarely reflected on anything; introspection seemed a waste of time to him. He avoided reflection the same way he avoided scenes.

Still, today he'd had the past thrown in his face, in the shape of his wife and daughter. He couldn't avoid *thinking* at the moment.

He took a deep breath, his eyebrows descending into a frown

as he contemplated the end of his marriage to Rachel. He had been traveling a lot. It had been business, but it had been a lot of fun, too. If he was honest with himself, he had traveled more than necessary, every chance he got. He'd been eager to take advantage of what he called "opportunities." He'd enjoyed spending time with his colleagues, establishing himself, not worrying about the limitations imposed by everyday life. Feeling like a professional in the business world.

Until that trip to Las Vegas. Las Vegas had been a colossal blunder on his part.

Yes, he knew why Rachel had not told him about her pregnancy when he returned from Las Vegas. As she said, they'd had a different sort of conversation to pursue. Back then, he would have made the same accusations he'd made today, even though he was perfectly aware that *he* had been the one pursuing external activities, not Rachel. Just as she had said.

Had Rachel somehow succeeded in telling him back then, would he have accepted the news? Very likely not. Very likely the scene, the breakup, would have simply been uglier. Regardless, he had lost the first four years of his daughter's life.

Michaela, who'd spent her entire life without him. He'd never seen her, never even suspected her existence.

Well, that's about to change, he told himself. *I'm a father, and I'm going to be good at it.* He felt a genuine smile tug at the corners of his mouth.

Lucas returned the photo to the safety of the envelope. He leaned back against the bench, raking his fingers through his hair in the way that had always suggested inner turmoil. He admitted to the tension he felt now, the sensation of ice-cold butterflies in the pit of his stomach.

Tense, yes, he was certainly tense. Poised for…something he couldn't name.

How would my life be if I'd spent the last few years with Rachel, raising our daughter?

The question sideswiped him. *I won't think about that.*

But he had a strong suspicion it would have been better than how he'd been living.

Chapter 3

Walking on legs of rubber, Rachel finally made it to her car. She tossed her briefcase onto the passenger seat and blindly reached for the bottle of drinking water she kept in the console between the front seats. A few deep drinks and a few deep breaths later, she started her car and pulled from the parking lot.

She was dismayed to notice the continuing tremor in her hands and the erratic pounding of her heart.

"*Bueno,* Rachel, what did you expect?" she spoke the words aloud, berating herself. "You haven't seen him in years. It was bound to affect you." She inhaled deeply, then blew out the breath, finding she was still inundated with Lucas's scent. "And, yes, the person you knew, the man you fell in love with—he's still there. He's wearing many layers, but he's still there." She couldn't deny that much.

Unfortunately, she also knew that the woman who had fallen in love with him all those years ago still lived in *her* somewhere. She, too, was deeply buried, but she had responded to Lucas nevertheless. Something she could not allow. The knowledge left her shaky and dangerously close to tears.

But Rachel Neuman never cried—she couldn't afford to

waste the energy. In any case, she would never show such weakness where anyone might see her.

Checking the time, Rachel decided to stop at home and see if she could manage lunch. She'd had merely a bagel and juice this morning, and that only because it had been forced on her by Linda Tafoya, the day supervisor.

Rachel Neuman, at twenty-seven years of age, was young to hold the position she held: head pediatric nurse at Phoenix Children's Hospital. When she had accepted her first position at PCH five years ago, night shift had been offered and she had accepted it. After a while she'd found it suited her. These days, even though she was head of the department, she continued to work the night shift.

Initially her remarkable academic record had caught the attention of the higher-ups at the hospital when they had interviewed her, but she had gone on to demonstrate thorough professional competence and a warm personal touch—a combination much valued in a nurse. She was adept at handling multiple tasks, monitoring health-care issues as well as those that dealt more with comfort and happiness. She fit in with both the staff and the doctors at the hospital, not to mention patients and their parents. She graciously coped with the dreaded administrative duties and paperwork involved in the job, as well. In any case, no one begrudged Rachel her position.

The upshot of this was that she worked a very long day. Her shift ran officially from midnight to 8:00 a.m. However, she usually met with patients, patients' parents and hospital administrators after that. Her bedtime was 4:00 p.m., so the intervening daytime hours were hers. To spend with her daughter.

Today, however, she'd had her meeting with Lucas at ten-thirty. She'd gone to her office promptly at the end of her shift, knowing she could use the personal quarters the hospital staff had set up for her there as a changing place.

It was a miniature home away from home, except for the absence of a kitchen. This was a factor in her recent weight loss, but not the only factor. Her hospital colleagues were aware of it, understood the reasons, but knew she couldn't afford to stop taking care of herself. Hence, Linda shoving a bagel in her face.

As she maneuvered through the traffic, heading out of

Scottsdale and into Phoenix, Rachel was disgusted to feel the sting of tears at the back of her eyes. Usually she was so successful at controlling things like tears.

She hadn't allowed herself such a release during her final year with Lucas, nor during the breakup or its aftermath. She hadn't cried as she struggled to become a single mother or as she had learned, in fact, how to *be* a single mother. She hadn't even cried when Dr. Paul Graham, director of the Children's Cancer Unit at the hospital, had told her Michaela's test results.

After all, he was really only confirming what she'd already known. She'd seen the symptoms too many times before, as a nurse. She had recognized what she was seeing; she'd known it was more than the flu. That's why she'd gone to Paul in the first place.

Dear sweet Paul, who'd been working at the hospital for nearly fifteen years before Rachel's arrival. He'd become her mentor, a guiding hand when she'd needed one. They had become fast friends, in addition to working together, sharing one of those rare and profound friendships that occasionally bless a person's life.

Rachel was utterly unaware of rumors that had their relationship heading in a different kind of intimate direction. Paul was old enough to be her father and Rachel viewed him in that light. He had helped restore her self-confidence when she had arrived, new to her career, newly pregnant and without a husband. He had helped her believe again, and she had secretly hoped he would help her believe this time, too—preferably by telling her that Michaela didn't have leukemia after all. Of course, he hadn't told her that. Rachel had known, really, that he wouldn't.

That day Rachel had fainted for the first and only time in her life. Paul had taken care of her, never mentioning her moment of weakness to anyone. It was something else to add to the list of reasons she was grateful to him.

Rachel knew what leukemia would mean. She knew it meant granulocytes, a certain type of white cell, were causing the problem. She also knew that chemotherapy would be the initial form of treatment and that it would likely be a rough experience for her little girl. And for her.

It had been worse than she'd expected. Michaela had lost

her hair almost immediately. Her nausea was intense and frequent. They could help her some with that, but it still left Michaela a very fragile, very weak little girl. Had Rachel not seen the procedure before, she would have found it hard to believe this state of being could in any way be connected to an improvement in Michaela's health. When the chemotherapy took longer to work than they had expected, Rachel had faced it stoically, refusing to let herself shatter, turning her energies instead toward supporting her daughter in any way she could.

Rachel had known that a bone marrow transplant would be a likely next step, and that identifying a suitable donor was crucial to performing the procedure. As a matter of course, Rachel had had herself typed, assuming she'd be an acceptable match for her daughter. When that had not occurred, she had assumed someone in the family would be suitable. That failing, she had bravely pursued the next possibility: she had initiated the search to identify other potential donors. She had worked diligently on finding a match for several months, watching her daughter's lurching progress through chemotherapy, when she had one day acknowledged that she had not succeeded.

She had also exhausted all of the obvious avenues for locating that donor, with one equally obvious exception. Lucas. Michaela's father. The one blood relative who, under normal circumstances, would have been one of the first to be tested. But these weren't normal circumstances.

By the time testing Lucas had occurred to Rachel, Michaela had been in the hospital for several months, undergoing all manner of treatment, and Rachel was living in her office. She had refused to take a leave of absence, knowing that she needed her work to help maintain a sense of normalcy in her life.

Once Michaela's condition had become apparent and the hospital staff had understood that Rachel wouldn't go home if it meant leaving Michaela at the hospital, they had called upon the administration to provide Rachel with a suitable refuge. No one debated Rachel's need to be near her daughter; supporting families in this way had long been incorporated as an aspect of care. They would definitely take care of their own. Moving remarkably fast for a bureaucracy, the hospital had reshaped Rachel's office. What had once been an area reasonably able to accommodate a desk, file cabinets and a few chairs had been converted into an acceptable, if small, living space.

Support was the thing, and everyone knew that.

No one had ever seen Rachel hit the breaking point, but they all suspected she was dangerously close. Except, of course, Dr. Paul Graham—who realized she had already hit her breaking point and was now running on empty.

Rachel had appreciated the renovation of her quarters. She had tried to let everyone know her feelings, but acknowledged that she wasn't very good at accepting help from others. Her *familia,* of course, were different from other people. They knew her better, and were able to anticipate some of what she needed from them. They could offer to help before she had to ask for it—and asking for help was foreign to her. That's why it had been so difficult to go to Lucas for help.

Part of the reason, anyway.

With Lucas it was something else again. Needing him was something Rachel had weaned herself away from. It was a survival technique that had developed slowly, but which had become firmly embedded in her way of life.

Turning to Lucas now was, quite simply, a violation of Rachel's current code. Everything in her resisted opening herself up to the man, showing him anything of herself that might look like vulnerability. Rachel needed to protect herself.

But, ultimately, what Michaela needed was more important than what Rachel needed. If Rachel had been slow to think of testing Lucas, it was because she'd had no concept—anymore—of turning to him. That, and she'd truly believed Michaela's treatment would follow the path Rachel had seen before.

It was traumatic enough, without adding other dramas to it. For Michaela, though, Rachel had managed to overcome her own nature as well as the hard-earned aversion to needing Lucas. As soon as the thought had occurred to her—as soon as she'd seen what should have been obvious—she'd asked him to help.

Sí, sí, Rachel admitted to herself, *today was nothing more than another difficult challenge on an ever-increasing list of difficult challenges.*

She thought of her visit to Lucas's office, remembering the

cold, though luxurious, stainless steel-and-glass decor. It seemed so impersonal to her, so spiritless, so sterile. That Neuman Industries was in the architectural field was surprising.

Not that Rachel had ever really been tempted to do otherwise, but seeing those surroundings reminded her that she was happy she'd followed the career course that was natural to her. As a nurse, especially in pediatrics, heart-wrenching tragedy was not unknown. At the same time, however, Rachel found that the best of human courage and compassion were found there, as well. She'd always been drawn toward nursing, but had known it was the right place for her the minute she had started working as a medical trainee at the University Health Center when she was only eighteen.

No, she admitted, *I knew it was right before that or I'd have never set foot in the center. I knew it when I helped* Papá *at the veterinary clinic.*

And yet...Lucas had never noticed. He hadn't seen her "big picture" at all.

As she made her way through the Phoenix traffic, a slight smile played around her lips. She thought about her phone call yesterday, when she'd made her appointment with Lucas. The receptionist she'd spoken with had been at a loss for words when she'd identified herself as Lucas's wife. Clearly, the woman had joined the company after the demise of the Neuman marriage. Obviously, Lucas didn't promote himself as a married man, not that she would have expected him to. After all, it had been Rachel who'd wanted to make the marriage work. It was Lucas who...well, who hadn't.

How had their special relationship slipped through their fingers? She had believed in it, in *them,* so completely.

Why had things gone wrong? Now there was a question. One she couldn't afford to think about right now. She had no answers.

She turned off of Sixteenth Street, just north of McDowell Road, into the area where her town house was located. Technically, it was considered a garden home, part of a new planned community built in an older section of Phoenix, but one designed according to the city's older flavor. The idea behind these communities was to draw young families from the suburbs, encouraging them to live in Phoenix proper. To sweeten the deal, the city also helped sponsor low-cost loans so that families that might not otherwise be able to own a home could buy one in these communities.

Rachel had lived with Rick, her brother, for the first few months following her break with Lucas. She had heard about these communities, recognizing them as the best kind of place she could provide for her daughter. The locations appealed to her, as well. Working at a hospital in the city meant that she appreciated the idea of living there. She had begun to put aside every cent she could for a down payment. Once her family had caught on to her plan, they had helped her. She had been ready for home ownership far sooner than she had hoped. In fact, she had had time to settle in before Michaela's arrival.

Each home boasted a small, private courtyard that opened onto the shared community "green" and facilities. The homes were clustered in pairs, each one sharing a wall with one other home. Rachel's was one of the smaller choices: two bedrooms and two bathrooms upstairs, with an additional 1/2 bath downstairs. She had an open, bright kitchen with an eat-in dining area, as well as a great room, rather than separate living, family and dining rooms. It wasn't fancy or extravagant, but it was perfect for Rachel and Michaela. It felt like home.

These days she was doing the best she could financially. It wasn't too bad. Her job was a good one. She was well paid and had considerable benefits. She would never be rich in her field, but then she hadn't chosen nursing for the money.

Pulling into the driveway of her cream stucco home, she pushed the button on the remote garage door opener and drove into the garage. She kicked off her shoes as she stepped inside and picked up the stack of mail her neighbor, Tanisha Davis, had been bringing in. Tanisha was also a single working mother, and she and Rachel had a solid friendship.

Sorting through the mail, Rachel mechanically threw out the junk and filed away the bills. It was twelve-thirty now, so she decided to fix lunch for herself before returning to the hospital.

A glance in the fridge revealed it was virtually empty. Rachel gingerly peeked into a tub of cottage cheese, noting it was beyond its use-by date, and hurriedly tossed it into the trash bin. She then eyed the splash of milk remaining in the jug and decided to use it since its date suggested it was still fresh. She grabbed a can of tomato soup from the cupboard and prepared it to heat on the stove.

Rachel ran upstairs, knowing she needed to gather some clothing to take with her to the hospital. She smiled at the piles of clean laundry her mother had left on her bed. *What would I have done without* Mamá *to help me?*

Or, to be fair, what would I have done without everybody's help?

If she continued to think along these lines, Rachel would be crying soon. She felt weak today, worn out from meeting with Lucas. She could understand the weakness, but that didn't mean she had to give in to it.

And yet, she was so tired. So tense inside.

She shook off the thoughts and stripped off her suit, carefully hanging it in the closet. She pulled on pale blue jeans and a T-shirt in primary color stripes. She slipped on her sandals and reached for a small suitcase at the top of the closet. Quickly she loaded it with clean undergarments and headed back down the stairs. She poured her soup into a large mug and returned to the living room. Settling on the couch, she whispered a brief prayer and began sipping.

Thoughts, emotions, memories. They were bombarding her. This time she would be unable to stop them.

Things had gone so wrong. But what choice did I have? How long was I supposed to take it, try to ignore it, pretend it didn't matter to me? After all, Las Vegas had been the last *straw—it hadn't been the only straw. There came a point when enough was simply, truly enough. Right?*

Ayuda, she knew, *ayuda* had saved her then. It continued to sustain her now.

Ayuda, that particular Mexican form of "circling the wagons" to support, aid and protect anybody considered part of the group. It existed, of course, in any culture, but it was an ever-present force in the Mexican mind-set, simply more visible at some times than at others.

Rachel's *familia* was a large group. Of course, it included grandparents, parents, aunts and uncles, her brother—the obvious people. Some members were called cousins and were actually related in traditional ways. Others were called cousins simply because it was a convenient title and the actual relationship was too complicated to explore. *Familia* extended to certain friends and friends of friends, and to those who married into it. Rachel's father, Mike Shannon, was one such member, affectionately referred to as *el gringo*. This title acknowledged his non-Hispanic background, simply, easily—but it also marked him as someone included in the *familia* by choice.

Rachel's *familia* had watched her marry outside their circle, welcoming her young man because she had chosen him. He had been brought in unreservedly, had been granted a place within their group because of his connection with Rachel. They had watched the early happiness, shaking their heads in bewilderment over how such a fine young man could have sprung from such cold, overbearing, narrow-minded people as his parents.

They continued to watch as Lucas had veered away from life with Rachel. Rachel had never said anything, and, out of respect, they had never mentioned it to her. But they knew she knew.

When the day came that she appeared at her brother's door, he knew exactly why she was there. Rick had been ready to help her, just as anyone in their circle would have been. Quickly news of her wounded status had spread, and family and friends had rallied around her. They had, in fact, circled the wagons—kept her safe until she was ready to face the world again. Because her state was regarded as unresolved, they remained on high alert where she was concerned. They knew she needed room to appear independent, to save face in public, but they also knew they had to be ready to support her.

In earlier times Lucas Neuman might well have found himself on the wrong end of violent vengeance. In the eyes of Rachel's people, not only had he betrayed her—he had deceived the entire group. In doing so, he had demonstrated his lack of character. Instead of violence, however, they elected to monitor his activities. They talked amongst themselves, quietly, gradually spreading word of Lucas Neuman beyond Rachel's immediate group. Of course, Arnold Neuman had already made a questionable name for himself. It was no great difficulty to suggest, with a shrug, *De tal palo, tal astilla.* An apple never falls far from the tree.

Rachel would have been surprised had anyone told her they

kept tabs on Lucas and that they knew exactly what he'd been doing since she'd left him. She tried not to think of him at all.

She had loved him deeply and completely. He had loved her in return. Whatever she had questioned—and she'd had many questions—she had never doubted that he loved her. That's why his behavior had been so hard to understand. He had just drifted away, following his parents and Alana, almost like a sleepwalker.

They had been happy together at first, she and Lucas. They had led a simple life, largely because they hadn't had enough time or money for anything complicated. They had both been university students, living in a dumpy little apartment within walking distance of the campus. Others in the complex had "partied hearty," staying up late, carrying on. But Lucas and Rachel had lived quietly. Sunsets had been nice for them. Ice cream on Saturday mornings had been nice. Spending Sundays in bed, or hurrying to make morning classes because lovemaking had gone into overtime—that had been nice, too. Grocery shopping and laundry duties had been times to spend together, not chores. Music had always been there; they'd enjoyed dancing, even when it was just the two of them in the kitchen. *Especially* when it was only the two of them in the kitchen. They'd laughed together, they'd had private jokes. They'd been in love, but it had been more than that. They had matched each other. And there had always been a sense of a future together.

Rachel had believed she knew Lucas, knew who he really was, right to his core. Even when things had begun falling apart, she had been able to see the person he was. Deep inside. Down to his soul. Just as he had been able to see hers.

Maybe we were too young, Rachel considered, swishing the dregs of her tomato soup. She'd only been nineteen, Lucas, twenty, when they'd married. Too young was a possibility. It was a major objection offered by Lucas's parents. But that, Rachel knew, was only because it was a socially acceptable thing to say. The real problem was that Rachel was not, and could never be, what the Neumans wanted for their son's wife. Specifically, she was not Alana Winston—a woman who had been groomed for just that role. Or for a role just like it, anyway. And she'd had her sights set on Lucas for a long time.

Alana Winston was everything Rachel was not. Most importantly, in the Neumans' opinion, her pedigree was impeccable. Rachel's was not. After all, Rachel's mother was Hispanic. She had been born in Mexico, and happily acknowledged that she had as much family living on the American side of the border as on the Mexican side. She spoke Spanish and she'd taught Rachel and her brother to speak Spanish, as well. Her father, a white man, had done nothing to discourage their ethnic tendencies—he even seemed proud of them. As far as the Neumans were concerned, that was nearly worse than the existence of the ethnicity in the first place.

To Arnold and Sophie Neuman, it didn't matter that Rachel's parents, Michael and Gloria Shannon, were well-educated, hard-working, caring individuals. In fact, that they *had* to work was another negative as far as the Neumans were concerned. Gloria was a teacher with a preference for teaching kindergarten. Michael was a veterinarian. Perhaps the Neumans would have been sufficiently impressed had he been a doctor who treated humans, rather than animals. But he wasn't, so it was a moot point.

As for their opinion of Rachel, nothing could win her an objective audience with them. Not her natural beauty. Not her quiet intelligence. Not her zest for life. Not her gentle competence, her genuine compassion or inner strength—the very qualities sustaining her as a single mother and as head pediatric nurse.

They held inflexible ideas about her correct place in society and it wasn't as Lucas's wife. She was suitable mistress material.

Alana, as Lucas's wife, would have understood a mistress. She'd been raised to understand that.

According to the Neumans, as a minority, Rachel should have been appreciative of such a desirable position. The Neumans had tried very hard to instruct Rachel on her "proper place." Rachel had rejected their reasoning, had found their demands unacceptable. Yet she had felt pressure to somehow get along with them. They were her in-laws after all.

Lucas had never understood why Rachel didn't want to be around his parents. He'd been confident that if she'd spend time with them, she'd come to like them. She just needed to give them a chance. If she would do that, he had said, his parents would come around and like her, too. Lucas did not understand prejudice, having never been on the receiving end of it. Rachel had been incapable of making him understand, had eventually quit trying.

Eventually Rachel had quietly tried to avoid Lucas's parents more and more, whenever possible. To manage this, she had begun to withdraw from the social life she shared with Lucas. She had hoped to nourish their private life. Except that their private life, their relationship, had begun to disintegrate slowly, bit by bit.

"Well, I'm not withdrawing now," she stated, clattering her spoon into her now-empty soup mug. "This isn't about me, about whether or not I'm comfortable. This is about Michaela. And if that makes Lucas uncomfortable, well, that will make two of us. It's about time."

Her reverie was interrupted by the sound of the doorbell. Answering its summons, Rachel found herself confronted by the dazzling smile and click of beaded braids that accompanied Tanisha Davis everywhere she went.

"Hey, there," Tanisha said in greeting.

"Hey," Rachel answered. "What brings you here?"

"Are you kidding?" Tanisha's eyebrows descended in mock disapproval as she breezed into Rachel's home. "I've been in this house lately, more than you I might add, and I know what the food supply looks like." Holding up a grocery bag that Rachel hadn't noticed, Tanisha continued, "I've brought tostada stuff. It's quick and it will be better than anything lurking in this house. And you a nurse." Tanisha tsk-tsked at Rachel. "You should know better. When food starts to come back to life, when it can move all by itself—you really shouldn't be eating it. It's a basic rule."

Rachel laughed and followed her friend into the kitchen, acknowledging that Tanisha spoke the truth. Or very nearly the truth, anyway.

Within minutes, busily filled with chopping vegetables and warming refried beans, the table was spread. Rachel couldn't help noticing how much more appetizing this meal was than her tomato soup had been. Not to mention that being with Tanisha always relaxed Rachel, since she knew she could drop her guard and be herself.

Of course, Rachel thought, smiling to herself, *the person who can fool Tanisha has not been born, so there's really no point in trying to be anything less than open with her.*

"Why are you home today?" Rachel asked, conversation rolling naturally and comfortably between them.

"Oh, well, it's my weekend, you know," Tanisha answered.

Tanisha, in order to avoid working off-shifts, had elected to take a schedule with rotating weekends. Therefore, rather than a Saturday-Sunday weekend, she sometimes had other combinations. In this case, it looked like Tuesday-Wednesday.

"And Vanessa is with Wayne?"

"Yeah," Tanisha agreed, nodding her head, her beads rustling in her hair. "I have to admit, once we worked it out, he's pretty sympathetic about the weekend time. He has alternating shifts, too, so we try to give Vanessa time with each of us on our weekends, but we try to give each other a free weekend now and then. We've been able to reduce day-care time for Vanessa, which is great. Not that it was easy to get it worked out." Tanisha was shaking her head vehemently now, lending emphasis to her words, the beads increasing their gentle rhythm.

Rachel had never pressed Tanisha for the details of the situations, grateful that Tanisha had never pressed her either. Frankly, she was reluctant to risk asking anything that would change that. Rachel had never been inclined to complain about what life had thrown her—living it was all she could do. She assumed Tanisha had a similar philosophy.

Always, it had been enough that they were both single mothers of young daughters, doing their best. In that, they had much in common.

However, Rachel now considered the possibility that knowing how someone else had coped might be valuable information. Comforting, even. It was the reason for support groups, she reasoned.

Suddenly Rachel wanted to know more about Tanisha's details. "How did you work it out?"

"Well—" Tanisha pondered a minute "—first, I had to let go of Wayne, I guess. I had to accept that he didn't want to be married, or at least not to me. But he did want to be a father. Once I got used to those basic facts, things went a lot better."

"He didn't want to be married?"

"No. Well...I mean, I didn't either, exactly. We were just, you know, *seriously* seeing each other, not dating anyone else. But we sure were not thinking about making babies. Then, when I realized that we *were* making a baby, whether or not we planned to be, well, that's when we got married. No argument on that. But after a couple years, it was pretty obvious that Wayne really didn't want to be married. I fought that. I didn't want to give up, you know? I thought a marriage, no matter how bad, was better than no marriage. And I didn't think ours was that bad. So, eventually he was moving out and filing for divorce and I was a nutcase over it. I was *not*—" she emphasized the word with a severely arched eyebrow "—very nice about it." Tanisha shrugged, exchanging her harsh expression for a relaxed one. "But eventually I admitted to myself that it was losing the marriage that upset me, not losing Wayne. I liked him well enough, but—" she shrugged again "—I was not consumed with love for the man. Passion, oh, yeah. That part we did right, which is what got us together in the first place."

She punctuated her story with a laugh. "But I wasn't in love with him. He wasn't in love with me. That was never really part of our marriage. So I finally let go. And now Wayne and me, we're friends. I would have never believed it, but we are. And that's the best we can do for Vanessa, which is the important thing, anyway."

"Do you ever miss it? Being married, I mean?" Rachel wasn't sure where the questions were coming from.

"Lord, yes, I miss it. I don't miss Wayne, mind you, not anymore. But I miss being part of a couple. I'd like to have that again. You know what I'm saying?"

"*Sí, sí,* I think I do know." Rachel nodded. "I'd say I miss being part of a couple, too. I guess some people see freedom in being single, but for me, to always be making decisions by myself, to never have anyone to share things with, good or bad...that gets old."

"I hear that," Tanisha said in agreement, her ebony eyes watching Rachel, missing nothing. "And that's the weird thing with Wayne now. We are both so much parents. If it has to do with Vanessa, I'm not alone. We are totally, completely partners as parents. I just can't believe it sometimes.'' Tanisha raised her eyebrow meaningfully, signaling her upcoming questions. ''What about you? Do you have someone to parent with you now?''

Rachel gave a start, surprised by Tanisha's inquiry. ''You mean…Lucas?''

''Is that the man's name? I always wondered.'' Tanisha was nodding, her hair beads rustling again.

''*Sí,* his name is Lucas.'' Rachel sighed deeply.

''And how did your meeting go?''

''You know about that?'' Rachel had told very few people about this morning's meeting. She couldn't remember discussing it with Tanisha. It had been arranged quite suddenly.

''Oh, yeah. Your *mamá* and me, we talk.''

''Ah, *bueno.* I see.'' Rachel smiled, then sighed again. ''I guess it went well.''

''He's going to help?''

''Mmm-hmm. At least, he's going to be tested. This afternoon. I just have to hope he'll be compatible. And then that he won't chicken out, once he knows what he'll have to do.''

Tanisha regarded her friend, noticing how pale she looked, seeing the signs of strain in her face. ''And how is the *mamá*—you, that is—how are you doing?''

''Me?''

''Yes, you.'' Tanisha laughed, pointing her index finger at Rachel, her sparkling burgundy fingernail the perfect complement to her mahogany skin. ''I have to think it was not the easiest way to spend your morning.''

''That's true enough,'' Rachel said, a weak smile touching her lips. ''I'm okay, I guess. Very anxious about the testing. And, yeah, as you said, I have definitely had more fun.''

''Was he nasty to you?''

Tanisha's insight startled Rachel into honesty. ''*Sí.* At first. Then again, this was the first he's ever heard of us having a daughter, so he was bound to have a strong reaction.''

Tanisha raised her eyebrow again, Rachel's admission not being what she had expected. ''So…Lucas, is that his name? He didn't know about Michaela?''

Rachel shook her head.

''Lord, girl, you did drop a bomb on the man,'' Tanisha said, chuckling briefly. "Does that mean...the two of you haven't seen each since...how long?"

"Five years, basically."

"Mmm-hmm." Tanisha pondered this, then looked directly into Rachel's face. "So, how are you, then? Really?"

Another long sigh escaped Rachel. "I've been better. It wasn't exactly my best day."

"Well then, it's a good thing I came over and gave you a decent meal. You have to go back in and face this man, right?"

"*¡Dios mio!*" Rachel exclaimed, standing abruptly. "What time is it? He's got a three-o'clock appointment. I've got to get back to the hospital! I need to spend some time with Michaela!"

"It's two, Rachel, you've got plenty of time if you go now."

"Are you sure? This—" she motioned toward the kitchen table "—needs cleaning up."

"Go, you," Tanisha said smiling. "I've been here more than you lately anyway. Your house knows me. I'll clean up, lock your door. Take any decent food home with me. You just go."

And Rachel did. Before she got to the part where she had to acknowledge that her husband's touch still made her melt. That his touch could make her think of things other than helping Michaela. She could have never lied to Tanisha about that, she was certain.

Indeed, it had not been her best day. And it wasn't over yet.

Chapter 4

Lucas Neuman was completely, utterly out of his element. And he was not happy about it.

He'd had a vague idea of where the Phoenix Children's Hospital was located. Didn't everybody? So, without checking the address or consulting a map, he'd driven to the area he had in mind, only to find himself facing the Samaritan Medical Center. Eventually, putting his faith in the posted signs, he came to suspect that the children's hospital was on the same grounds as the medical center. Hadn't Rachel said something like that? He thought so. And he eventually discovered it was true. But the damage had been done—his mood was turning ugly fast.

He had parked where indicated, then taken the elevator to the appropriate floor. At least, he hoped it was the right one. He certainly didn't want to stop and ask for directions, but he didn't relish the idea of wandering through the hospital hoping to eventually find his way.

Stepping into the corridor as the elevator doors opened, Lucas felt a momentary rush of something close to...panic. He didn't like hospitals, anyway. Who did, right? But he couldn't control what went on in a hospital, he probably couldn't even *understand* what went on in a hospital. And today's visit wasn't a social call.

He was nervous about that, too. How should he present himself? Charming or aggressive? Aggressive or charming? He tried to decide on a plan of attack. Selecting a strategy might afford him some degree of control. He knew full well that his control was slipping, that he was about to teeter into the discomfort—okay, hysteria—that hospitals engendered in him. He had to find an advantage for dealing in this foreign place.

As he moved down the corridor, toward a large reception desk, he was startled at the comfortable environment he encountered. Soft lighting kept the area bright, but not overbright. Flower arrangements and painted murals added subtle, cheerful color. Silently bubbling aquariums full of colorful, slow-moving fish served as focal points in the various seating areas. Seating areas, Lucas noted, where the chairs looked like something a person could actually sit in.

Glass partitions marked off patients' rooms, allowing for privacy without sacrificing the open feeling. Lucas could see that miniblinds would be pulled when full privacy was required. Yet somehow, despite the low-key and easy atmosphere, Lucas also felt the efficiency and sharp attention that permeated the air. He felt it keenly.

Charming or aggressive? He smoothed imaginary wrinkles from his impeccably tailored clothing, forced the frown from his forehead. And his mouth. This time, to hide his discomfiture, he chose charm. Confident charm. That—and his professional aura—should do the trick.

"Hello," he said, flashing a smile of even white teeth at the nurse's assistant sitting behind the reception counter. "I'm to see Evan Campbell at three. I'm early. I would like to look in on Michaela Neuman." Saying the name was bizarre in its newness. Even Rachel hadn't put the two names together. It shook him.

"Well, sir," the young woman sputtered, "Michaela... she's...she's not in her room right now. She's with her mother." She was clearly torn between her sense of duty to Lucas and that which she owed to Rachel and her daughter. She pointed toward a nearby corridor. "You could wait over there if you like, so you'll see them when they get back."

Lucas glanced in the direction she'd indicated, feeling the annoyance rising. He didn't find these answers acceptable. *What the hell does she mean, Michaela is not in her room? How could she be off somewhere with her mother?*

"Where is Michaela? I thought she was too sick to go anywhere." He injected sufficient sneer into his voice to suggest that he was questioning the young woman's competence. Or honesty. Or someone else's—like Rachel's.

"I've tried to explain, sir...." Her voice trailed off.

"Excuse me, Kristen," came another voice, "do you need some help?"

"Thank you, Nurse Linda," the assistant responded, her relief evident. "This gentleman has an appointment with Dr. Campbell, but he is asking to see Michaela Neuman as well. I've tried to explain."

"That's all right. I'll talk to him."

Lucas noticed he was being discussed as if he weren't there, a treatment he found supremely insulting. Any effort at charm was abandoned.

"Yes." He directed himself toward this newly arrived woman, assuming she had some degree of authority. "I want to see Michaela Neuman, but I'm told she isn't here. How can that be? Where would she go? If she really is so sick—"

"Don't doubt that for a second, Mr. Neuman," the woman said sharply. That she used his name surprised Lucas; he knew he hadn't yet revealed that bit of information.

Seeing that he was taken aback, Nurse Linda continued, "Oh, yes, I know who you are. Furthermore, I know why you're here. I'll answer your questions. But make no mistake, Mr. Neuman—Michaela's welfare is my first concern. I don't know that you and I share that bond. Now, come with me."

Lucas struggled to maintain his stern exterior and prevent his genuine, warring emotions from taking over. He couldn't swallow his sense that Rachel had played him for a fool—and yet, that didn't seem like Rachel.

Not seeing any other option, he did as he was told. He followed the nurse to a seating area off to the side of the reception counter.

"Your explanation?" he prompted, aggression in full swing, rudeness fast approaching.

She turned to face him. "I'm Linda Tafoya, head nurse during the day. I won't say it's a pleasure to meet you because that would be a lie. You see, Mr. Neuman, I really do know who you are."

Folding her arms across her body, she said, "I consider myself Rachel's friend. And Michaela's, too. I know how important your visit today is, no doubt better than you do. Of course Michaela is here, in the hospital. She hasn't been anywhere else for longer than I care to consider. She is too sick to go very far and you need to realize that right now, before you stay one second longer. She isn't in her room right now because, every afternoon, Rachel takes her from the ward—just down the hall—in order to spend some personal time with her. We support what she's doing and we go out of our way to grant her that privacy, to respect that privacy."

"Oh, I see."

"No, I'm sure you don't. But you will. She usually comes back by about two-thirty, which would be any minute now. Because I know they're wrapping it up, anyway, and because I know why you're here, I will let you in on their private retreat. Respect it for what it is."

Lucas was sure that Linda Tafoya was very nearly the same age as he, she was not particularly tall, she was attractive in a neat, organized way. Nothing about her was imposing, but he couldn't ignore the note of command in her voice. She was in charge. "Okay."

She stared at him a moment longer, sizing him up, Lucas could tell. "Right," she said, pointing toward another corridor. "There's a lounge area, three doors down on the right. It's a bit like an atrium—you can see into from the hallway. You'll know it when you see it. Tell Rachel that Linda sent you."

She nodded in the designated direction and left him alone. He stood then, noticing a sign posted by the door next to him. It read, "Rachel Neuman, RN Head, Pediatric Nursing."

Lucas was stunned. His eyebrows returned to their frown position. Rachel had not explained what she did for a living and he hadn't exactly explored the question deeply. Now he had the answer.

Recovering from this revelation, he began to move down the corridor.

He counted the doors, stopping when he reached a glass enclosure. The area was pleasantly lit—possibly by skylights. He could hear—and now see—birds playing in the fountain that sat outside the glass, in the enclosed courtyard. He pushed open the door, scanning the seats. He spotted Rachel immediately. She sat with her back to him, her mane of chocolate-colored hair still caught in that morning's ponytail. He could hear her voice, murmuring softly, not able to distinguish the words but suspecting she was telling a story.

She held a child on her lap—Michaela, he knew. He couldn't see her from where he stood. He could only see part of a shoulder, a typical looking shoulder except for the IV pole positioned behind it. He could see that the pole was actually attached to what looked like a child's stroller, rather than to a wheelchair. But the child was definitely on Rachel's lap.

He approached them quietly, almost reverently, finally understanding that he was violating something personal—something that, until now, had never had anything to do with him. His bravado collapsed. He couldn't breathe—again. He was pulled toward the scene, toward Rachel and Michaela, by a force he wouldn't contemplate.

''*Y todos vivieron muy felices.*'' Rachel finished her story, one she had created especially for Michaela. In this story, as in all of those Rachel told, everyone lived happily ever after.

Rachel sighed, pulling her daughter into a more comfortable position on her lap, resting her own head lightly against Michaela's.

It was then that she saw him. Her eyes widened in recognition, her pulse quickened in a reaction she was powerless to stop.

''Hello, Rachel,'' he whispered, ''Linda sent me.'' He'd had no intention of explaining his presence that way. Somehow, unconsciously, he had known it was the right thing to do.

''Hello, Lucas. We were just having our story time.''

He came around in front of them, his eyes intent on the child, his heart thundering in his chest. He squatted down in front of them in the stance of a baseball catcher.

''This is Michaela,'' Rachel said, gently stroking the delicate fuzzy head that rested against her shoulder.

"Hi, Michaela," Lucas answered, his voice breaking, his mouth dry.

"¿Quién es, Mamá?" The child looked at her mother, quietly curious, waiting for an explanation.

"El se llama Lucas, Michaela, *pero es su padre, mija,"* Rachel replied gently.

Lucas caught his breath. While his knowledge of Spanish was shaky at best, he knew he had just been introduced to his daughter. He didn't speak, knowing he couldn't trust his voice, knowing it wasn't his turn to speak yet.

Michaela regarded him solemnly, as only a child can. She took in every aspect of his appearance. *"¿Por qué..."* she began.

"English, *mija,*" Rachel reminded her. "He doesn't speak Spanish."

Michaela changed track, easily resuming in English. "Why is he here?" Again, the honesty of childhood sparkled.

"He's going to see if he can help you." Michaela didn't question what Rachel meant by this. Evidently, the little girl knew what kind of help she needed.

"He looks like me on the outside, *Mamá.*" Lucas noticed that, although she spoke English, Michaela retained the Spanish pronunciation of *Mamá.* It was, of course, part of Michaela's heritage. It was natural to her.

"Yes, Michaela," Rachel answered, "he does. We need to know if he's like you on the inside, too."

It was that simple, Rachel thought. *And that complicated.*

Lucas's head was reeling. It was all so much to take in. Bone marrow transplants, which they abbreviated as BMT, were a new concept in his world.

"We need to draw a blood sample," Dr. Campbell advised Lucas. "Rachel tells me you would prefer a DNA-based test, which is my preference, as well. Without giving you all the boring details, I'll just say that we tend to get more accurate information more quickly when we use the DNA test over the serology test. There are three levels of investigation we do on the sample. In your case—" he handed him a paper which Lucas recognized as a consent form "—we'd like permission to run all three levels straight away. We know our chances of a match are strong with you, and if we proceed this way, we'll have the information that much sooner.''

Lucas nodded, thinking it couldn't really make any difference to him. He understood, however, that urgency was involved, that speed could make a difference to Michaela.

''Furthermore, if you are a match, we'll want to get you in as quickly as we can. There's no point in dragging it out.'' Dr. Campbell handed Lucas several brochures. ''These have diagrams and such. I would recommend that you look at them. The donor procedure itself is not the worst thing you'll ever experience, but it isn't the most comfortable, either.''

He went on to describe how the bone marrow would be extracted from Lucas's hip under a local anesthetic. He would be able to stay in the hospital overnight if he wanted, but he should anticipate a certain degree of tenderness in the area afterward and should not plan to drive himself home.

''How will Michaela get the transplant?'' Lucas wanted to know.

''Well, I'm not her doctor. You'll want to talk to Dr. Graham for the specifics of Michaela's case.'' Dr. Campbell removed his glasses and was pinching the bridge of his nose with his fingers. ''That said, the recipient usually receives it through an IV. The chemo she'll have prior to it will be worse for her than the actual BMT procedure. But she will be fragile for some time afterward. Essentially, she'll have no immune system and she may very well have side effects from the chemo again.''

''So,'' Lucas pondered aloud, ''this is what Rachel meant when she said it would get worse before it gets better.''

''Probably,'' Dr. Campbell agreed, reaching to push the buttons on his intercom. ''Yes, Kristen, this is Evan. Is Paul Graham around?''

A few seconds later he spoke into his phone again. ''Yes, Paul. Evan here. Listen, Lucas Neuman is in my office, talking to me about the bone marrow transplant. Do you have a few minutes to talk about Michaela?''

Scant minutes later another man let himself into Dr. Campbell's office. Lucas found himself standing and shaking hands with Paul Graham. Paul was blond and blue-eyed and noticeably fit. He had a gentle manner, but Lucas felt himself squirm under the intensity of the man's blue gaze. Lucas had no idea how old the man might be; his appearance gave nothing away.

"I've got brochures for you, too," he began, handing Lucas another handful of leaflets. "These give some general reference information, but as far as Michaela is concerned, well…hers has not been an easy case. She didn't respond as quickly to chemotherapy as we might have hoped. AML, the kind of leukemia Michaela has, tends to spread to organs throughout the body. The longer it takes to get remission to occur, the more likely this kind of spread is. That's why her BMT is so important. On the one hand, it's not an unusual procedure at this point in treatment, but she needs it more than most. Without it…" He shrugged, letting his silence finish the sentence.

They had talked for a few more minutes, Lucas understanding that either doctor would be available to discuss the situation with him again, if he felt the need. Lucas was also aware of their disapproval—a very sure knowledge that they didn't like him, despite having just met him.

The busyness outside Dr. Campbell's office briefly dazzled Lucas and it took him a few minutes to get his bearings. Then he decided he wanted to look in on Michaela and maybe speak with Rachel again.

His attention was diverted, however, by a cluster of people moving along a corridor and coming to a halt at the reception desk, a few feet away from him.

"Muchas gracias, Doña Raquel, muchas gracias."

Lucas watched as a woman clutched Rachel's hands, offering her thanks. She was Hispanic, her jet-black hair showing a few impressive streaks of white, her black eyes sharp and bright with unshed tears.

"De nada, señora." Rachel answered, continuing on in hushed Spanish tones that Lucas could neither follow nor understand.

"What's the commotion?" Dr. Graham's voice came from behind him, followed quickly by a chortle of laughter.

"Ah, yes," Dr. Campbell said, smiling at Lucas, nodding his head toward the ruckus. "Today, Tómas goes home. He is a fan of Rachel's, I'm afraid."

Lucas searched the cluster of people, seeking someone who

might be considered a patient. He finally spotted a boy, perhaps thirteen years old, sitting in a wheelchair, a hand and a leg encased in plaster. *Or fiberglass, or something,* Lucas corrected. *Whatever they make casts out of these days.*

The young boy, blushing furiously, clearly had eyes only for Rachel. She handed him a bouquet of balloons, speaking to him in Spanish, and posed for a picture with him. Lucas supposed the woman must be the boy's mother.

Lucas's first glimpse into Rachel on the job left him uneasy—and grudgingly respectful.

The group eventually arrived at the elevator, freeing Rachel to make her way over to Lucas when she saw him.

"Hello," she said, smiling lightly. "How did your meeting go?"

"Fine, fine," he answered. "I met Dr. Graham as well as Dr. Campbell. Dr. Graham is Michaela's doctor for...this?"

Rachel nodded.

"Right," Lucas resumed. "Anyway, they gave me my marching orders and a whole lot more, right here." He held up the handful of papers. "I'll be back in the morning."

"I might see you then," Rachel said, making to leave.

Lucas's hand shot out, as if to grab her, a motion she evaded. "Um, wait, Rachel." Now that he had her attention, he wasn't sure what to say next. "So you're a nurse." It wasn't particularly elegant or profound, but he had succeeded in extending the conversation.

"Yes."

"How long...how long have you worked here?"

"This is the first and only place I've ever worked Lucas. I've been here five years."

"Five years," he repeated stupidly, understanding the significance of that time period. She had obviously started working here just when they had separated. When she'd finished school.

"Yes, Lucas. I interviewed for a position while you were in Las Vegas. It was one of the things I was doing...*that* week. I took the position as head a couple of years ago. I certainly wasn't hired as head."

Lucas knew he would reflect on this information at another time. At the moment he didn't want to leave Rachel. He needed another topic to postpone his departure. "That group that just left?"

She nodded again.

"She called you Donna something? What was that about?"

"Sort of," Rachel said smiling. "*Doña Raquel. Doña,*" she emphasized the pronunciation of don-ya, "is a title we use sometimes. It goes with first names. Raquel is Rachel in Spanish." She shrugged. "I am called that a lot, actually. Many of our patients speak Spanish—sometimes they speak virtually no English. But even if they speak English well, if Spanish is their mother tongue, it's more comfortable for them to use it during a time of trauma. And, of course, trauma is not unknown here."

Lucas absorbed this information. He had never thought about Rachel using Spanish—not really. He knew, of course, that she was bilingual. He knew that she spoke Spanish with her family. He'd just never considered what that meant. That she could choose either language at any given moment to communicate.

"Was that all?" Rachel was asking.

"No," Lucas said, running his empty hand through his hair. "I was actually wondering if I could see Michaela again."

"Sure, Lucas," she replied promptly. She scrutinized him for an instant, then came to a decision. Shrugging again, she continued, "I think you're getting an idea of her situation, so if you want to go, I'll take you."

Rachel motioned toward him, and he followed her. He caught a breath of her vanilla fragrance. He hadn't thought of it in years, not until she'd come to his office this morning. Yet he'd never really forgotten it, either. Silently he noticed that his body recognized it as well.

Standing in the doorway, Lucas watched as Rachel went over to Michaela and kissed her forehead. He could tell they were exchanging quiet mother-daughter words, but he couldn't pick up what they were saying.

Of course, if it's Spanish I won't understand, anyway, he observed silently, knowing he could not share this angle of their relationship. He'd have to create his own place with Michaela. And with Rachel, if she'd let him. He wasn't sure what he meant by that.

Suddenly, it seemed to Lucas, Rachel lifted her head and motioned for him to enter the room. Holding Michaela's hand, she said, "I thought you might want to tell her about tomorrow."

Lucas nodded, taking her lead. "Um, yes, I would," he answered, marveling that he sounded so unsure of himself. But then, he wasn't exactly overflowing with confidence right now. Nothing inside these hospital doors could be described as his comfort zone.

"Well, Michaela," he began, noticing that Rachel had withdrawn to a discreet distance, allowing him a few private moments with his daughter. "I'm going to have some tests in the morning." He paused, wondering if that was an acceptable term to use with a child of this age. He had no experience with children to guide him. Remembering how Rachel had discussed the situation earlier, he said, "Yes, tests that will show if we match each other enough so that I can help you."

"I hope you match me," Michaela said simply.

"Me, too," Lucas responded, realizing it was true, amazed that he could feel so intensely about something so completely new to him.

Rachel moved back into the room then, leaning over to kiss Michaela's forehead. *"Hasta mañana, mija. Buenas noches."*

"Sí, Mamá. Buenas noches."

Surprised—and surprised that he had understood the exchange—Lucas asked, "She goes to bed so early?"

"Well, she sleeps a lot whenever she can. She tends to get tired easily. But, it's actually *my* bedtime." She laughed at his surprised expression. "My shift starts at midnight, Lucas."

"You can kiss me goodnight, too, *Papá,*" Michaela suggested.

Lucas's mouth dropped open. He again experienced the breathlessness that had plagued him all day. He managed, however, to lean over the bed and kiss Michaela's forehead just as he had seen Rachel do.

Walking down the corridor, Rachel turned to Lucas. "I'm sorry about that, if you felt put on the spot. Michaela doesn't understand the shock I'm sure you're feeling, so I hope you allow for that. I can have her call you Lucas, though, if the father title is just not—" she waved her hand in the air, trying to make her meaning clear "—something you're comfortable with."

"No—" Lucas shook his head "—no, *Papá* is fine. Strange," he acknowledged with a smile, "but I think I could get used to it."

"If you'd rather be Dad..."

"Oh, no," Lucas responded immediately. "The Spanish seems to be natural to her."

"Yes, it probably is. I mean, in my family we do use Spanish with each other, probably for our names more than anything. She may never have heard a father called 'Dad,' now that I think of it, not by anyone she actually knows." Rachel pondered the possibility for a minute. "She has cousins and extended cousins, and they may all say *Papá.* I'm not sure." She smiled softly. "I just meant that I know the concept has to be strange to you, so if you'd rather she use a word that's more natural to you, I could have her say Dad."

"It's okay, Rachel," Lucas said, realizing it was the truth. "I can be *Papá.* If that's what Michaela wants."

"Bueno." She nodded at him, stopping in front of her office door. "I guess I'll see you tomorrow. Probably, anyway."

Lucas knew he was being dismissed, but he wasn't ready to leave yet. "Wait, Rachel," he began, running a hand through his hair, letting it rest on the back of his neck. "Could I come in for a minute?"

Rachel was taken aback by the question, and it showed. "I guess so," she said hesitantly. "But, well, I usually call it a day around three and it's already after four, so it really can only be for a minute."

She pushed open the door, standing aside so Lucas could enter.

"How long does it take you to get home?" Lucas could not contain his curiosity about Rachel's lifestyle.

"What do you mean?" Rachel wasn't following his line of questioning, being so accustomed to staying at the hospital that it never occurred to her that anybody would think she did otherwise.

Lucas squirmed, unsure how he could rephrase his question so that it sounded appropriate. "I was just wondering...you said it was bedtime for you—after bedtime I suppose. But you're still here and I was just thinking you still had to...that there was still the time it takes you to get from the hospital to your…house—'' he hesitated on his word choice, not knowing if that was an accurate word ''—and that would mean you wouldn't get to bed for even a longer time.''

''Oh, I see what you're asking.'' Rachel's expression cleared. ''I don't go home often, Lucas. The hospital staff has built an addition for me, a bit of private quarters, so that I can stay at the hospital round the clock. I can go to bed as soon as I walk through that door—'' she pointed ''—and crawl into the bed they've tucked in there.'' She walked farther into the room, starting her hot water kettle, knowing tea would help her relax, regardless of the caffeine factor. ''I went home today for the first time in several weeks, just to exchange dirty laundry for clean. I guess I sort of live at the hospital these days.''

Fleetingly, Lucas wondered where home was for Rachel.

Looking around, Lucas also noticed how Rachel's office suited her. He remembered her criticism of his own office years before—that it had been impersonal and cold. While her office felt like an office and still, in fact, felt like a hospital, Lucas had to admit it was more welcoming than his. Compared to his luxurious surroundings, Rachel's office was spartan. He suspected, however, that the artwork and dried flowers were her choices—or that of her friends who had prepared this place for her—and not the efforts of an interior decorator who'd never met her. Which was the case with his own office.

Her diploma and other awards were posted on the walls, but numerous personal photos adorned the area, as well. It was as homey as a hospital room could be.

''Rachel,'' he said, turning back to face her. ''I guess I just want you to know that I'm glad you came to me about this. I understand you didn't have much choice, but I also know you might have believed I would be…less than cooperative about it. You could have explored legal avenues first rather than just trying to talk to me. You could have easily decided to keep our lives separate. I'm glad you took the chance. And I really hope I'll be able to help her.''

Wringing her hands, Rachel said, ''Somehow, Lucas, I really believe you will. I mean, some family member just *has* to be compatible.'' Rachel knew desperation had crept into her voice but she couldn't help it. ''And no one in my family suits.''

''You've all been tested?''

"Oh, yes," she said, nodding solemnly. "It stands to reason that your family will have the match, and you're the most likely of them all."

Just then a voice came through on Rachel's intercom. "Rachel?"

"Yes, Hannah?" Hannah was one of the reception attendants.

"I'm sorry, but...it's Kerry Ann Parker's mother. They're going over tomorrow's details and she's—"

"I understand. I'm coming, Hannah."

"Aren't you off duty?" Lucas asked, thrown off by her acceptance that she couldn't say no.

"Technically, of course." Rachel smiled softly. "In reality, never." Lucas saw her fatigue despite her attempt to conceal it from him. "It's the nature of the job, Lucas. It doesn't have limited business hours." She reached into a closet that Lucas hadn't even noticed before and pulled out a white lab coat. "I'll try to hurry. I would think you'd understand extended working hours."

She dashed out and Lucas was left alone in her office. He knew what she meant: he'd always tended to work long hours himself. He'd rarely, if ever, declined the opportunity to work beyond regular office hours, although he suspected Rachel's motivation was different from his. Making more money seemed an unlikely contributing factor for her.

Trying not to snoop and yet knowing that was exactly what he was doing, he moved toward the shelves that held numerous framed photos. He recognized Michaela in various stages of infancy and toddlerhood. His eyes were drawn to one in particular, which he picked up. It was clearly a newborn Michaela, held by her exhausted but proud mother and a man. Looking closer, Lucas realized it was Rick, Rachel's brother.

"So he was with Rachel when Michaela arrived," he whispered. "Of course, it would have been better had it been me." He wouldn't analyze the thought. And Lucas refused to acknowledge the fact that, had it been another man, someone besides her brother, someone he didn't know, he would have been upset. Very upset that Rachel had found someone else to share such an intimate moment with.

Lucas glanced at the remaining photos, finding pictures of

Rachel's family in a variety of casual and formal states. He found a formal photo of Rachel in graduation gear, apparently delivering the commencement address for the school of nursing. He looked closely at the photo, observing the honors colors she wore.

She was valedictorian. First in her class. That's why she's giving a speech.

Needing to know more, he picked up the photo. There it was, engraved in the frame. May 13. He'd been in Las Vegas. Rachel's graduation, being top of her class, speaking at the ceremony—reasons she'd had for staying in Phoenix that week. Reasons why she hadn't wanted to go to Las Vegas with him. He hadn't known and he hadn't been there for her. He'd gone to Las Vegas without her.

He set the photo back down. He leaned forward enough to read the dates of the framed documents on the wall.

"I took the National Licensing Exam at the beginning of the week. May eighth to tenth. A grueling, horrible time. But good. Like boot camp, I suppose, in a way. And yes, I graduated that week. I interviewed for this job. I found out I was pregnant. I tried to tell you it was an important week for me. It was. Anything else you'd like to know?"

"I wasn't prying, Rachel." Lucas had heard an edge in her voice. "But I guess I am trying to put together the pieces of this puzzle that I've walked back into the middle of."

Another photo had caught his eye: toward the back, but still visible, sat a formal shot of their wedding. Involuntarily he reached in to pick it up, then looked at Rachel with questions clouding his gray eyes.

Meeting that look, Rachel sensed which photo he held. She knew what he needed to know. "I've never hidden your identity from Michaela. I never wanted it to seem like you didn't exist or that I was anything less than proud of her parentage. I wanted her to be proud of it, too. I wanted her to always know that she is the result of love, and that nothing changes that fact. I've kept pictures of you around. She's started asking why you don't live with us, but she never had to ask what you looked like or, worse yet, whether she had a father. She always knew. I hope it's helped to keep her…secure."

"So she knew who I was today, might have recognized me?"

"Probably. She certainly wasn't surprised when I explained who you were."

"I noticed that. I just thought maybe kids…took information like that more easily than adults. I'm not around kids much—at all, really—so I don't have much to go on."

Rachel smiled. "They probably do roll with things easier than adults. But Michaela knew she had a *Papá,* somewhere."

Involuntarily Rachel stepped forward, gently lifting the treasured portrait from Lucas's hand and returning it to its spot on the shelf. Immediately she wished she had resisted the impulse—her stomach fluttered, she was too close to Lucas. She had brushed his fingers, she could still feel the tingle on her skin. Lucas filled her senses, overwhelmed her senses. Lucas was everywhere, everything.

Glancing toward his face, she caught her breath. He was reaching toward her, tucking a wayward strand of her hair behind her ear. Except that he wasn't really. His hand crept around to the back of her head, resting on the nape of her neck.

No, she realized suddenly, *he's taking out the barrette.*

Which he did, dropping it on the desk behind her, his hand returning to her hair, freeing it to cascade through his fingers. Stroking her hair, caressing the chocolate silkiness, both his hands buried in its depths, turning her head toward his, tipping her mouth to meet his.

Claiming her mouth, gently in a short taste at first, returning immediately for something deeper, seeking something deeper still. Finding it. Rachel moved to fit against him, her mouth first, then the rest of her body, molding itself against him in an instinctive caress. Her hands found their way around his waist, pulling him to her, suggesting another kind of fit that their bodies instinctively remembered, too. His hands in her hair, his mouth finding the delicate spot at the base of her throat, an involuntary gasp coming from Rachel's lips.

And another gasp, one filled with quiet despair, very nearly a sob. Her hands pushing against his chest, forcing some distance between them.

"Why did you do that?" she whispered, her eyes wide and shining topaz.

Blinking at her, Lucas took a few seconds to respond. "Why did I do that? What do you mean?"

"This—" she let her hand flicker between them "—why did you...kiss me?"

Lucas smiled, a smile that reached his eyes. "I'd think that was obvious. I did it because I wanted to. Didn't even stop to think. I guess it just felt natural." *What was there to explain,* he wondered.

His smile widened, his focus shifted. "I love your hair," he murmured. "I always did. Oh, yes, Rachel, I did it because I wanted to. Definitely. I still do."

He reached for her again, his fingers seeking the satiny strands.

Rachel shied away, knocking his hand away. "Please... don't. Please don't touch me...again."

"Why not? This wasn't just about me, Rachel. I initiated it, yes. But you responded. You wanted it, too. Until you started thinking about it. Then you wanted to stop. What would be so wrong with me touching you again?"

His voice was a slow caress, running across her senses.

Rachel didn't answer right away, but she pulled away from him. She continued to meet his gaze.

Finally she said, "I can't do it, that's all. Please...just respect what I'm saying. Don't touch me again."

Frustration and confusion nipped at Lucas. "Rachel, I didn't plan that. That's been building between us all day, ever since you walked into my office today. Why not just enjoy it?"

She sighed, suddenly sad. Suddenly weary. "Look, Lucas. It just happened. Okay, I accept that. Our bodies remember the chemistry or something. Whatever. It can't happen again. I'm not made that way. I'm just not."

Lucas wasn't sure exactly what had gone wrong, but he knew he was being dismissed. Again. Despite this final setback, he felt warm inside.

When he left, his step was lighter, his mood was lighter. A lot of good had happened today, after all. Even if this last bit with Rachel confused the hell out of him. He could overlook that and concentrate on the positive the day had brought.

He never saw the single tear that trickled down Rachel's cheek—or that she angrily smudged it away with the back of her hand.

As soon as the door closed behind Lucas, Rachel turned back toward her sitting room. She picked up the remote control for her little TV. Sitting down on one of the couches, then curling her legs beneath her, she clicked on some show, just for the noise, and blinked until the tears backed down.

She'd told Lucas it was past her bedtime—and it was—but she hadn't explained that there was little point in trying to sleep just yet. These days she rarely slept for more than three or four hours at a time, and always restlessly. That was when she was lucky enough to actually fall asleep.

Dios, she thought, *when was the last time I really slept?* She couldn't remember. But it had been a while ago.

In a way, she hated sleeping—dreams came then. Dreams of things she preferred to forget. Dreams she preferred to avoid.

So it was better to focus on the TV program, without concentrating on it, until she was too tired to keep her eyes open. If she stayed here on the couch, rather than trying to lie down in her bed, it was possible that some sleep—however limited—might come.

Chapter 5

The next morning Lucas drove to the children's hospital with confidence. He strode into the building, this time knowing exactly where he was going. He was proceeding nicely, quite satisfied with himself.

Until that damn needle had come in his direction.

"Relax, Mr. Neuman, this will just be a little stick," the nurse was saying as she jabbed the needle into his arm and began juggling various tubes and vials.

Lucas turned to the logical part of his brain, the part of his brain that could remind him this was only a blood test. Perhaps the longest blood test ever administered to a human, but a blood test nevertheless. After all, he reasoned, he wasn't exactly squeamish. He was reasonably brave.

But, God, this was taking forever. Surely they weren't going to take all of his blood?

"There you go, Mr. Neuman, all finished," the nurse chirped. "Just hold that cotton there for a minute. Would you like a glass of orange juice? We have some muffins also."

"No, no." Lucas waved away the offer, rolling his sleeve down and buttoning the cuff as soon as the adhesive bandage was in place. "I need to be going." Standing quickly, Lucas found himself abruptly returning to the sitting position.

"Would you like to reconsider the offer?" The nurse smiled as she handed him a glass of orange juice. "Most people feel a little woozy after the more extended blood work. Donating blood, for example, has the same effect."

Grateful for the offer, now that he saw the wisdom in it, Lucas took the glass and downed the juice. Just as gratefully he accepted the blueberry muffin the nurse extended his way. Unbelievably, he actually thought he could feel the nutrients—and sugar—hit his system. He'd wait a few more minutes before standing, though. Wait until he had his "land legs" under him again.

As he proceeded toward the elevator, he suddenly felt a rock-hard hand descend upon his shoulder, halting his progress.

Turning toward that hand, seeing a familiar face, Lucas's first impulse was to smile and shake the man's hand. It was Rick, Rachel's brother, a man Lucas had always considered his friend. They had always gotten along together, had good fun together. But Rick was clearly not intending to reminisce over their friendship now.

"I understand why you are here, Lucas. The entire family knows why," he said gruffly, "and we appreciate that. Forgive us if we don't appear to welcome you." Lucas thought he detected sarcasm and a certain level of bitterness. Something he'd never heard from Rick before.

"But," Rick continued, emphasizing the word, spitting it at Lucas, "Rachel has already suffered too much at your hands. You have hurt her more than any one person should have the power to do. *Dios de mi vida,* do not hurt her—or Michaela—again. Do you understand me?"

Rick's body shook with suppressed rage, his hands, having let go of Lucas's shoulder, clenching and unclenching by his sides. Lucas fully understood that had they not been in such a public place, he would have been on the receiving end of Rick's fist by now. Still, his words sounded like a plea.

"I don't know what happened to you, Lucas. Our family liked you. I don't know if you changed or if you just tricked us." Rick stepped away from him, silently instructing Lucas on the meaning of the words *if looks could kill.*

"Your father is a bastard, Lucas, a first-class snake. I thought better of you."

Rick stepped back, as if intending to walk away, then thought better of it. "I never understood why you carried on like you did, Lucas. If you were wanting out of the marriage, a divorce would have been a lot fairer. It would have still been painful, but it would have been decent. What you did was...low." He shook his head sadly. "You romanced Rachel, convinced her, convinced all of us, that you truly loved her. That you recognized what a special woman she is. Then you deserted her without actually letting her go, started strutting around like a *pelado,* with that *woman—*" he sneered it into an insult, his words still clipped by anger "*—that* woman on your arm, setting up your *casa chica* in Rachel's home. Why did you do that? What kind of man would do that?"

Lucas opened his mouth, ready to explain that he hadn't actually, truly *done* anything, that things had just worked out that way. Seeing Rick's black eyes glittering with rage, he thought better of it. Rick wasn't going to accept that explanation.

"You humiliated Rachel, Lucas, very publicly. People noticed what you were doing. Did you ever think of that? It wasn't just that Rachel had to live with it—she also had to face that other people knew what you were doing. Did you ever consider what she was going through, how she felt, while you were off...carrying on? And then she went through hell trying to put her life back together. Has she told you that?"

Rick didn't wait for an answer. "No, she wouldn't have. She doesn't talk to anybody about it. She holds it all inside." He paused, weighing his words. "She came to me at first. She lived with me while she was putting the pieces back together. She stayed until her town house was ready. She rarely spoke about you or anything that had happened, but I knew she needed help and she'd come to me. I did what I could. She was a shell of her former self, Lucas. She's never been the same. You did that to her."

He glanced away from Lucas, apparently having said more than he'd intended. He shrugged his shoulders—it was too late to take it back—so he forged ahead. "It was another month or so before she even told me she was pregnant, but she had known for a while. I think she only told me when she was starting to show, when she knew she couldn't hide it anymore. I was her coach when Michaela came, a proud moment for me. I am close to the *niña.*''

He stepped closer to Lucas, their noses only inches apart. ''Rachel loved you, Lucas. Hell, I think she still does, but wouldn't admit it for anything. It's buried very deep, if it still exists. You will never know what it cost her to turn to you for help now. None of us will. Rachel never asks for help. And to need you, of all people. *Dios mio,* I can only imagine. She doesn't trust you, Lucas. She can't. You dismantled her faith in you, piece by piece. For a while, I think her faith in herself was destroyed, too. Something in her—'' He stopped short, shaking his head, more sad than angry now. ''It just died afterward, after she moved away from you. It's closed off. She's not the same woman. She tries to hide it, but those of us who love her...well, we know what we are seeing.''

Lucas had no response for this. Again, he acknowledged that Rachel seemed different to him, too. She did seem...detached, he decided. Although not exactly. Controlled, maybe. He'd assumed, to the extent he'd thought about it, that this was simply due to coping with Michaela's illness.

So, yes, she's changed. Haven't we all?

But to swallow Rick's accusations would mean he was responsible for the state Rachel was in. No. Lucas halted his train of thought. He was not responsible for Rachel. Rachel was a grown woman. She had left him. That was the simple fact. And he couldn't undo the past, anyway. What's done was done.

''She needed you for this. She had to turn to you.'' Rick paused, inhaling a shaky breath. ''Don't hurt Rachel again. Don't hurt Michaela. If you have it in you to behave as a decent man, do it now.''

Rick left then, going down the hall, to a destination that Lucas couldn't identify. Once the elevator arrived, Lucas hurriedly stepped into the relative safety of its cubicle.

Glancing at his watch as he pulled into his parking space, Lucas was relieved to see it was not yet ten. He wouldn't be late for his father's weekly status meeting. He wasn't ready to explain anything to anyone just yet, and an explanation would have been expected had he been late.

Stepping off the elevator, he went straight to the conference room without stopping at his office, taking his briefcase with him.

"Good morning, Jennifer," he said, pausing briefly at his assistant's desk. "Anything that needs attending before the ten-o'clock meeting?"

She smiled prettily and shook her bleached-blond hair. "Nothing that won't keep."

"Great," he answered. "Oh, if I get a call from a Dr. Campbell, I want to take it." He'd given the doctor his cell phone number and hoped he would use that instead of his office number. However, Lucas didn't want any chance of missing the phone call when it came.

"Of course," she responded, her curiosity obvious. Lucas had no intention of providing more information than that, however.

Once inside the conference room, Lucas set his briefcase on the table in front of his chair. He then made his way to the refreshment table, something he never did, bringing coffee and a cinnamon roll back to his place.

The room filled quickly after that. Much to his displeasure, Alana took a seat next to him. She turned to him, smiling and inquired, "Have a busy night, Lucas?"

At his blank expression, she leaned forward, her breasts brimming over the arm of her chair. "You're needing so much sustenance this morning, Lucas. I was simply wondering why—wondering what you did to work up such an appetite this early."

"Not the way you're implying, Alana." His voice was clipped, his manner curt. He noted dispassionately that this time the voluptuous presentation of her body was doing nothing for him. He was relieved. At least he was in control where Alana was concerned.

Or didn't need to be, because he simply didn't feel anything for her.

After yesterday's kiss, Lucas knew it was Rachel his body was responding to. *Best not to think of that,* he reprimanded himself. *You don't need any embarrassing reactions during the meeting.*

He waved off the cigar extended toward him, content with his coffee and cinnamon roll.

"Of course, I know it had to be some other way, Lucas," Alana whispered, reaching forward to wipe a nonexistent crumb from the corner of his mouth. "You weren't with me last night, so it couldn't be a hangover from a night of...passion. Could it?"

"Good morning, everyone," Arnold Neuman's voiced boomed across the room as he eased his bulk into his chair, preventing any response Lucas might have made.

"Good morning," they chorused.

"Okay, we'll start by going over progress on existing developments, then proceed to the Mercado complex set for Chandler. Then," Arnold paused for dramatic effect, "we'll discuss this year's company retreat."

Cheers and raucous laughter met this announcement, just as Arnold had anticipated. His beady black eyes gleamed their satisfaction. Lucas, however, was finding it difficult to feel enthusiasm for the company retreat or for anything else on his father's agenda.

His mind kept wandering to the expected phone call from the hospital, and to the stack of information burning a hole in his briefcase, the one from Dr. Campbell and Dr. Graham. He'd meant to start reading it last night, but had fallen asleep in front of the television. Music from a blaring commercial had awakened him just after midnight.

As he thought about it, Lucas admitted that he had simply received too much new information in one day, starting with the reality of a daughter. Or maybe it had started when he'd noticed Rachel's name in his appointment book. He still couldn't decide when his life had turned surreal. He wasn't sure where the new information had ended, either. Or if it had ended yet. But sometime late last night, his brain had hit overload, and he had been unable to approach the packet.

Today, however, he was alert. He was ready to discover and digest more about what Michaela was facing. *Michaela.* He smiled to himself. *Three days ago, I didn't even know she existed. Today, I'm calling my daughter by name.*

Vaguely Lucas noticed his father had wrapped up the segment on current projects and had launched into his spiel regarding the proposed Mercado project. Lucas knew he needed to follow the discussion, but found his thoughts returning to Michaela. And to Rachel.

Thinking again! But...he thought of them anyway, the women in his life. No doubt that Michaela was his daughter—he knew because he fully realized that Rachel wasn't the kind to fool around. *No,* he admitted, *Rachel wouldn't have done that.* And for some reason the knowledge comforted him.

"What do you think, boy?" his father's voice interrupted Lucas's thoughts.

"About the Mercado?" Lucas stalled for time, feeling like a seventh-grader caught sleeping during history class.

Deciding to be honest, for once, Lucas gave an answer he knew would not be well received. "Well, Dad, actually, I don't like it. It's an uninspired design in a location that doesn't need another structure of that type. It has no personality, no style. Nothing to distinguish it from dozens of other shopping centers in the Phoenix area." He took a deep breath, forging ahead with what he had started, mentally noting the stunned silence his remarks were producing. "It's not a smart location for what you have in mind. It would be the fourth such center within a two-mile radius. I have to question who researched it, because the inappropriateness of the location should have screamed out." Looking straight at his father, Lucas continued, "I can't support it, Dad."

"Well," Arnold blustered, his face reddening by the second, "maybe you and I will need to talk. Your objections are duly noted. What commentary do you others have?"

Lucas had never publicly contradicted his father's plans before. He'd tried offering his true opinions when he'd first come to work at the company, only to quickly discover that opinions other than Arnold Neuman's were not welcome. Figuring that he had a lot to learn, Lucas had shut up and started learning. He kept his ideas to himself, even when he believed his father was making a mistake. However, he had not felt comfortable with his job at Neuman Industries in some time. It didn't fit him any longer. Maybe it never did.

He knew his father wasn't happy with him. There would be fallout. But, remarkably, Lucas found that he didn't care.

On cue, Lucas's colleagues rushed to stroke Arnold's ego, assuring him that they supported his project. Lucas had known they would.

But soon Lucas's thoughts returned to Rachel and how it had been when they first met, when they first got together.

He'd been in his second year at the university, involved in a dual-degree program that allowed him to obtain both a bachelors in business and an M.B.A. He hadn't really minded doing a program in business, knowing it would be useful in some way. His father had refused to consider that he do anything else. Lucas hadn't confronted him about it. Instead, he'd quietly added a minor in architecture to his program, despite the university's distaste for minor concentrations.

Lucas had wanted to create and to restore. Architecture had been his dream. He'd expected to have the chance to design and develop buildings when he worked for his father. He hadn't expected endless cookie-cutter work, where remarkably similar projects were stamped out as quickly as Arnold Neuman could arrange it. Lucas had said it about the Mercado: there was no style or personality in anything Neuman Industries produced. Maybe that wasn't a problem when one was dealing in parking lots, as his grandfather had done, but with buildings…Lucas had just expected so much more.

Briefly Lucas thought of Diego Fuentes, whom he had met in school. Diego, Rachel and her brother, Rick, Lucas had discovered, considered themselves to be family—although Lucas knew better than to try to figure out the actual family ties. More than likely, there weren't any. It was their perception that made them family—or *familia,* as he knew they called it. Nevertheless, they were close friends, and Lucas had become part of their group.

Lucas and Diego had met in an architecture course, quickly discovering that they shared views on what architecture should be, how it could enhance a community. They had worked together on numerous term projects, always earning top marks for incorporating community and environmental considerations in their plans. After graduation Diego had taken a risk. He had started his own company, Fuentes de la Juventud. Their work was so…renowned, Lucas supposed, that even the non-Spanish speakers in the industry knew that the company name meant Fountains of Youth, using Diego's last name as a play on words.

Hell, Lucas thought, *they even knew to pronounce the* j *like an* h.

Diego's first love, even during school, had been restoring old properties rather than designing original projects. Lucas remembered that Diego had actually been a history buff, at least where southwestern America was concerned. His company promptly established itself as *the* firm to enlist for restoration work. Gradually they had extended their expertise to designing and developing, too. Lucas couldn't think of a single branch in the field that Fuentes de la Juventud didn't cover these days, although they seemed to limit themselves to the southwestern states.

The company had earned a solid reputation for doing exactly the kinds of work Diego had envisioned as a university student. The kind of work that Lucas had also envisioned. Diego's path hadn't been as comfortable as the one Lucas had followed, but it was paying off in ways that Lucas could only dream of these days. No cookie-cutter designs for Diego Fuentes.

Something had prompted Lucas to call Diego several weeks back. It had been their first contact in years. Lucas had no idea, really, why he'd made the call. But he had. He hadn't had anything in mind to talk about, either. Predictably, trying to talk had been rather awkward, and they had finished by scheduling a time to go golfing. That was neutral ground for both of them.

Lucas had missed Diego, although he balked at acknowledging it. They had taken such different paths. Now they would cross again. And now Lucas had a certain sense of anticipation about their outing.

I'd better check my schedule, Lucas thought urgently, *see when that is exactly.*

Fuentes de la Juventud, a company with a conscience.

The thought brought Lucas back to Neuman Industries. He didn't believe that his father allowed a conscience to influence his projects in any way. Arnold Neuman did whatever it took to get the result he wanted, often ignoring background research if it didn't mesh with his desires. Lucas was sure this was the case with the Mercado.

In his cynical moments, which were frequent these days, Lucas had begun to wonder why they bothered to conduct the research, given that it did not appear to enter into the decision-making processes in any way. He knew certain legalities demanded background research—on paper, at least. Increasingly, Lucas had the uneasy feeling that his father would also ignore the legalities themselves, if they displeased him. Arnold liked to cut corners.

Lucas's dreams had still been intact when he'd met Rachel. He had still believed he would do great things. She'd been an undecided major, working at the University Health Center. They'd dated for an entire year before they decided to marry. They had been young, but they had known they were right for each other.

Or at least, Lucas reflected, *we believed we were right for each other.*

His parents had desperately, frantically opposed the marriage. Despite all their dire warnings, Lucas had married Rachel. He had loved her. He had only felt complete when he was with her. And once she'd left him, he had never felt complete again.

Rachel's family—her parents and brother—had been cautiously optimistic and supportive of their marriage. They had made Lucas feel welcome and had invited the couple to join them in various family activities. Lucas had learned how to fish with them, even how to clean the fish.

Now there's a thing you haven't done for a while, he mused.

They had been happy in their marriage at first. Rachel had continued to work, although she loved her position at the Health Center so much, it almost didn't seem like a job. Lucas had never before considered that she was serious about her work, he could concede now. Clearly, she had made a career choice and he hadn't noticed. Lucas had pursued school full-time, his father providing a living allowance that, when combined with Rachel's meager income, had been enough for survival. Lucas felt justified not working, knowing he could finish his degrees more quickly that way, and knowing that he would be able to pay his father back once he went to work at the office.

Their first home had been a small studio apartment, filled with old, secondhand furniture. They were living within walking distance of campus, and generally walked to and from their classes together. Public transportation was unreliable or nonexistent, so they had purchased an ancient used car for forays beyond campus. Their idea of a vacation had been to see how far they could go on one tank of gas.

So simple, he thought, smiling. *We were so good together then.*

School had been a serious commitment for them. They had both been driven to perform well, but had always made time for each other, always tried to support each other when studies became a heavy burden. They'd managed to turn to each other, sharing their love, sharing simple things and sharing exceptional sex.

She was so passionate and intense about everything, lovemaking included.

Lucas remembered very, very well.

"It isn't just our bodies, Lucas," Rachel would say. "It's our souls joining, too."

And he had believed her. It felt like that to him, too.

Yes, the marriage had started well enough. Then Lucas had finished school and everything had changed. In one year it had disintegrated.

Moving into the corporate world had had its effect on Lucas. He felt he owed his father…something, and Arnold started to collect at the graduation party. His father had called it a combined graduation and welcome-to-the-company party. That was his explanation for including Alana, and everyone else from the office, while excluding Rachel. Lucas had never explained that to Rachel. She'd never known just how many people his father had seen fit to invite while leaving her off the guest list.

Lucas had felt awkward about all that, maybe even a little ashamed. But explaining the details to Rachel just wasn't something he'd felt capable of doing. He'd have needed to confront his father first, and he wasn't about to do that.

So he'd followed his father's wishes and gone to Cancún, with Alana and not Rachel. That trip set the pattern from then on. Alana was good company. The two of them had ended up staying in Cancún for a full week, while the others had returned home after a few days. Lucas couldn't explain why; it just happened that way. Travel of that kind, staying at a resort where everything he could possibly want was readily available—it had been a new extravagance to him and he'd decided he'd earned it.

In the first rush of making "real" money, Lucas had found ways to spend it. Having money that was *his,* that he had earned, had opened up new possibilities. Upon his return from Cancún, without Rachel's knowledge, Lucas had chosen a condo in Scottsdale. Alana had been with him the day he'd heard about it and she had gone with him to inspect it. She said it was exactly the sort of upscale place a young executive should be living in. Lucas signed the papers on the spot.

Later, when he told Rachel what he'd done, it was the first time he could remember that they actually argued about something. The graduation party had hurt her, but she had accepted it quietly. The condo had enraged her. She'd hated the place. Rachel hated that it was in Scottsdale, an impressive address Alana had said, but to Rachel, it meant she could no longer walk to campus. Instead, she would have to drive. In fact, she drove the old, battered car while Lucas tooled around in his new Lexus—a vehicle presented to him by his father to "polish his image."

Reluctantly Lucas now acknowledged that he hadn't considered Rachel's needs or preferences in that decision. *I should have known that anything Alana loved wouldn't suit Rachel,* he thought. *And I should have known better than to let Alana choose a home I expected to share with Rachel.*

Not that he had explained to Rachel who had helped him select it. No, Alana had made a point of telling her.

Lucas compressed his lips, years of training guiding his thoughts, leading him to tell himself what he had been repeatedly told—that Rachel could have tried to fit in with his new life. He'd only been asking for her support, and she had refused to give it. She wasn't cut out to be a corporate wife, just as his parents had said.

"Well, Luke, what do you think?" Alana's voice startled Lucas so that he jumped. Her hand rested on his thigh, suggestively close to his crotch yet hidden from view by the table. "Maybe you and I can share a cabin, hmm?"

"Share a cabin?"

"Yes, silly," she purred, easing her fingers up his leg. "Weren't you listening? Our corporate retreat this year is a Caribbean cruise. Ten days, nine nights. We could have a very good time, don't you think? We've never done a cruise before."

"And we won't be doing one now, Alana," he responded, removing her hand from his body, pleased that her effort was leaving him cold.

"Dad," he called out above the excited chatter. "I won't be attending this year. In fact, this is a good time to announce that I'm going to take some personal time off, starting immediately. I'm not sure how long I'll be away—" he rose to his feet, briefcase in hand "—but I will let you know as soon as I know."

Suddenly Lucas understood he would be devoting time to his daughter. Getting to know her. Maybe there'd be a way to get to know his wife again, too. His decision made, he walked to the door.

"Son—" his father's voice bounced off the walls "—you'll be explaining yourself to me."

"Yes, Dad, sometime I will."

Sitting at home, Lucas felt the truth begin to sink in.

"Cancer. Leukemia is a kind of cancer." Lucas said the words aloud, remembering that Rachel had said that very thing—but somehow the seriousness of her statement hadn't reached him. He understood it now.

After his father's status meeting, Lucas had left the office. He had stopped to bring home a three-meat submarine sandwich and now sat planted on his couch, sandwich remnants and bits of information packet scattered around him.

He had begun reading somewhat distractedly, part of his mind thinking about his lunch. The brochure had his full attention now, however. Words like *chemotherapy* and *radiation* kept jumping up at him. They weren't new words to him, of course. He was sharp enough to know they had something to do with cancer treatment. They had just never applied to someone he cared for before.

Over the next hour, he began to understand a little of what was really going on. He came to understand the critical role of bone marrow therapy in treating leukemia. He also came to understand how significant a suitable donor was in order for the procedure to be conducted.

He pored through the pages of explanations on tissue typing and donor matching. The brochure spelled it out: once BMT was determined to be possible, the patient would undergo intensive chemotherapy in an effort to kill the diseased bone marrow, after which the healthy donated bone marrow would be administered through an IV. In time, as the new bone marrow took hold, her immune system would recover and the leukemia would be cleared from her body.

Michaela would lose her hair again, what little delicate fuzz she had. And until the BMT took effect, she would be very fragile. She would need protection of the most intensive sort.

As he continued to read, he came to the section on AML where he was reminded of something else, something that both Rachel and Dr. Paul Graham had mentioned briefly. AML, he saw, tended to spread to major organs. He didn't want to contemplate this possibility with Michaela. The BMT just had to work.

Running a shaky hand through his hair, Lucas leaned back against the couch, closing his eyes. He felt utterly drained and powerless.

"No," he spoke aloud, "I may not be powerless. If I'm a donor match, there is something I'll be able to do."

Suddenly he caught an image of Rachel. The air zipped out of his lungs.

She would have received the diagnosis alone. She had coped alone and withstood what must have seemed like an onslaught of bad news. She had been tissue typed, only to learn she wasn't a match. She'd had her family typed and not found a good candidate in the bunch. She'd registered with donor registries. She'd arranged a donor drive. And she'd done all this, watching her child weaken due to the illness and also due to its treatment. All the while she'd known about the risk of the cancer spreading.

Lucas had always known Rachel was strong, but this was proof. As if he needed it.

She'd received the diagnosis alone. She had coped alone.

Until now. He was in the picture now and he could share this.

He had a responsibility—the word he hated, but the truth nevertheless. He could do better. He could start acting like a father, being there for his child the way he always should have been, making sure she had the support of two parents.

I can do this. I want to do it. I can be good at it, dammit.

Loving his daughter, loving Michaela, had come to him easily—quickly. Immediately, really, upon seeing her photograph and the obvious truth it reflected.

Lucas felt sure that Rachel wouldn't keep him from Michaela, not now. She had wanted him to know his daughter, had seen to it that their daughter knew who her father was. Rachel wouldn't hinder a father-daughter relationship, she would encourage it.

But what about Rachel herself? What about things between the two of them?

Clearly, the physical side of their relationship could still work. Had Rachel not shown reluctance at a key moment, Lucas was sure they would have consummated their relationship. Again.

And it would have been extraordinary.

Lucas couldn't remember the last time the scent of a woman had spawned desire within him. He couldn't remember the last time a kiss had left him desperate for more. Or when burying himself in a woman had seemed like the most necessary thing in the world.

It hadn't just been him, either. Rachel had wanted it, too. He knew it. He knew Rachel too well. She couldn't hide it from him. He'd felt the fire in her kiss, dammit. The longing in her body the minute he'd touched her.

It was natural, what happened between them. It always had been.

So why the reluctance?

She'd never been hesitant with him before. She'd been open and spontaneous and…wonderful.

It didn't need to be different now. They could recapture that, surely. Briefly Rick's words came to him: that something in Rachel had died when she'd left. If Rick couldn't figure it out, could he?

Whatever it was, they had to get past it. He had to convince her. Because he wanted her. And because then they could act like a family, something Lucas suddenly realized he wanted very badly. He didn't want them to act like divorced parents dealing with joint custody and visitation arrangements.

Hell, now we could actually become divorced parents. Lucas didn't like the thought, even though he'd suggested it to Rachel in anger—was it just yesterday?

Yet to be with Rachel and Michaela was the first thing that had felt right to Lucas in many years.

Rachel placed *The Cat in the Hat* on the seat next to her, gazing down at the child sleeping in her lap. She fingered the dark fuzz on Michaela's head, knowing that it would disappear again soon.

But that would be a good thing at this point, Rachel. It would mean Lucas is a donor match.

That was the irony of the thing. Michaela's hair would go if they were lucky enough to find a donor and could proceed with the BMT.

Rachel sought to reassure herself, knowing that watching a child suffer was the worst thing a parent could endure. She bent forward a little, just to where she could rest her head against that of the drowsy child. Rachel felt drowsy, too, but then, it *was* nearly her bedtime.

Lucas approached the atrium, confidently this time, yet quietly. He already understood that this was a haven for Rachel and Michaela, and that regardless of the role he might be able to play, it wasn't his right to intrude on this.

Standing in the doorway, he caught his breath. This was their first encounter since he'd decided he was going to be a *real* father, among other goals.

He was bound to feel…different. He stood watching. Watching Rachel gently stroke the child's face. Watching as her swirl of chocolate hair fanned out around them, acting like a shield between the child and the outside world. He supposed, in a way, that had been Rachel's function for Michaela. He scuffed his shoe on the floor then, making enough noise to announce his presence.

Rachel tipped her head slightly, until she had located her visitor. She'd known who it was, of course. Her personal radar didn't identify anyone but Lucas this particular way. She smiled softly, mouthing "Hello" at him.

Following her lead, he whispered, "Hello," and entered the room, heading toward them. He bent down to kiss Michaela's fuzzy head, surprised to find the gesture had occurred by itself, with no planning.

He reached out to caress Rachel's cheek then, a gesture that also occurred involuntarily. That she flinched away from him before contact was made was not what he would have hoped for.

He sat down, choosing a seat across from Rachel and Michaela.

"She is beautiful," he said awkwardly, although truthfully.

"Yes, she is," came Rachel's response. *"La niñita más linda del mundo."*

Lucas leaned back in his chair, clasping his hands behind his head, stretching his legs out in front of him. Rachel watched him curiously, privately appreciating the lean length of his body. Whatever he'd been doing these past few years, he hadn't gone soft.

"What does that mean?"

"What?" Having been absorbed in her perusal of Lucas, Rachel didn't understand his question.

"What you said then...*más linda* something."

"Oh." She smiled. "I didn't realize I'd said it. *La niñita más linda del mundo.* The most beautiful little girl in the world. But not just on the outside. Inside, too. You'll see that, one day." She hoped. Fervently.

He nodded, maintaining his relaxed, stretched-out position. Much to Rachel's discomfiture.

Hesitantly, forcing herself to look away, she asked, "You were able to schedule a blood test?"

"Yes," he said. "I had it done this morning."

"Oh." She was surprised. "We should know soon, then."

She smiled and admitted, "I guess I expected to see you when you came in for it. Then again, it gets hectic some days."

Abruptly Lucas leaned forward, elbows on his knees, resting his head on his clasped hands. Rachel sensed he wanted to speak, so she waited.

"Rachel, how did you know?" he finally asked.

A bewildered frown puckered her forehead. "What do you mean, Lucas?"

Sighing heavily, running his hands across his face and up into his hair, he backtracked. "I've spent the day reading the packets Dr. Campbell and Dr. Graham gave me. I'm finding out everything for the first time, and it's not the lightest reading I've ever done. You were told some time ago and I guess I'm wanting to understand, you know, how you found out—what made you start asking questions." He paused.

"I see," Rachel said, adjusting Michaela in her arms, talking softly so as not to disturb her. "Well, the first signs looked liked the flu. Nothing unusual at first. Then I started to realize that the flu wouldn't last as long as her symptoms. She was excessively tired, drained. Her joints would ache." She swallowed. "That was about six months ago. Maybe more. I've sort of lost track of the time." She took a deep breath. "Then I noticed she was bruising at the least little touch. I was...I was pretty sure about it then."

"Why?" Lucas demanded. "How could you know like that?"

"Lucas," she began patiently. "I'm a nurse. It's not the first time I've seen those symptoms. Unfortunately—" she grimaced "—it won't be the last, either. I knew what it looked like. I had the means to find out for certain, quickly. Of course," she added ruefully, "I hoped I was overreacting."

Lucas digested this, thinking her profession probably had helped, that the diagnosis would likely have been made early due to Rachel's watchful, professional eye. "So you brought her to PCH?"

"Yes," Rachel agreed. "As I said, I had my suspicions about what was wrong. I knew who to talk to, what had to be done for a diagnosis. We started chemotherapy very quickly, but as you know, it didn't help quite as we had hoped. BMT is the next step, if we can find a donor. But you know that, too.''

Her voice trailed off, and Lucas understood why.

''Rachel,'' he began gently, ''you know you'll have to take a leave of absence eventually. You'll need help. You'll have to take care of yourself, too.''

She didn't respond for several minutes. When she did, she kept her eyes trained on the window behind Lucas. ''Immediately after the procedure, she'll be in the hospital, more or less in isolation. It's called reverse barrier nursing, where the patient is kept isolated in order to protect her, rather than to protect everyone else from what she has. Her immune system will basically be destroyed, so she'll need the protection. Once it starts to rebuild and her numbers are high enough—that sort of thing—she'll be able to go home to live quietly as she regains her strength. To recuperate and convalesce. Then, particularly, I will need to be with her. I won't be able to work. I will need to take leave. I just haven't worked out how I'll do that, exactly.'' She sighed.

Knowing this was his opportunity, Lucas reached toward her, touching her hand. ''I'd like to help you, Rachel. I'd like to share it with you, handle things together. I'd like to act like a father.''

Rachel smiled, feeling a floating sensation in her stomach—a lightness that was foreign to her.

''I can't make up for all I've missed. I know that. But I can do better from now on. I can be there. We can work out the details later, but I'm telling you my intentions. I want to act like a father, Rachel. I want to *be* a father. I really want you to understand that.'' He had grown more confident as he spoke, knowing this discussion was nothing but an introduction to the subject.

Rachel nodded, momentarily unable to speak. She stared at Lucas, the only man she had ever loved, the man who had given her Michaela. Not for the first time, she wished things had been different.

''I'd be glad to have someone to share this with, Lucas. Of course I've had lots of family and friends helping me, doing whatever they can, but…none of them are her father.'' She sighed. ''I can't lie. It's been difficult. No, that doesn't even begin to explain it. Being so helpless. To be doing everything I could possibly do and yet see, with my own eyes, that it wasn't enough. Mostly—'' her voice wavered ''—mostly, I don't let myself think about...what's actually going on. I just...do what has to be done. I just live in the day....'' She let her voice trail away, a voice made husky by the tears she swallowed, tears that she wouldn't allow.

Lucas's gut lurched. Was that guilt he felt? Yes guilt, but mixed with fear for his daughter—and compassion for Rachel. ''I won't say something stupid like 'I understand.' I can't even begin to imagine.'' That was certainly the truth, Lucas knew. ''I realize that you've dealt with...some devastating realities alone. That is a fact that I wish I could change. But it will be different from now on. I will do better. I will be there. Okay?''

She nodded, not trusting her voice. She'd have a lot to think about later. Much later. She couldn't risk the vulnerable feelings that wanted to surface. Not right now. Later.

Silence ensued then, each of them lost in their own thoughts.

Looking at Lucas, Rachel finally asked, ''Would you like to hold her?''

''Yes.''

Carefully Rachel maneuvered her sleeping daughter into her father's arms. ''She's not heavy,'' she said.

Rachel sat down again, her regard steady on her daughter and her husband. He flicked a glance at Rachel, just long enough for her to see the darkening of his gray eyes—a sure sign of strong emotion. She saw him swallow and knew he was experiencing the unspeakable awe that comes from holding one's child for the first time.

Rachel, too, knew that feeling. Only, she had experienced it four years ago.

They sat there together for a while, not speaking, not needing to. Then they took Michaela back to her room and settled her in for the night.

Chapter 6

Her shift finally over, even with the extra bits that always followed it, Rachel decided to take a quick shower before changing clothes. While her life these days always had a slightly surreal edge to it, so much of her time being spent at the hospital, she tried to make a distinction between when she was officially on duty and when it was her own time. Casual clothes sometimes helped that illusion.

"Rachel!" The urgency in Lucas's voice conveyed itself to her immediately, chilling her, freezing her, sapping the color from her face, activating her on-demand self-control. "Rachel!"

She could hear him clearly, which led her to believe that he must have stepped into her office. Surely he wouldn't yell like that from the reception area?

She snapped off the water, toweling herself dry quickly, slipping into her jeans and rosebud-print blouse. "*Momentito,* Lucas!" she called back, unwittingly using Spanish, the language that often came to her when her emotions were frayed.

Taking a cleansing breath, she stepped into the office section of her quarters, still toweling her hair dry. "I'm here, Lucas. What is it?"

"Have you heard?"

Her face was carefully blank, prepared as she was for news she didn't want to hear. This was a routine she knew only too well—false, outwardly convincing calm.

"Of course you don't know yet." The words bubbled out of Lucas. He was clearly thrilled about something. Rachel let go a deep, slow breath, and with it, some of the tension that Lucas's voice had initially caused her.

This wasn't the look of a man bearing bad news.

He came toward her, taking the towel out of her hands, grabbing her by the shoulders, crushing her against his chest. "Rach, I'm a match!"

Pushing him away, her heart pounding, desperately needing some space, she looked at him dumbly. "A match?"

"Yes," he said, pulling her against him again, rocking her, spinning her in a dance she couldn't feel. "The results came through early this morning. I can donate. Dr. Campbell called me about seven-thirty. Does the man ever sleep? Anyway, I got dressed and came right over. I wanted to tell you, face-to-face, not just over the phone. Do we tell Michaela now? What do you want to do?"

"Gracias a Dios," she whispered, pushing herself free of him, hugging her arms around herself, shakily touching numb fingers to her cheeks. "Are you sure? Really sure? Evan called you? He said you can donate?"

Puzzled, he responded nevertheless. "Yes. Yes. Isn't that what I'm saying?"

Rachel tried to pace, but her jelly-filled legs wouldn't cooperate. She was shaking, couldn't make it stop. She reached for her cell phone, punching the number that would call Evan, getting through on the second ring. "It's true, then, Evan? Really?"

He confirmed it for her, and she started trying to punch out other numbers. *"Dios,"* she muttered, "I can't push the buttons."

Lucas took the phone from her, setting it down on the table. "Rachel," he said, grasping her hands—hands that were ice-cold and still shaking. "Hey, sweetheart, relax." He knew this was adrenaline, pure and simple, and that Rachel needed soothing. Shock could be that way.

Rachel could not allow the contact, wrenching herself away from him. "I've told you not to touch me!" she gasped, then turned, nearly running from her office.

Ostensibly she wanted to confirm the other arrangements. After all, it was important that things were handled properly. The donation procedure did have to be arranged. Michaela's pre-BMT chemo had to be arranged. There was a countdown of sorts involved before the new marrow could be administered; it was a highly sequenced process.

Still, that didn't explain her panic, her sense that she simply had to escape. Escape Lucas?

And Lucas knew it. She couldn't fool him. Moments later, when she returned to her office, she didn't know what to say to him. How could she possibly explain? And he'd cornered her. Or at least she'd felt cornered.

"Why, Rachel? Why do you act like my touch is something you simply cannot tolerate?"

"Because I can't tolerate it, Lucas."

"But you can. You more than tolerate it. You respond. That's just it. You do respond. Why shouldn't you? We're normal, healthy adults. We have a history together. You admitted that the chemistry is still there. What's the problem?"

"I don't know how to explain, Lucas," she offered a little desperately. "I'm not playing games. That's not my way. But...physical things...don't happen for me. I can't do it." She ran a trembling hand through her hair. "We'll be seeing each other, yes. If you're going to be in Michaela's life, we will see each other. But I can't pretend that everything between us is okay and normal, like nothing...happened...before."

"We wouldn't be where we are, Rachel, if *something* hadn't happened between us before."

"Yes, I know. But I can't take up where we left off, Lucas. For me, there's a lot that's unresolved between us. Sex won't fix that. And I can't be...a convenient diversion for you, either. Just because we're going to be together, at times, doesn't mean I can...be with you that way, too. You've gained a daughter, you can be a father now, but—" she stopped, shaking her head "—I haven't actually regained a husband. Not really. And I'm not the type who can separate sex from emotion. Sex isn't casual or recreational for me."

Lucas began to feel angry. "When I came to you this morning to tell you about Michaela, I wasn't thinking about sex. That was a different kind of emotion entirely."

"Yes, yes it was. I'll accept that. But I can't turn to you for my emotional support, either, Lucas. I don't know how. I've been alone a long time, dealing with things. My self-reliance was hard-won, and it won't disappear overnight."

"Okay, I accept that," he said, echoing her words.

He left it at that, which she was thankful for. They had a lot to work out, but she wasn't ready to try yet. Everything was still too raw. And she had Michaela to deal with, as always.

"*Bueno,*" Rachel told the darkness, "I can't sleep. Fine. I admit it." Glancing at her bedside clock, she noted that it was just after six-thirty in the evening, so the darkness was still somewhat artificial.

She sat up in bed, pulling herself to sit cross-legged. She'd been trying to fall asleep for several hours, tossing and turning. Insomnia was no stranger to her. In fact, it had become her constant companion lately, so this wasn't exactly unusual.

But it wasn't just insomnia this time. She was simply too keyed-up to sleep. Too many jumbled emotions.

Replaying the day surely for the millionth time, Rachel found herself stuck on the moment Lucas had stepped into her office. How her fear had turned to joy so immediately. She still couldn't quite believe what was happening, including the intense presence of her husband in her life again.

Her thoughts kept going around and around.

The best news was that Michaela would get the treatment she needed.

The next best news was that Michaela would have a father in her life now.

And, if Rachel was honest, learning to share parenthood with Lucas wouldn't be the worst thing she'd ever done. Not easy, but worth it. She'd told him she couldn't give up her self-reliance lightly, and she knew that was true. Even in this case, when the other party was Michaela's father, Rachel knew it would be difficult to share. No matter how welcome it might be.

That was one of the conflicts she faced. She missed being part of a couple—she'd told Tanisha that. She did miss it. She was alone too much, she was too isolated. As a woman, not just as a mother. But letting someone else in—or more precisely, letting someone *back* in—was no simple thing.

Rachel had learned to turn inward, to keep to herself whatever she was feeling. Releasing her grip wouldn't be natural. It wouldn't be quick. She could see that already.

She hadn't been involved with anyone since Lucas, although she'd had opportunities. She had simply been unable to participate in a relationship that headed in a physically—or emotionally—intimate direction.

How could being together again be so easy for him? Had Lucas actually been unhappy in their marriage? He'd never said so. He'd apparently been content, having his cake and eating it, too, as the saying went. That would explain why the transition back to seeing each other was simple for him. He was capable of things she couldn't do.

Even his touch threatened her. It threatened to stir emotions that she couldn't allow to be disturbed. For Rachel, it was a form of survival. Lucas would have to respect that.

But right now, Rachel couldn't sleep. All this craziness was keeping her awake.

Joy was there, joy at Michaela's best chance. Hesitant joy, now that the initial rush had worn off and Rachel knew what lay ahead. Michaela's next experiences would likely be even worse than the ones she'd had so far. Could any mother ignore that? Rachel knew she couldn't, even though she understood better than most that this really was, all things considered, Michaela's best chance.

About Lucas as a father—well, Rachel could tell that his joy and relief for Michaela were genuine. Rachel had no doubts about his desire to help Michaela—or about his sincerity in wanting to be a real father to her.

But Rachel had locked away so much when things had ended with Lucas. It had taken all her strength to admit defeat in their marriage. She had suffered in her decision to hope for the best when things began going wrong, and she had suffered when she finally knew she couldn't tolerate it anymore. That realization, that decision, had been as much for her unborn child as it had been for herself. Certainly, she had known that she wanted better for her child than what Lucas was offering then.

She had wanted what Lucas was offering now. For Michaela.

Images of Lucas and Michaela—a recovered Michaela—together, doing father-daughter things both thrilled and tormented Rachel. Of course she wanted a normal father-daughter life for Michaela. She was secure enough in her relationship with her daughter that she didn't fear Michaela would somehow prefer Lucas to her—although she knew how charming Lucas could be and he certainly didn't have the financial restrictions Rachel had. That was another detail that would have to be addressed.

What worried Rachel was that it would be so easy to pretend they were a normal family, doing normal family things. So easy to believe it. And she must not. She couldn't risk her emotions—her heart—in that way.

It wasn't a game. At least, not to Rachel. Marriage—her marriage to Lucas—it meant something to her.

A floating feeling was back in her stomach.

Sort of like feathers, blowing around inside me, stirring and rippling, she decided, then laughed aloud.

Dios mio, *Rachel, you're describing excitement and it sounds like you're describing nausea. You are sometimes too much of a nurse.*

But the feeling continued and so did her thoughts. Could she handle Lucas in her life, somehow live with it for Michaela's sake?

"But then, maybe Lucas doesn't have that in mind," she muttered, even though her conscience prodded her for such uncharitable thinking. For now she needed to let herself continue in that vein. "For Lucas, 'being there' for Michaela could mean handing money to me, then taking her out for grand adventures in the tradition of good-time daddies who share nothing in the daily responsibility of their children."

She bit her lip. Lucas wouldn't do that sort of thing. That was her old pain, her old disappointment, her very serious problem with trusting Lucas, rearing its head. That reaction protected her against the vision of the three of them playing happy family. Sharing decisions, good times—not just tough times—with their daughter. She knew it couldn't be like that.

They'd been living separate lives for five years. If she hadn't shown up at his office, they would still be living separate lives. Nothing would have changed. That he seemed attracted to her physically meant nothing. Especially to him.

A thought came to Rachel: *What if there's someone else in his life? Didn't he ask me, first thing, if I was ready for a divorce?* Dios mio, *what if he is ready?*

Rachel didn't care to examine that question. Glaring at her clock, she considered calling someone—someone who could help her get out of the funk she was in. *Mamá?* Her brother? Tanisha?

That brought to mind what Tanisha had said about working things out, how she and Wayne had done right by their daughter. What were her words? *I had to give him up.* Or something like that. That had been the key for them. Maybe it was the key for Rachel also.

Tanisha had admitted to herself that love wasn't what their marriage had been about, and once she'd let go of that notion, she'd become friends with her husband. Ex-husband. And they'd worked things out. This all sounded very good, like a reasonable blueprint to follow. Except for one thing. Rachel couldn't say her marriage hadn't been about love, because it had been. And she was very afraid that for her it might *still* be.

Rachel fluffed up her pillow and lay down again. She had only three hours before she needed to get ready for her shift. She shut her eyes, knowing she had little hope of sleeping during that time.

Chapter 7

Easing his sore hip onto the couch, Lucas slowly dropped into a semireclined position. The site where they had taken the bone marrow was sore. No doubt about it.

They had warned him that the discomfort—hell, the pain—would be worst when the full effects of the epidural had worn off. He figured that had happened by now. Hopefully the pain wouldn't get worse than this.

The procedure had been conducted early in the morning and gone pretty much according to the textbook descriptions he'd received. He'd been given the option of staying the night, but had decided against it, eventually taking a taxi home. Once his legs had been able to function, he had looked in on Michaela and then taken a moment to tell Rachel it had been done.

Wincing as he stretched his leg, he reached over to pick up the pills Dr. Campbell had prescribed, eyeing them suspiciously. Lucas held a deep distrust of painkillers—his partying had never gone in that direction.

Discarding the pills, he reached instead toward the case of beer he had placed on the table, ripping it open and selecting a can. At least with alcohol he knew what to expect. Opening the can, he took a long sip of the cold beverage and automatically reached for the package of cigars lying next to the beer. Smoking when he drank had become a habit for him, one he hadn't noticed until this moment. And at this moment he didn't want a cigar. Not at all. In fact, he realized, he hadn't wanted a cigar since the morning Rachel arrived at his office. This was the first pack he'd bought since then.

He tossed the unopened package back onto the table and drank again from the can. He sincerely hoped this approach to painkilling would take the edge off the throbbing in his hip.

Michaela's treatment was going according to plan, her pre-BMT chemotherapy having been completed and her body nearly ready to receive the transplant. The doctors and Rachel seemed pleased with her progress, but Lucas was deeply shocked by what he had seen.

Michaela looked horrible, he thought. He remembered his reaction when he had first seen Michaela's catheter, the little device piercing the delicate skin of her chest and semipermanently attached to her body. His horror had been total. He understood the catheter's role now, that everything Michaela needed—including the chemotherapy drugs—could be administered through it, providing some relief from frequent needle pokes.

But at the time he had been overwhelmed. Rachel had grabbed his arm and pushed him into the corridor with a strength that had stunned him. She had been furious, a rare occurrence. Even more rare, she had touched him, albeit in anger.

"Don't ever let her see you react like that, Lucas," she had spat at him, never mind that she was whispering. "I warned you that things could get ugly. The doctors and the information packets said the same thing. Michaela can handle everything if she knows everyone around her can handle it. We have to be matter-of-fact, even if we don't feel it. We have to be strong for her. If you can't cope, stay away."

She had thrown his arm back at him and stalked back toward Michaela's room, the tension visibly leaving her body as she crossed the threshold. That had been a test for Lucas. He had composed himself and returned to his daughter's bedside. He desperately hoped nothing else would tempt him to react in a similar way. Strength was taking on a new meaning.

Chemotherapy really did produce side effects, and those side effects could be brutal. He was seeing this firsthand, for the first time. Michaela, who had been thin to begin with, seemed to have lost more weight. She was paler than she should be. And, of course, she was bald. She didn't even have eyelashes or eyebrows. Lucas hadn't expected that. This change—the hairlessness—had seemed instantaneous to him. Literally, that one day, her hair was simply gone, although he couldn't be sure if it had really happened like that.

In response, he was thinking about shaving his head. He didn't know if this would call unwanted attention to Michaela's state, or if it would demonstrate solidarity to her. "Maybe I should ask Rachel about it," he pondered aloud.

His thoughts drifted to the encounter he'd had with his brother-in-law. Lucas had tried to shake it off, but parts came back to him and wouldn't leave him alone.

The hell of it was that Rick was right, at least partly. Lucas had never put any value on how Rachel felt about his behavior or how other people might view it. Mostly because Lucas himself had never really thought about it. He had just done what was expected. Or, at least, what was expected by his parents. Certainly not what was expected by Rachel.

Lucas reached for another can of beer.

Voices in the corridor outside his apartment caught his attention. Moving to sit up, he immediately fell back to the couch, his head fuzzy and his hip throbbing. Glancing at the table, he realized he had already made his way through more cans of beer than he'd thought, and had consumed very little food to supplement it.

The voices in the hall made him look up again, just in time to see his parents walk into his condo. Cursing the day he'd given them a key, he smiled and said, "Good evening, Mother, Dad. What brings you here?"

"Are you drunk, Lucas?" Although she didn't add it verbally, Lucas could hear the tsk-tsk in his mother's voice.

"No, just a little fuzzy."

By way of response, she hmphed at him. Eyeing him critically, taking in his condition, she said, "We're here to get some straight answers from you, Lucas, so if you're in no shape to give them, say so now."

"Straight answers?" *Good God, what's on their agenda to-night?* Lucas could only wonder.

"Yes, son," his father's voice boomed at him. Arnold Neuman had already grabbed a beer for himself and was opening the package of cigars Lucas had discarded earlier. "You've not been yourself lately, what with missing work, this 'personal leave' thing, questioning my decisions in front of the rest of the staff—"

"Not to mention Rachel having the gall to show up at the office," his mother said. "I can't imagine what possessed her to do that." She shuddered. "And then finding you here, like this—" she wrinkled her nose "—when you should have been at the office today. Yes, Lucas, we want to know what's going on. It's time for some explanations."

"Well, Mother, Dad," Lucas said, "if you want to ask questions, go ahead. I'll answer if I can or—" he paused, surprised to realize that he was challenging them "—or if I want to."

"Well, you see, Lucas," his father resumed, "we've been having you followed."

Lucas's eyes narrowed but he said nothing.

"Yes, we felt it was our responsibility. We needed to come here with as much information as we could gather—ammunition, if you like—so that you wouldn't be able to lie to us."

"I've never been in the habit of lying, Dad. As I said, if I can see where what you want to know is any of your business, I'll tell you."

"Well, Lucas, let's start by saying that we know you've been going to the hospital. We want to know why."

Inwardly Lucas groaned, briefly acknowledging that his father hadn't been bluffing.

"Are you ill, Lucas?" Something in his mother's voice made him meet her eyes. She was standing still, keeping her distance from both Lucas and his father. Lucas caught a glimpse of something in her face—was it fear? Whatever it was, for an instant she did not look like the cool, cultured, distant woman he knew as his mother. Lines of concern, of worry, showed on her face. Despite the efforts of one of Phoenix's best plastic surgeons to remove any trace of age from Sophie Neuman's face, it had briefly shown.

Deciding to go for the truth, Lucas said, "I have a child."

For a second both parents were stunned. They were speechless. His father released a long plume of cigar smoke, then went remarkably pale. Clearly, this answer had not been anticipated.

Various emotions warred with each other on his mother's face. Lucas suspected real emotions were in conflict with the emotionless persona she had learned to wear.

"A child!" she finally breathed, clasping her hands in front of her. "How perfectly delightful! Did you hear that, Arnold? I'm a grandmother. Finally!"

Arnold Neuman grunted, his facial color returning only as two red splotches on his cheeks. Sophie Neuman was now wringing her hands, but Lucas had to admit that she seemed genuinely pleased. Like a child who'd just been allowed to buy cotton candy at the circus.

Sophie began to chatter. "Well, Lucas, who is she? Who is the child's mother? There's no reason you shouldn't marry her, you know. In fact, it's so important that you do. It's simply the best thing. We don't need months of planning to present an appropriate wedding, under the circumstances. After all, your first marriage was the big 'do.' A second marriage, well, it's simply tacky to make that into the grand event that a first marriage requires. Although, of course, Pauline Hendrickson did that for her daughter. But, really, it was just awful. Pauline acted like the first wedding had never occurred, like Marilyn was a blushing bride who deserved to wear white—and everyone there knew she'd only been divorced a few weeks and that her first wedding had been less than a year before. Why, Alice Johnstone said some of the gifts from the first wedding weren't even out of the boxes yet—not to mention that her new groom had been the best man at the first wedding." She shuddered for dramatic emphasis. "No, I wouldn't want to do anything so classless, but we could do something small and tasteful, maybe even at home. And then have a large reception, down at the club, Arnold, and introduce the child and the new bride to everyone—"

"Mother." Lucas cut her off, not wanting to hear any more babble about weddings. "Mother, I'd have to get a divorce from the first wife before I take a second wife." He paused, watching as his words took effect. "And since Rachel is the child's mother, and the marriage still stands, I don't see the need to do anything.''

Silence again dropped over the room.

''Are you saying that you're still married to Rachel?'' his mother whispered.

Lucas nodded.

''So you are saying that you and Rachel have a child?''

Again Lucas nodded.

Getting to his feet, Arnold Neuman approached Lucas, his fury bursting from every red pore, his black eyes boring holes into Lucas's soul. ''Now listen here, boy,'' he began, stabbing his finger in Lucas's face, ''I know that when Rachel came to the office the other day, that was the first time you'd seen her in many years. I know that.''

''How do you know that?'' Lucas wasn't sure he wanted to hear the answer.

''I keep up on your activities,'' his father stated unabashedly. ''I know you like a pretty face and a well-cut body from time to time. Or at least you used to. Beginning to wonder what's wrong with you in that department. Don't see you with women much these days—'' He stopped, apparently realizing that his audience wasn't interested in that line of discussion. ''But more to the point, I know that Rachel hasn't been in your bed since she walked out. God only knows who she's been with—not too careful about where they get it, those kind—but I know she hasn't been with you. *You* haven't been with her. I'd have put a stop to that in a hurry, yessirree. I'd have got her away from you. Just like I did before. So, if she's turned up with a baby, we both know the kid can't possibly be yours. She knows it, too. You haven't been with her in years, boy. So, we can fight her with every legal angle we can come up with, something to force her down where she belongs, something to make her realize that she shouldn't have crossed swords with me, that she should have accepted her place, accepted what was offered to her all those years ago.''

His black eyes were gleaming. He obviously relished his plans. ''She never did get it. But neither did you. She wasn't for you. You could have kept her around, in luxury if she wanted. You could have had her and Alana both—you just married the wrong one. That'd've been a great setup for you. I bet that little Rachel's something—''

''That's enough, Dad.'' Lucas cut in, hearing for the first time the strange mixture of contempt and desire in his father's voice when he talked about Rachel, wondering if his mother could hear it, too, wondering if Rachel had ever heard it. ''You're assuming she's presented me with a baby, which she hasn't. The little girl is four. There is simply no question that she is mine.''

Recovering quickly, his father said, ''Then we'll hit Rachel with every possible legality to get custody of the kid—''

''No, Dad, we won't. We will not threaten Rachel, with legalities or otherwise. She is the mother of my child and will be treated with respect. By both of you. As will the child.'' He felt protective of both of them and saw no reason for things to go down an ugly path.

''We could offer her money, Lucas.'' His mother's voice was quiet.

''For what?'' Lucas couldn't help snapping at her.

''For the child, of course. To give you the child to raise, to break the influence of her family and to get Rachel out of your life. Finally.''

''But we'd have to demand proof of paternity—''

''We will not try to buy the child from her,'' Lucas interrupted. ''Rachel's a good mom to her, and I wouldn't let anyone say otherwise. I would fight you, Dad. And I do have proof of paternity. In a number of forms, not to mention the fact that she looks like me.'' Lucas ran a hand through his hair and tried to ease the position of his hip. He reached for a can of beer, noting that his father was already making his own dent in the supply. Lucas set the can back on the table. He had dulled the pain in his hip, and had no interest in a round of drinking with his father.

''So the child is a girl.'' His mother's whispered remark was so soft that Lucas almost didn't hear her.

''Yes, my daughter is named Michaela,'' Lucas supplied. He took a deep breath. ''You need to understand, perhaps, that Michaela is not well. She's been, well, living in the hospital really. I've been visiting her regularly ever since Rachel came to the office.''

"Ah," his father said knowingly. "So, you didn't know about her. This kid is *news* to you."

"I didn't know about her before, that's true. I'd like to think I would have made some different choices if I'd known about her. But I'm not sure I would have. I hate myself for that, but it's the truth." Running his hand through his hair again, he continued. "This morning, I donated bone marrow for her. I'm the only compatible donor they've found, and that, Dad, is very compelling proof of paternity. If I needed it, which I don't."

Adjusting his hip again, he said, "So, yes, Mother, I probably am a little drunk. But it's an effort to dull the ache I've got in my hip where they took the bone marrow from. As an alternative to that bottle of pills—" he motioned toward the table "—that the doctor gave me. It's not because I take time off work in order to lie around, drinking the afternoon away. It's medicinal." He smiled thinly. "And that's something Dad can't claim."

Lucas looked at his parents then, knowing he was perhaps seeing them for the first time in his life. He could see what everyone else saw in his father. What Rachel had seen, what her brother, Rick, had obviously seen, as well. Arnold Neuman was a cold man. He thought of his own interests first. Hell, maybe he *only* thought of his own interests.

His father had never treated his mother very well, Lucas knew that. He'd known that as a child. When he'd been old enough to have an inkling of comprehension about sex, he'd understood that his father had not found fidelity in his marriage necessary on his part. Discretion wasn't exactly his strong suit. Some years later Lucas had realized that his mother had been fully aware of his father's infidelity, and that she had tolerated it because—why, exactly?

Because she'd been raised to believe that a "good" marriage was her crowning achievement in life. And that *good* meant a husband with the right status, preferably with money. It had nothing to do with love, or even friendly feelings towards the life partner. Lucas had never accepted that definition of a good marriage. It was why he had married Rachel. Suddenly he needed to know—he needed to ask something he'd never actually asked his parents before. He needed to hear the words, point-blank.

"Why have you always objected so strongly to Rachel as my wife?"

His parents exchanged glances.

"Because she was wrong for you, Lucas. She wasn't one of us. Given her background, she never could be one of us." His mother stated her answer calmly, coolly. She was again wearing the mask that Lucas knew only too well.

"Why not?"

"Why not? To begin with, they were *working class,* dear. It was in her mentality." Sophie shook her head, her blond highlights shimmering slightly in the fading light. "That's why we would need to assume responsibility for the child, Lucas, immediately. We can't change what she actually is, but we can teach her to be something else."

"Did you hear what you just said, Mother?" Lucas was incredulous. He'd *known,* of course, how they felt, but he'd never heard it stated so boldly. Or maybe he hadn't listened quite like this.

His mother just looked at him blankly, so he changed tack. "Dad's from working class, too, Mother. Why is that okay?'

"Because he rose above it, dear. The need to work, the manual level of work, *that* went out a generation or so ago. We can teach your daughter—it can be learned." She smiled benignly.

Dismissing Rachel's parents' occupations, veterinarian and schoolteacher, as manual labor wasn't appropriate, but Lucas decided not to pursue the point. His parents wouldn't get it, anyway.

"And, besides, boy, I come from solid German stock. So does your mother, with that little bit of English mixed in. We've got something to work with, you know, genetically speaking."

"Rachel is *Mexican.*" Sophie said the word as if it were a disease—quickly, distantly—as if she were afraid of catching something if she held it in her mouth too long. "She was always lovely in an unrefined way, but that was exactly the problem. She had no sophistication, no *understanding* of things. A corporate wife, a society woman, needs those qualities. Just look at Alana. Alana was raised with the proper values."

"In other words, she understands how to be an ornament.

That she should never bother anyone with thoughts she might be having, that it's better to simply pander to her man, saying whatever she thinks he wants to hear. Or what might impress other people. She dresses well, knows the right people—but never stops to consider if any of that matters to her. It's enough that someone else told her it matters. She's a socialite, with the emphasis on *light.* In her color and in her mind."

"Why, Lucas, what a cynical thing to say." Sophie was taken aback. "I'm a corporate wife, Lucas. I'm a society woman. I know my place, my role. Do you see me as an ornament, someone who is nothing but a man's accessory? A socialite?"

Lucas studied his mother a moment before answering, noticing her bubble of coiffeured ash-blond hair, her perfectly applied makeup, her exquisite jewelry that served as the ideal complement to her casually understated designer pantsuit.

"Yes, actually, Mother, it is how I see you. You are an asset to your husband. And you would never suggest that you had an independent thought, one that wouldn't agree with your husband's position. Yes, that's exactly how I see you."

God, he thought, *maybe I am a little drunk. Surely it's alcohol that's loosened my tongue?*

"Well, Lucas," she said, "you couldn't be more wrong. I just know who—and what—I am. I wouldn't try to be something I'm not. I wouldn't try to force myself on anyone outside of my proper place. Unlike Rachel. She had nerve, but that's all I'll say for her." She picked up her purse. "I think we still have plenty to discuss. After all, if you have proof this little girl is your daughter, we're her grandparents. We should have access to her, if not control over her. But I think it's time we left you alone for the evening. I'll just go powder my nose, then I'll be ready to leave. Okay, Arnold?"

She disappeared down the hallway, having chosen the most delicate phrasing for her activity. As always.

Arnold drained his latest can of beer—Lucas wondering briefly if his father intended to drive—and leaned forward in his chair, toying idly with the empty container. "I know what you saw in Rachel, my boy. Any real man would see it. You married her, made her my daughter-in-law, but...well, I didn't feel fatherly toward her. No I never did. She's the kind of woman a man can't help but notice. That fiery Latin temperament.'' He paused, shaking his head in admiration. ''Mexican women, they're taught to be that way. It's in their blood of course, but they are *taught* to please a man—''

''Dad, I told you already not to talk about Rachel like that. I am married to her. She is the mother of my child. Don't talk about her like she's...cheap. She isn't.''

''Now, don't work yourself into a lather, boy. I'm just saying that, as a man, I see certain qualities in Rachel—you know, that I appreciate certain of her attributes.'' He paused to examine the label on his beer can, thoughtfully, speculatively. ''Yessirree, I appreciate her.'' He took another deep look at his empty can, then finally set it down.

Lucas examined his father, noting there was a gleam in his eyes that Lucas didn't like. It was too soon for it to be solely alcohol induced. ''A woman like your mother, Lucas,'' his father continued, ''she's just not going to understand the appeal of a woman like Rachel. A man, though, yeah, he will. He'll want what she's got. Still,'' Arnold sounded philosophical, ''you screwed up when you married her. You could have kept Rachel around—I've told you that before. There's ways. Hell, I sure wouldn't have let her go. Couldn't blame you for wanting her.''

Arnold turned conspiratorial. ''I know something about Mexicans, too, you know. I know what they're like. In fact, we had a maid one time—Rosa was her name. Now she was delightful. She was with us for several years, until your mother put a stop to it. Said I could do what I liked, but not under her roof. So Rosa had to go. I was more careful after that.''

Horrified, Lucas realized he knew who his father meant. He remembered Rosa, wondered how willing a partner she had been. She hadn't been much older than Lucas himself.

''But you don't marry them, son. That's not their purpose.'' He winked at Lucas. Sophie returned just then and Arnold stood up.

''Look,'' Lucas said, feeling compelled to state his position, ''whatever you think of Rachel's family tree, keep in mind that my daughter shares it. You'll be polite about it.''

''Lucas, please understand we only have your best interests in mind. You have to be careful, concerned about your heirs,

Lucas. That was truly the main reason you shouldn't have married Rachel. But—'' his mother inclined her head ''—there is a child now, a child you are willing to claim, so we'll have to do what we can to mask her…heritage.''

''No, Mother, we will not mask her heritage. I am not ashamed, in any way, of Rachel or Michaela.''

''Blood will tell, son. You've been sprung from our line. You'll see right. You have before, after all. You've just got stars in your eyes because of this kid. That'll fade.'' Arnold held out his arm to escort Sophie to the door. ''Don't bother to get up. We'll talk again when you're feeling more yourself.''

He was alone again. The silence was deafening. It made his thoughts seem louder. Again he wondered about Rachel and his father. He had known prejudice existed, but it had never occurred to him before that part of his father's bias was sexual. Had he ever acted on the attraction? Lucas couldn't consider it.

Rachel was on his mind again. Rachel had changed. Rick had said so, had given examples. Had blamed Lucas for those changes.

But Rick had mentioned something else, too, something that gave Lucas pause. Rick had said that the changes in Rachel weren't obvious on the outside. But that those who loved her could see the difference. He, Lucas, had seen the difference, almost immediately.

What did that mean?

Chapter 8

"So, Rachel," said Dr. Paul Graham, "is Michaela settling into her new abode?"

Rachel was sitting with Michaela, watching her daughter sleep. Her new abode was the private room where she would be staying following her BMT procedure, until she was sufficiently recovered to go home. Traffic from other patients, staff and visitors, would be minimal, and those would did enter would be required to wear protective clothing—including face masks—for Michaela's benefit.

"Yes," Rachel answered, "I think she knows this is her place for a while. She's just so..." Her voice trailed away as her eyes wandered back to her sleeping child.

"I know," Paul said, patting Rachel on the shoulder.

The bond between Paul and Rachel was strong. Paul was an attractive man, his fitness and blond good looks suggesting he could easily be younger than his fifty-two years. But Rachel had never noticed that. She simply saw Paul as her friend, had immediately placed him as a sort of adopted uncle—as *familia.* Michaela, as young as she was, understood *familia,* and knew that Paul belonged there, too.

"Everything's set to begin in the morning, Rachel." Paul

moved to stand in front of her. "Rachel, look at me." She turned her head, and he continued. "You know that you are not working tonight. You must sleep. You will sleep."

"Yes, I know," Rachel said, nodding her head slightly. She knew Paul was talking about more than just this night. "I know I need to take some leave, Paul. I've arranged it, but I've also left an option to work if I really need to. Working has saved my sanity through this, and I may need that again."

Sensing that Paul was about to argue with her, she continued quickly, "I know I can't be her primary nurse, Paul, even when she gets home. I know I'll need to sleep sometimes. My family will help me. They always have. But I need to get through this a little bit at a time. I have to deal with the moment as best I can. Anything else has to wait."

Paul looked at her thoughtfully, then nodded. "Okay, Rachel." He leaned over to kiss her forehead. "I'll leave you to it, then. Get some reasonable sleep tonight. I mean it." His smile removed the sternness from the words, and yet—he did mean it. Rachel knew it.

Not for the first time, thankfulness rushed over her. The circle of family and friends who had stood by her and helped her was special indeed. She knew some very good people.

As Paul moved toward the door, Rachel glanced behind him into the reception area. A commotion had caught her eye. As she made sense of the situation the color drained from her face.

"No," she whispered, jumping to her feet and pushing past Paul, out of Michaela's room, automatically shutting the miniblinds on her way out. "*Dios mio,* no. No, no, no, no."

She yanked the mask away from her face, nearly running to the reception desk, a worried and baffled Paul right behind her.

"No!" she cried, her voice strangled, as she approached. "No. These two people—" she motioned toward Arnold and Sophie Neuman, who stood with Lucas beside the reception counter "—these two people are not allowed in here. Paul—" she turned to face him "—I'm not joking. They will not be Michaela's visitors. They will *not.*"

"Of course, Rachel," he responded without hesitation.

"Oh, now, girl." Arnold's voice rumbled over everyone else. "No need to act like that. We're family and we're here to see that child. You can't stop us. We've got rights. You should know that.''

''Actually, Arnold, I can stop you. And I am.''

''Don't push me, girl.'' Arnold waggled a finger in Rachel's face.

Slapping his hand away, Rachel said, ''Do not threaten me, Arnold. Do not even pretend to touch me. Do you understand?''

Looking at Lucas, who had apparently brought his parents, she said, ''In my office, Lucas, now. All three of you.'' Looking at Paul, knowing his support would be needed to resolve the situation, she said, ''Please come, too.''

Once inside her office, Rachel made the necessary introductions. ''These are Lucas's parents, Paul. Arnold and Sophie Neuman. And they are not to visit Michaela, not under any circumstances.''

Arnold moved closer to Rachel, sliding his arm around her shoulder. ''Now, now—''

With a finesse that could only come from long practice, Rachel whirled out of the attempted embrace, her hand shooting out to smack Arnold across the face. ''I told you, you lecherous pig, do not touch me. I have tolerated a lot from you, Arnold, and we both know it. I refuse to put up with you anymore. Do you understand? No more.''

Looking at Sophie, including her in her remarks, she said, ''I don't owe you two anything. I know you're not here because you suddenly have warm, grandparently feelings for my daughter. The last thing she needs, the very last thing she needs, is to be paraded in front of anyone like some sort of zoo animal. I will not allow it.''

''Don't try to throw your weight around, girl,'' Arnold began. ''You don't have that kind of power.''

''First, Arnold, my name is Rachel. Secondly, I do have that kind of power. Thirdly, I am using it. You will not be granted access to Michaela.''

As Arnold began to sputter again, Paul cut off his attempt to speak. ''Actually, Mr. Neuman, Rachel's right. She is the patient's parent. She is also head of nursing at PCH. She has that power, Mr. Neuman. As Michaela's doctor, I wholly support Rachel's opinion on that matter. She is exactly right. The patient's well-being is my first concern. If Rachel believes your presence would be counterproductive, then you won't be allowed in.''

''Now, really,'' Arnold boomed, his finger wagging in Paul's face this time. ''I'll talk to my lawyer about this.''

''You're certainly at liberty to do that, Mr. Neuman. However, you will find that the courts are very reluctant to authorize anyone to threaten a patient's well-being, particularly when the patient is a child. They follow our counsel in these matters. This type of situation is not new to us, Mr. Neuman, but it appears to be new to you. You do not understand your position.''

Now Rachel was facing Lucas. ''And you! *Dios mio,* Lucas, what were you thinking? No, wait—'' she held up her hand, traffic-cop fashion ''—I know better than to ask you that—because you never think, do you? Why should you bother to think when you have your parents to do it for you?''

Rage that had been bottled up for years was spilling out. ''You waltz in here, proclaiming you want to do right as Michaela's father and then you do this? Is it possible, somehow, that you do not understand Michaela's situation? Why the hell would you bring them—'' she gestured accusingly at his parents ''—two people who have never caused anything but strife between us? Why bring them here, so that they can terrorize our daughter the way they have always done me? Think, Lucas, for once. See what's actually there! Take off those damn blinders!''

Rachel heard her own voice, stunned that the words could fly from her mouth so quickly. They were words she had never uttered before. But they had festered for many years. And she had never felt so angry in her life.

''Do you realize why you brought your parents here, Lucas? Do you understand why?''

''Rachel—'' Lucas tried to speak, but Rachel was having none of it.

''Lucas, you brought your parents here because it was easier than telling them no. It was what they wanted, and you always do what they want, no matter who it might hurt.''

She was panting, her color high and her eyes flashing. And she was on a roll. ''For you, it's easier to do what they want than it is to challenge them. Easier to go along with whatever they say than to think for yourself. Easier, easier, easier.'' She broke off on a sob. ''Why did you bring them here?''

''Rachel, I didn't bring them here.'' Lucas's words were soft.

Rachel looked at him, glanced at his parents and Paul. ''What...what did you say?''

Picking up on the bombshell effect Lucas's statement had had on Rachel, Paul herded the Neumans out of Rachel's office.

''I said—'' Lucas was watching her closely, knowing this was important ''—I said that I didn't bring them. I arrived here this morning to find them already here. Arguing with the reception staff,'' he added wryly.

Rachel felt the air *whoosh* out of her body, felt her knees go week. ''I need to sit down,'' she whispered, blindly reaching toward a chair from her dinette set.

Appreciating that Rachel needed a few minutes to compose herself, Lucas moved toward the tea-building area in Rachel's office and began the preparations for a cup of tea. He knew—he *remembered*—not only that Rachel tended to unwind with a cup of tea, but also how she preferred to prepare it. He smiled with satisfaction, pleased at the discovery.

''Here,'' he said, extending the cup toward her, warmed by the surprised thanks he saw in her eyes. It had been a long time since he'd been able to read her feelings there.

Rachel sipped for a minute, still shaken—not only by the Neumans' presence in her territory and Lucas's apparent innocence in the event, but by the strange familiarity of the current circumstances.

''I swear I had nothing to do with it, Rachel. I wasn't exactly pleased to find them here. I do understand—not as much as you, of course—but I do understand that Michaela has special needs right now. And that my parents can't contribute anything positive.'' They had made that quite clear to him last night, but Rachel didn't need to know about that conversation.

Rachel let out the breath she had been holding, willing calm to seep back into her. Her face still felt hot. She could feel sweat trickling down her neck, yet she felt chilled. At least she had stopped shaking.

''I wouldn't have done that, Rachel.'' He sat down at the

table, directly across from Rachel. He looked her in the eye. "Wanna tell me about it, Rachel? What brought all that on? Why'd you go ballistic with my father like that?"

Rachel shook her head, bewildered. "I guess I needed to say some things…that I've never said before."

"Can't argue with that, I guess." Truth be told, Lucas was reeling from what he'd witnessed.

Rachel had always been passionate, yes. But it was a rare thing for her to be anything but generous in her dealings with people. Lucas wanted her to trust him, to see him as someone she could talk to. Again.

"Look, Rachel, maybe it's all gotten to be too much. Maybe you're at your breaking point."

"My breaking point?" She was sideswiped by the remark, incredulous at its absurdity. "My breaking point? Maybe it's all gotten to be too much? What the hell are you talking about?" Anger was resurfacing, words were boiling again. "*Dios mio,* Lucas, I hit my breaking point a long time ago! It didn't matter, I had to keep going. What you are seeing—this is my life you're looking at, not my breaking point!"

Discomfited, Lucas said, "You just don't usually…do anger in public."

"Oh, right. And you'd prefer that it stay that way." Rachel stirred her tea vigorously. "I'd forgotten how important it is to avoid scenes."

Lucas blushed. He couldn't deny it. She knew him too well.

She touched her mug to her lips, sipping, seeking a return of the calm she'd temporarily experienced. They had things to say, the two of them. She decided to broach the first matter of discussion, the most important one. "You know that Michaela's BMT is ready to begin?"

He nodded.

"I'll be here. Will you?" She was asking if she could rely on him, theoretically, anyway.

"Yes."

"*Bueno,*" she breathed a sigh of relief. "My family will be around, as well. You understand that your parents aren't welcome?"

It was a question that needed an answer, Lucas realized that. "Yes. I know."

"Okay, then."

Rachel considered the next topic.

"I know we've kind of meandered along, you and me, without—" she pondered how to phrase it "—without establishing rules of conduct. Whatever you and I decide to do, we do it to support Michaela. Your parents are not the central point. Michaela is. Their rights as grandparents are not an issue at the moment. Michaela is the only issue." She met his eyes. "How long have they known?"

"Since last night." Lucas decided she needed to know. "Learning about Michaela has had an impact on me, Rachel. My parents noticed and they decided to hire an investigator, see what I've been up to. They came by last night to confront me. I told them then."

"They hired an investigator?" Rachel was incredulous. "You are joking, right?"

"No, I'm not."

"I see." She laughed humorlessly, as something occurred to her. "That must have been some conversation."

"Why do you say that?"

Rachel made to drink from her mug again, returning it to the table when she noticed it was empty. "Tell me, Lucas, just out of curiosity, when they found out about her, how many disparaging remarks did they make regarding her bloodlines?"

Lucas sucked in his breath.

"I thought so." Standing up, walking toward her window, she continued. "So, Lucas, why did they come today? What did they want? Evidence for a smear campaign against me? Do they think Michaela is someone else's or do they believe she's yours? In other words, do they want to get her out of your life or do they want to take her away from me?"

Lucas caught his breath, shocked that Rachel knew, she *knew,* what his parents had had in mind. It would serve no purpose to try to defend them.

She fingered the curtains. "How do you feel about their arguments, Lucas? Am I in for a fight?"

"No, Rachel. I wouldn't do that. I'm here now, I'm part of the equation. But she belongs with you. Please trust me on that."

"Well, frankly, Lucas, that's asking a lot. I've learned from our past together that when your parents' wishes come up against mine, your parents win. They wanted something from you, you delivered it. It was a knee-jerk reaction. A habit. It has nothing to do with thinking. You've never had the nerve to stand up to your parents. Not ever."

"Maybe that's changed."

She turned around, looked him straight in the eye. "Why should I believe that?"

"I'm a father now, Rachel. Or at least I know I'm a father now." He noticed her wince, knew she felt some guilt about that. "I told you that that discovery has made a difference to me. I want to do whatever it takes to help her, to have a relationship with her. With my daughter." It still made him tingle to say those words.

Rachel noticed.

"So," she began, "maybe you've answered your own question, the one you asked about my going ballistic with your father." She had his attention now. "Somehow, all those years, Lucas, I couldn't—or wouldn't—defend myself against him. But when I felt like my child might be the target I never gave any thought to whether I would protect her. I just did it. Even though that meant touching him." She couldn't suppress the shudder the thought gave her.

They were silent for a moment. This was intense as well as tricky ground to cover.

"What about..." Lucas tried his best to broach the subject tactfully. "What did you mean about not needing to put up with them anymore?"

"Well, we're not actively married, Lucas. They aren't my in-laws in a true sense. Their status as grandparents doesn't merit discussion. And that being the case, I don't have to get along with them anymore. I've already tolerated more than was fair. I don't owe them anything. I tried to live with it, Lucas, I really did. Especially when you seemed to be blind to it. What could I do? They're your parents." She took a long, deep breath. "I've held that in for a long time. That's probably why it felt so good to smack your father. It's been building up for years."

Lucas suspected he would not like where the discussion was heading. He knew his parents had not been good to Rachel. He had known about their prejudices, although he'd never overtly challenged it before last night. He hadn't exactly been blind to it, as Rachel suggested, but he hadn't done anything about it, either. Not that he was proud of it, but it was true.

And now, while he felt queasy about the next information, he knew he could not hide from it any longer. He would have to push her this time.

"Blind to what, Rachel? Tell me."

Something in his voice compelled her. She took a deep breath. "In the past, at various functions, when you were off networking with Alana, your father stayed behind to entertain me. Are you sure you want to hear this?" She met his eyes. He nodded. "Why do you think I came to hate those events so much?"

"Well, you always said it was because you couldn't stand society politics."

She nodded her head. "Yes. And I did hate that. But mostly, Lucas, I was desperate to avoid your father. And he was at his very worst when I was alone with him in public."

"What do you mean?"

"*Bueno,* Lucas, if you want to know...in the workforce, they call it sexual harassment. With a family member, they call it something else."

She'd never actually voiced this information. The words had never left her mouth. Not for anyone. But it was time. The words would not be withheld any longer.

Shuddering involuntarily, she spoke, almost to herself. "At first I thought it was accidental. He would claim it was accidental, the way he would bump into me or rub against me. He'd touch me, you know, like a normal person does, then it would slide into something else and he'd apologize, but..." She shook her head.

"I thought I had to be imagining it. He would corner me, Lucas, just out of sight of anyone else. At those events, when we'd be left alone at the table. Or he'd ask me to dance. Very public, but all the while...he was talking, holding me too tightly, too close. Yes—" she was nodding her head "—he did corner me. He would call me on the phone, Lucas. I actually met him for lunch once, at the beginning, before I understood. I believed he just wanted to get to know me a little. That's what he said.''

Her voice hardened. ''I didn't realize he had arranged for a suite at the Hyatt and that not only did he expect me to fall into bed with him, he expected me to be thankful and happy for the opportunity. He said he would set me up in my own place, that I'd have everything I could possibly want, that he would stay with me whenever possible. That Sophie wouldn't mind. That you wouldn't mind, either. He even brought me some kind of legal document, Lucas, spelling out what he'd give me, just so I could see he really meant what he said. I guess he thought I'd like that.''

She sighed. ''Even after you and I were married, he kept at it, saying he'd be happy to…share me with you. He said he'd take what he could get.''

Lucas's pallor gave away his horror. It couldn't be true, and yet… ''I don't believe you.''

''Yes, you do. You don't want to, but you do. I can see it in your eyes, Lucas.'' And she could. His gray eyes were utterly black with emotion at this moment. ''You believe me.''

Not waiting for a response, she went on. ''Why do you suppose he thought I'd jump at what he offered? He, well, both your parents, believed I was not only too low on the evolutionary scale to marry the likes of you, but that my lowly status relegated me to the whore class, Lucas. Your father wanted to elevate me to 'mistress to rich white man,' thoroughly believing it was his right to do so and that I would consider it a privilege. *Dios mio,* but he is a fool.''

Eyeing Lucas, her contempt for his father showed in her eyes, bringing shadows to the gold. ''As you may realize, my Mexican heritage is at the root of his opinion. It's a bit like the lord of the manor claiming rights with the servants.''

Lucas flinched as he remembered his father's boast about Rosa.

''He really didn't understand that I wasn't interested. When I continued to refuse, he turned ugly. Well, uglier.'' She laughed humorlessly. ''He said you would never need to know that I was with both of you. He said he could understand that you might not want to give me up. He—'' she bit her lip ''—is apparently genuinely attracted to me. I believe that much is true. I think he has never forgiven me for refusing him. He became hostile toward me.''

Lucas knew he had paled even further, that the shock he was feeling showed. ''If this is true, why didn't you tell me any of this?''

He asked the question but knew she spoke the truth. He knew that his father had expressed more than idle interest in Rachel in their very recent conversation. In fact, he had expressed desire for *her* as well as what seemed to be desire for revenge.

''I wanted to tell you, Lucas. I tried to. But listening to my criticisms of your parents was never high on your agenda. Maybe I should have insisted, but it embarrassed me. I felt guilty, kept wondering if I'd done something to ask for it somehow. I kept hoping he'd stop, that he'd leave me alone eventually. I just tried to stay away from him, from both of them actually.'' She played with the spoon in her empty teacup. ''I don't know what your mother thinks of it, although I'm sure she knows. But I've never been inclined to chat with her.''

Rachel went to fix herself another cup of tea. Carefully, studiously, she poured the water over the teabag, eventually adding honey and milk. ''Michaela is also Mexican. Your father will never be decent to her. Your mother follows him. I can only draw on my experience—and that hasn't been very good.''

''You believe there is a connection between your heritage and Dad's…behavior.''

''I'm certain of it.''

''Everything about them not wanting us to marry, my father's…interest in you, the way they treat you, the way you think they'll treat Michaela. You believe it's all racial.''

''Not for me, Lucas. It's racial *for them.* I'm pretty comfortable with my background. Your parents are less receptive.''

She walked back to the table where Lucas still sat. ''What I don't know is how you feel. You've never said.''

The question jolted him. ''Are you asking me if I agree with them?''

''*Sí,* I suppose so.''

Should he tell her about his recent conversation with his

parents? That he had disagreed with them, defended Rachel and Michaela? Had he left Rachel so unsure of his opinion?

"*Por Dios,* Lucas," Rachel snapped when no response was forthcoming. "Surely you aren't still wondering if my heritage matters to them? When they make snide remarks about my background, exactly what do you think they mean? When they get to talking about pure bloodlines, what the hell do you think they're referring to?" She paused, her gaze direct. "Would you agree that your parents were highly opposed to our marriage?"

"Yes," Lucas inclined his head. "They were. Still are."

"*Bueno,*" Rachel said, clasping her hands together in a mock-praying pose. "Do you have any theories about why that is?"

"You weren't what they expected me to marry."

"Well, that's an understatement." She thought back, bringing back a moment from the past. "Did you know that your mother tried to convince me to sign the marriage certificate using only my middle initial? She said 'Juanita' was just too ethnic. If people saw *that,* she said, if they heard me say *that* when we took our vows—well, then everyone would *know.* People could accept the name Rachel. Rachel was classic, she said. But Juanita showed the truth about who I was. I refused her request."

Lucas felt his eyes widen. He had never heard that before.

"Your parents have very definite ideas about people's places in society. Do you agree?"

He shrugged, but nodded. "Okay." They had given him lessons in this subject. The real problem, he was beginning to see, was that he'd never considered the consequences of their prejudice. He'd discarded their commentary as something he had no use for. But maybe, just maybe, his silence had looked like agreement.

Rachel, however, was not privy to Lucas's thoughts. "Do you know where my place is, according to your parents?"

In spite of himself, he blushed. He couldn't pretend he didn't know, not anymore. He couldn't meet her eyes as he acknowledged, "Yes, I know."

She regarded him steadily, waiting for him to continue, content to let the silence grow.

"Okay, you weren't…wife material." He glanced at her,

wondering if that would be a sufficient admission for her. "They expected me to marry Alana. Or someone just like her, I suppose." He shrugged.

"And why was that?"

"Because she was what they expected. You...weren't."

"Why not?"

"Because," he began, realizing he didn't really know where to take his explanation, but sensing that Rachel wasn't going to make it easy. "Not just because you're Mexican. There were other reasons." No matter how angry his father had made him, Lucas couldn't stop defending his family. Maybe that, too, was a knee-jerk reaction.

"Oh?"

"They did keep saying we were too young."

"Yes."

"Well, okay then, you weren't from our...class." He cringed at the word. It was a little too close to the racial point. "You weren't raised for...for the role a society wife would have to fill. You didn't conduct yourself that way." *God, that sounds even worse, as if she lacked manners or something.*

"Of course, Lucas, the society-wife bit. A stunning living trophy who can bat her eyelashes and play hostess—and talk fluff. Alana is prepared for that. I'm not. I'm not glamorous or elegant, and I don't care about designer clothes, jewelry or cars. I have my own definition of 'having the right friends, knowing the right people.' I think for myself."

She paused, looking up, wondering if he was getting this. He met her gaze. He nodded. She nodded, too, and continued. "I don't come from money. That could be considered one aspect of background. My pedigree isn't what Alana's is. But that isn't all of it, is it, Lucas?"

She stood up, beginning to pace. "The problem was never simply all the things I am not. The real problem was what *I am* instead. Being Mexican, it's part of who I am. No big deal for me, but I know prejudice when I see it, Lucas, when I experience it. Michaela deserves better from her grandparents."

She stirred her tea, not really wanting to drink any more of it.

Taking a deep breath, she returned to her chair. "As long as we stayed away from them, we were fine. We had our own ways, together, you and I. Good ways. But gradually you started spending more time with them, without me, and with Alana. It made a difference. You see, Lucas, despite all their efforts to drive me away, they didn't succeed—but you did. *You* succeeded. You followed whatever your father said, did whatever he wanted you to do. You just…drifted away from me until you couldn't see me anymore.''

''Rachel, it wasn't like that.''

''Wasn't it? I left the marriage, Lucas, but you deserted the relationship. You chose a successor while I was still there. You put her in my place.'' Sadness had crept into her voice. ''I was alone, just the way your mother is. The difference is that, having not been raised to accept that sort of thing, I walked away. She's lived with it, accepted it, for…how long? Maybe for the entire marriage? I couldn't do that, Lucas, I just couldn't. To their way of thinking, I deserved far less than Sophie had. It just never occurred to me that you shared their views. Had I ever suspected that, I would never have married you. I thought you were different.''

Suddenly Lucas was desperate to say what he should have made clear a long time ago. ''Rachel, I never shared my parents' opinion about you, your status or your…background. You need to know that. Hell, I would have never allowed…'' He shook his head ruefully. ''But I did, I guess.''

''Like I said, maybe I could have insisted you listen. Maybe I could have been more diplomatic.'' It was an olive branch, extended as a peace offering. Both of them knew it.

Lucas ran a hand through his hair, belying his outward calm, hinting at his internal confusion. ''I also admit I have a hard time thinking about prejudice the way you're describing it. I…don't relate to it. I don't feel it. I don't have negative feelings about your heritage or about Michaela sharing that heritage. Really. I just don't look at people and evaluate them that way. I never did.''

Rachel regarded him carefully. She didn't really think Lucas was prejudiced. She thought it more likely that he had been so well cocooned in a world that didn't experience it that honestly he didn't understand what prejudice could look like. He was—or had been—horribly naive about such things.

No matter what her anger or wounded heart tried to make

her believe, she knew Lucas, knew him deep down. If he had ever judged people based on anything less than their own attributes, their own personalities and self-worth, she would have known. She would have known.

"I believe you."

He smiled, a weight lifting from him. She smiled back. It was a step in the right direction between them.

A buzz from Rachel's phone interrupted them. She pushed the appropriate buttons, waited for the voice on the other end.

"I'll be right back, Lucas. Paul needs me for a minute."

When Rachel returned to the reception area, she spotted the Neumans. They had apparently not left yet. Arnold was standing at a window, gazing out at the parking lot, a cup of coffee in his hand.

"Rachel," came Sophie's tight voice, startling her. She approached Rachel cautiously, taking great pain to choose the right words. "I apologize if we have...intruded. But, please...would we be able to see the child? From a distance?"

Taken aback by Sophie's hushed tone, Rachel hesitated. She eyed Sophie carefully, cautiously, as one would examine a coiled snake. Despite her misgivings, Rachel sensed a war of emotions battling it out inside the older woman. Somehow Rachel knew what it had cost Sophie to speak up. Regardless of her flawless, impeccable appearance, Sophie Neuman was not calm.

Welcome to the club, Sophie, she thought. Rachel took a long time in answering.

"Rachel, tell me to go to hell if you want. I would understand, actually." Sophie's smile was brief, tentative. "But I had to ask. We've come this far."

Wondering if she was making a mistake, yet somehow attuned to the older woman's genuine need to see her granddaughter, Rachel pointed to Sophie. "You, you *only,*" she stressed. "Come with me."

Avoiding any glance in Arnold's direction, Sophie nodded and followed Rachel toward another hallway.

Replacing her mask over her nose and mouth, Rachel walked into Michaela's room, closing the door behind her. Moving quietly, she pulled back the blinds that covered the glass partition separating the room from the corridor. Gently she lifted

Michaela into her arms, into a sitting position. Michaela mumbled something, but didn't wake. Rachel kissed her daughter's forehead through her mask, then glanced toward the window.

Confident that Sophie had had a reasonable glimpse of her granddaughter, Rachel lowered Michaela back to the bed, rearranging her bedding and closing the blinds.

Stepping back into the corridor, Rachel glanced at Sophie, who merely nodded in response. Rachel returned to her office, not waiting to see what the Neumans were doing. Collecting her mug from the table, she dumped the dregs of her tea into the sink, debating whether she wanted to fix another round.

"So, Rachel," Lucas's voice was slow and languid, slowing the air molecules to the speed of honey, prompting an immediate throb of response in Rachel.

It made her jump, nevertheless. "*Dios mio,* Lucas, you scared me. I didn't realize you were still here." Her breathing had quickened, along with her heartbeat.

Noticing this, he smiled slowly at her, took a step toward her. "So, then. I guess that leaves one other thing." The caress she remembered so well was in his voice, the blackness of his eyes had changed. "What about us, Rachel?"

"Us?"

"Yes, us." He chuckled softly as he extended his hand toward her, seeking her hair. He could smell her—vanilla. Vanilla and spice and something else, something Rachel. Her own scent. The one he had missed, even without knowing it.

One hand was in her hair then, tipping her face toward him. With his other hand he stroked the curve of her cheek, watched as the rhythm of her breathing changed yet again. "What are we going to do about this, Rachel? This thing between us..." He pressed himself against her, letting her feel the state of his body, his readiness. It could happen so fast, he marveled, when Rachel was near.

I want her so much.

He bent lower, so that his lips brushed her cheek, in place of his fingers. "You smell so good, Rachel, you feel so right..." And she did. Absolutely perfect. His arms stole around her, pulling her against him tightly, leaving no room for doubt. She fit him. Perfectly.

"Damn you, Lucas! I've told you no!"

When she began to resist, he sought a way to soothe her. He wanted this so badly. Wanted her so much. He knew she felt the same way. He just needed to remind her. "Rachel, it's okay. This is us, sweetheart. It's okay."

"No, Lucas! It's not okay! Maybe it never will be." That was the sad truth she could not hide from.

He felt her turmoil. He didn't understand it, but he knew it was real. His arms dropped to his sides. Rachel wrenched herself away from him, nearly tripping on the little table in her rush.

"I've told you I can't do this, Lucas."

Her back was to him, her arms wrapped around herself. He realized then that she was fighting tears, that sobs were racking her body. Or was she just gulping in air, trying to get control? He couldn't be sure.

He moved toward her again, needing to extend…something to her. "Rachel, I don't understand. I'm sorry, whatever I've done here, I'm sorry." He struggled for words. "I feel so close to you, Rachel. The physical—it's part of my response to you. I only have to be near you."

A shudder went the length of her body, an involuntary response to his need. A need that spoke to her at a deeper level than she could accept.

She shook her head. "That's fine for you. But I'm not you." Despite her physical reaction, she knew this was true. "I told you before—our history, being normal, healthy adults—that's not enough for me. Please, Lucas. Try to understand. My guard is up. I don't know if that will ever change. Just don't touch me. I can't take it. I really can't." Her breathing had slowed down. Her composure was returning.

Involuntarily Lucas reached toward her again. When he saw her hold her breath, he let his hand drop to his side. Not knowing what else to do, Lucas gave a little wave of farewell. And left Rachel alone. He was more confused than ever.

But that was nothing compared to what Rachel was feeling.

Chapter 9

The dream came again when she tried to sleep. Or rather, the *dreams.* Dreams that had plagued Rachel for years. Dreams of being cornered, abandoned. Of wanting too much, of wanting something that always seemed just out of her reach. Of emptiness, of the unknown, of what she couldn't quite see. And an understanding that she had to move toward it, anyway.

Sometimes she awoke on a sob. Sometimes it was with a stifled scream. Sometimes it was with the sense of falling.

Exhausted, Rachel pulled herself to a sitting position in her bed. Pushing her damp hair away from her face, she expelled a long, shaky breath.

She would prefer insomnia. At least with insomnia, she had some control over her thoughts. Dreams demanded a response; they required that a person follow. Sometimes even after waking. Which was what was happening now. Even though she was awake, Rachel couldn't avoid thinking about the dream.

It was all being stirred up again. Lucas's presence was bringing back all the old pain. She could keep the hurt pushed down, buried someplace where she couldn't feel it, most of the time. But in her dreams, it had returned.

That awful night. That awful *year* that had culminated in that awful night.

Only a few months into her marriage, Rachel couldn't help feeling that Lucas had come to prefer Alana or, at least, Alana's company. Lucas called that ridiculous. He couldn't see that Rachel had cause to think that—and that many other people thought it as well.

Okay, Rachel could acknowledge now, maybe she'd been a little jealous. But not of Alana exactly. Jealous of the *time* Lucas spent with her. Jealous that he seemed to enjoy the time he spent with Alana and thought that time with Rachel was...owed. That being with Rachel was no longer the preferred choice.

Things had added up. The graduation party had mattered. The condo purchase had mattered.

Nothing she'd tried had worked, nothing could get through to Lucas. She couldn't reach him no matter what she did. Eventually she began to turn her pain, her loneliness, her disappointment, her humiliation, inward. She quit trying to connect, to fix things. She quit allowing herself to feel.

And after the Las Vegas trip, she knew there was nothing left.

Las Vegas. True, Lucas had asked her to go with him, the only time he had ever invited her to travel with him. But it had been a week of life-altering events for her, events that belonged to her. A week when she couldn't go with him. Lucas hadn't listened, hadn't believed her, hadn't caught on that something important was happening for Rachel. He simply reminded her that she was a failure in supporting his career and had stormed out of the condo, suitcase in hand.

A week later, when he returned home, she had had such wonderful news for him. She was already dressed for bed, wearing a simple white eyelet nightgown she preferred during warm weather. Her silky, dark hair was free and loose, just the way he liked it. But the minute Lucas walked through the door, she knew that something was dreadfully wrong. For the first time in their lives together, Lucas couldn't meet Rachel's eyes.

"Is everything okay?" she'd asked.

"I'm tired, I guess," he said with a shrug.

She didn't push him for answers. She'd been bursting to talk to him, but he managed to cut her off.

"I think I'll take my bag to our room," he said, still avoiding her eyes. "I'll take a shower. Maybe that'll revive me."

While he was in the bathroom, Rachel began the familiar routine of sorting his gear for washing and dry cleaning. He'd wrapped a towel around his waist and walked from the bathroom, drying his hair with another towel. He paused when he saw her sitting on their bed, abnormally still.

"Did you have something to say to me?" she questioned quietly, but not quite a whisper.

"What…what do you mean?" he floundered.

"Oh, Lucas, please," she said, sounding tired. "Let's at least have some honesty. Here—" she lifted a shirt she held in her hand "—is a shirt smeared with two different shades of lipstick. Here—" she pointed absently "—is an invitation of sorts, written on hotel stationery, which I found in your jacket pocket, apparently sealed with a kiss by Cathy. Cathy, I notice, was not wearing either color of lipstick that I see on the shirt. And here—" she motioned toward the bed again "—would be a handful of condoms that I found in the inside jacket pocket. I've rescued them for you. Wouldn't want to send them to the dry cleaner, I'm sure."

She was rolling something back and forth in her hands but continued calmly, "I wasn't snooping, Lucas. I was just sorting, that's all."

She stood up, looking him in the face for the first time. "Did Cathy seal you with a kiss, too, Lucas? Or did someone else leave all those marks down your neck and across your shoulder?" Her voice vibrated with resigned sarcasm. And defeat.

"What do you mean?" he asked as he moved to look at himself in the mirrored closet doors. "Oh," he said, smiling sheepishly as he lightly touched the fading love bites. "I didn't realize I had them. But no, that would have been Alana."

"Oh, well, I see," Rachel said. "Excuse me, will you, Lucas?" Rachel, feeling strangely dead inside, stood and moved toward the bedroom door, turning as she remembered she held something in her hands. "Let me give this back to you," she'd said, hurling the small item at his head. "It was in your jacket

345 SDL DU6U　　　245 SDL DU7C

FIRST NAME　　　LAST NAME

ADDRESS

APT.#　　　CITY

STATE/PROV.　　　ZIP/POSTAL CODE　　　(S-IM-08/03)

Twenty-one gets you **2 FREE BOOKS** and a ***FREE MYSTERY GIFT!***

Twenty gets you ***2 FREE BOOKS!***

Nineteen gets you ***1 FREE BOOK!***

TRY AGAIN!

Offer limited to one per household and not valid to current Silhouette Intimate Moments® subscribers. All orders subject to approval.

pocket, too, nestled among the condoms. I'm sure I don't need it. But then, I don't suppose you need it, either.''

She'd left the bedroom, and Lucas looked at the floor, searching for the object that had missed his head only because he had moved quickly enough to avoid it. It lay on the floor next to the closet door track, sparkling vaguely in the muted light of the bedroom. It was his wedding ring. Only then did he notice that his hand was bare.

Shaken and not understanding why, he grabbed underwear and a pair of sweatpants, stumbling into them as quickly as he could. He heard familiar noises coming from the kitchen now: Rachel locating a mug, filling it with water, setting it to heat in the microwave, pulling a teabag from the canister, retrieving milk and honey to add to her tea, tapping her fingers on the counter while she waited.

He raced out of the bedroom, not sure what he would find, but expecting…something. Conflicted emotions roiled within him: fear, guilt, defensiveness, even triumph. He was oddly exhilarated, pumped up for a fight—a rarity in him. He was unprepared for what he encountered.

Rachel was sitting in a lounge chair near the window, her legs curled beneath her, quietly sipping from her mug. She looked out the window, not looking at him.

''I didn't actually have sex with Alana, you know,'' he burst out. ''I didn't.''

Her expression never changed, her gaze never wavered from some point on the horizon. Lucas couldn't be sure she'd heard him.

''Aren't you going to say anything?''

She answered by shrugging her shoulders. Then she spoke so quietly that Lucas had to lean toward her to hear.

''What would you have me say, Lucas? How does that make any difference?''

''What do you mean by that? I would think that the fact that I could have, that I nearly did, maybe I even wanted to, but I *didn't*—well, that should matter.''

Rachel shrugged again. ''Is that what you think, Lucas? That my reaction to this news should be gratitude? That I should be thankful to you for stopping short of…'' She couldn't say it.

She sipped her tea. She still didn't look in his direction. Her voice remained deathly quiet and calm. "No, Lucas, what matters is that you were in that position to begin with. Everything you've done lately, Lucas, it has not been the behavior of a man interested in honoring his wedding vows. If you didn't actually *violate* them, well, that doesn't mean abiding by them, either." She shook her head. "No, I really don't see where this fine line of distinction that you're trying to paint matters. The trust was bruised before, Lucas. Now it's broken. Fine lines of distinction won't change that."

She paused, continuing to look out the window, surprised at how calm she felt. Then she resumed in a voice that would have been soothing in other circumstances. "Lucas, tonight I'm forced to acknowledge what I've been fighting for months. Before this I hoped we could work things out. You've demonstrated very well for me, however, that I can quit hoping."

She sipped her tea in silence while Lucas began pacing. He had no idea how to respond. It wasn't like Rachel to be so indifferent. She was a serene person, able to deal calmly with whatever life threw her way. But still. Things were coming to a head, that was obvious. Under the circumstances, he might have expected anger. He would have known how to deal with anger, even if it had taken the form of an icy-cold shoulder. But this—this was resignation and he had no idea how to fight it.

And he had no idea what to say to break the silence.

Eventually Rachel turned to him. "Why did you marry me, Lucas?"

"What do you mean? What kind of question is that?" He was annoyed to hear himself snort. "Why do you think?"

"At the time, I thought you loved me. Any more I couldn't tell you." She shook her head sadly, turning her gaze back to the window, placing her empty mug on the end table. "Well, why, Lucas?"

"Because I loved you and wanted to spend my life with you! Is that what I'm supposed to say?"

"Only if it's the truth." She shrugged. Meeting his gaze as he stood paralyzed in front of her, she murmured, "Past tense, huh, Lucas? So, if you did feel that way once, when do you suppose it changed?"

She answered her own question. "It changed when you finished school, when you went on to bigger and better things in the business world and I was still a student. It changed with that damn graduation party, Lucas, when you came to me three days before the party I'd planned for you and casually informed me that I would have to cancel it. Why? Well, because Mother and Daddy had planned a party for you and you simply had to go. To Cancún. 'Oh, yeah, Rachel, by the way, you can't come.' The event, after all, wasn't intended for me. It was for you and other…important people.''

She shook her head, sad at the memory, disheartened by what it had meant, repeating how Lucas had explained himself. ''' You understand how it is, Rachel. I've grown up with Alana. We've known each other all our lives. It's natural that she and I would celebrate something like this together.' Can you believe you actually said that? I was your *wife,* Lucas, not a nosy neighbor or something.''

She took a deep breath, letting it out slowly. ''Yes, Lucas, that was the turning point.'' She gave a sad smile, nodding her head. ''Tonight is the end. I give up. I get your point. You win.'' She held both hands up in the air, palms toward him, in the traditional gesture of surrender. ''It's over.''

Finally she stood, walking to the kitchen and rinsing her mug. ''I'm going to brush my teeth, Lucas. You take the bed. I'll sleep out here on the couch.''

She'd come to his office for the first and only time the following morning. He had been stunned by her presence, shocked even further by her reason for being there.

''I've been to see a lawyer this morning, Lucas. I have papers for you to sign.'' She'd been cool and understated—but very, very clear. She wanted a legal separation, effective as soon as they could deliver the signed papers to the courthouse. One that would last a year before either of them initiated divorce proceedings.

Looking back, which Rachel rarely allowed herself to do, she marveled at the profound calm that had descended upon her that night. The acceptance. She had never felt surprised, really. Only disappointed and sad. She wondered about that, had finally decided that she'd been preparing for that moment during the entire previous year.

That profound calm had stayed with her. It had been a defense mechanism then; probably it still was. It helped her survive, rebuild, cope. First in dealing with Lucas, then with Michaela's illness. And everything else that she had experienced in these past five years.

She did occasionally wonder what had happened to the love he had felt for her. She believed he had loved her, once. She had certainly loved him.

''What is that expression?'' she asked aloud, suddenly back in the present. '''If you love something, set it free. If it comes back to you, it is yours. If it doesn't, it never was.' That's the way it goes. I guess we weren't meant to be.'' But it had felt as if it was meant to be. It still did.

At least to her.

She'd told Lucas she couldn't do casual sex—that she needed more. She'd been perfectly honest when she'd said that.

What she hadn't said was that she couldn't sleep with Lucas precisely because for her much more *was* involved. For Rachel, sex with Lucas could never be casual. And she couldn't handle what it would be.

She closed her eyes, only to feel hot, wet tears squeeze through her lashes and burn their paths down her cheeks.

''Damn,'' she whispered, getting up and going to the sink, splashing cold water on her face. She returned to her bed, trying to convince herself she would sleep now.

Lying on her back, she stared at the ceiling. She wished Lucas's face would quit dancing in front of her. And for all the reflecting she did—questioning what had gone wrong, remembering what had been good, debating her present life—she never addressed the one thing she had been avoiding all these years.

How did she feel about what Lucas had done? How had she felt at the time? How did she feel about it now?

She had locked away her feelings, cultivated an internal armor that housed emotions she had never been able to face. But these emotions were beginning to struggle for recognition now. She just hoped they didn't overwhelm her.

A bouquet of silk flowers appeared before Rachel. She started at its arrival, given that it had come from behind her, over her shoulder. She did, however, recognize the arm attached to the bouquet. Warm breath spread against the back of her neck, lips whispered against her ear. ''For you, my lady.''

Rachel inhaled sharply, attempting to step away from Lucas, only to find his arms closing around her waist. ''Lucas, please,'' she hissed, her panic rising even as something in her responded to the familiarity of those lips caressing her neck. Her heart skipped a beat, its rhythm thrown, as he pulled her close.

''Gladly, my dear,'' he answered softly, nuzzling against her. ''I wanted to bring you something pretty, but I remembered that real flowers aren't allowed in here.'' Lucas hoped she would appreciate that he had noticed the prohibition, that he understood that weak immune systems and natural plants didn't mix well.

''Yes, that's very nice, Lucas,'' Rachel whispered, struggling for composure, ''and they're lovely, but please let me go.'' She was polite but firm.

In his plan Lucas had viewed the flowers as a distraction that would help Rachel relax—relax enough that he could break the ice that separated them physically. Her reactions reminded him all too well of the black cat in the cartoons who was always squirming away from the amorous skunk. *Surely,* he thought, *I'm not so repugnant as a skunk.*

But his strategy was failing. They were in the reception area, a very public venue, so she wasn't yelling at him. She wasn't running away the way she had when he'd announced the blood test results. He could, however, feel the hammering of her heart and knew it was related to resistance, not acquiescence.

''Rachel, come on. We've got to get past this. I'm not going to hurt you. You must know better than that.'' He stroked her cheek, continuing to whisper in measured tones. ''I wouldn't hurt you.''

Her body stiffened. She drew in a deep breath. ''Why should I believe that?''

''Rachel, you're special to me—''

''Is that so, Lucas? Am I really? Or is this just a line you use?'' She plucked at his hands, unable to release herself and not willing to drop her flowers in the effort. ''Does it work?''

She didn't want to draw attention to themselves, but she was beginning to feel claustrophobic. She was beginning to need escape.

"Rachel, come on. Really, this isn't necessary."

"Does my lack of cooperation interfere with your goal, Lucas? And what exactly would that goal be?" She was angry. It couldn't be interpreted any other way. "I am not the type of woman who gets picked up in a bar. And this—" she waved her arm around somewhat discreetly, emphasizing their location "—this is not a bar."

Lucas recoiled at the venom in her voice. "Rachel, honey—"

"Don't do that, Lucas." She spun this time, breaking his hold. She'd had a bad night and she was touchy. She knew it, but she couldn't help it. "I am not the sort of woman you're used to. What can I do to make you understand that? I'm not trying to play hard to get, I'm not saying no when I mean yes. You live a different kind of life from mine, Lucas. I'm not judging it, but I can't live it. You had Alana—and whoever else was convenient and willing. I won't be put on that list just because I happen to be around. Get it through your head!"

She glared at him a moment longer, unwittingly punctuating her words with her eyes. Because Lucas saw them—wild and frightened—so unlike Rachel, he dropped his arms away from her and stepped back. This time he'd heard it. He'd seen it, too. The anger, yes. But something else. He finally got it: Rachel was wounded. Deeply. And that was his fault.

"Okay, Rachel," he said to her retreating back.

This time, pieces were starting to shift. He was finally beginning to understand.

But how to help her was another question.

It would take more than providing her with a distraction to get her through this. He knew that much…now.

Chapter 10

Lucas stepped back, watching his golf ball soar against the intensely blue Arizona sky. He'd become an avid golfer over the years, usually going out with people his father selected. Diego Fuentes, the man he was with today, had never been one of those people.

However, Lucas and Diego had golfed together many times back when they had been in school, usually at the university course during summer when the hundred-degree temperatures had sent the greens fees plummeting. Still, Lucas acknowledged, many years had passed since he had spent any time with Diego. Lucas quickly surmised that Diego had continued to play golf, as his improved skill was notable.

At first the two friends golfed amid a strained silence. Truthfully, it had always been their habit to begin golfing in silence, setting their concentration for the game that way. Today, however, the silence was not companionable.

"So, *amigo,*" Diego finally said, "why are we together again? Did you miss me suddenly?"

Lucas laughed, appreciating Diego's directness but unsure how to begin the conversation even with such an obvious invitation. He could sense Diego's reticence, a withholding of the warmth that had always colored their friendship, and Lucas couldn't really blame him.

"Not exactly," Lucas chuckled.

They continued to play, in silence, until Lucas finally spoke again. "How would you feel about taking me on at your firm?"

Diego's eyebrows shot up, nearly disappearing into the black darkness of his hairline. "*Bueno, amigo,* you have surprised me."

"Yes, well, I suppose so. Maybe I even surprised myself. That wasn't exactly what I expected to hear coming out of my mouth." Lately Lucas had been unsettled, confused on many fronts. It wasn't surprising that his subconscious thoughts would work their way to the surface, even without his permission.

"Did you mean it?" Diego asked, pocketing his golf ball after sinking his putt.

"Yeah, I guess I did. I haven't been happy working with Dad lately—damn, I'm not sure I've ever been happy there." Lucas removed his cap, running his fingers through his hair, then replacing the cap. "I've never been able to do the kinds of things I wanted, you know, things we talked about in school. I kept thinking I'd get a chance, once I'd learned the ropes. But I've learned the ropes and now I realize that Dad will never fund the kind of work I envisioned."

"So Lucas Neuman is disillusioned with his life?"

"Hell, yes, I'm disillusioned."

Silence returned as each man took his turn at the next hole. Getting back into the golf cart, Diego spoke. "You know, if you are disillusioned, maybe you have yourself to blame."

"What do you mean?"

Diego shrugged. "Just what I said. Bad choices don't lead to happiness. Because something is easy doesn't mean it's the best choice. In fact, it probably isn't. Sometimes a little risk is necessary to achieve something, and if you never take a risk..." He shrugged again. "You can only blame yourself for your choices, *amigo.* If you suffer now, well, it's what you deserve. You have earned it."

"Thanks, Diego. That's damn philosophical of you."

Diego smiled, not the least bit repentant at having made Lucas squirm. "It is how I live my life, my friend. Take today.

I haven't heard from you in years. You don't associate with my kind anymore.'' He paused, raising his eyebrows. The simple action told Lucas exactly what Diego meant by his ''kind.'' Lucas recognized the dare Diego had issued—the dare to deny the truth of his statement.

Diego continued. ''But did I ignore your phone call? Did I turn you down when you told me you wanted to get together, go golfing again? No, I did not. That was my first impulse, though. I thought if I wasn't good enough for you all this time, why should I suddenly care about why you wanted to see me? But I didn't follow that, *amigo.* That would not have made me happy. I would have still wondered. So I followed through on my responsibility to an old friendship.'' He smiled again. ''Of course, I was curious, too.''

Concentration on their putts was called for now, so silence resumed.

''You want to jump ship, is that it, my friend?''

''Dammit, Diego, I'm not sure what I want. I'm just trying to figure out what I don't want, trying to go from there.''

More silence.

''You know, my company is refurbishing, restoring, the area of Encanto Park. That's why I wanted you to come here today. This is the Encanto nine-hole course. Over there—'' he pointed northeast ''—is the municipal course that belongs to Encanto Park. So far, we've worked on this course. That one will be next. We're commissioned to work on the old houses, too. Encanto,'' he said a little dreamily. ''Enchanted place. That's what it means, *encanto.* Hopefully we can bring the enchantment back to Encanto. It's a grand old area and deserves it.''

Lucas looked around, able to see that the old course did indeed reflect the touches of loving restoration that Fuentes de la Juventud was known for. They kept a gentle hand, worked with what was there. Everyone in the industry knew it.

The game ended, both men calculating their scores and ribbing each other about it, just as they always had done, Diego emerging as the clear winner. This time.

''Come, *amigo,*'' Diego said, placing his hand on Lucas's back in a gesture of goodwill, ''let's go get some lunch, let you take a look at the clubhouse. We've been working on that, also.''

Once inside, out of the heat, they ordered their meals.

When chips and salsa arrived, Diego resumed, "You know, Lucas, my company does many things. We restore older buildings, World Heritage classified, that kind of thing. We do that throughout the American Southwest—Arizona, California, New Mexico, Texas, Nevada. We have offices in San Francisco, in San Antonio and in Santa Fe—and Phoenix, of course. We have an office in Mexico City and many projects in Mexico that we manage from there. My cousins, *comprende, mi familia,* they are in the business and run the other offices. The Phoenix office, it is the headquarters, and it's mine. I told you we are working on Encanto Park, trying to return it to what it was like in its glory days and maybe even make it a little better. But we always approach things with the idea of maintaining harmony. We turn down projects where we don't feel that is possible."

Lucas nodded, dazzled by this description of Diego's reality. He'd heard about Fuentes de la Juventud. He suspected Neuman Industries picked up many of the projects Fuentes de la Juventud rejected. It would figure.

"We have also designed and built a number of small housing communities in the inner city. Not just Phoenix, but San Francisco, Oakland, Sacramento, Albuquerque, even Tucson. We want to revitalize the areas that have been abandoned, bring people back from the suburbs. The city governments are usually very happy to help with this. They put up funds for loan programs. They rezone, they listen to the ideas for the whole community. They want to do more than just plunk down stylish houses. They want communities—grocery stores, schools and so on, so these families can live a good quality of life. We restore as much as we can. We try to use what's there. We design something new if we need to. It's a very satisfying arrangement. And it works because we've established a good reputation and we are committed to do our best."

Their food arrived and Diego paused as the items were arranged on the table. It had been a long time since Lucas had eaten real Mexican food, but he knew undoubtedly that the chimichanga that sat before him was as authentic as they came. Just as he knew that the green chili burro, enchilada style, that Diego had ordered would be on a different scale of heat than what Lucas had ordered. There was a reason chili peppers were categorized as mild, medium and hot. Hot took some getting used to. Lucas had managed it once.

As he ate, Diego continued talking. "We also do new projects—some shopping centers, business parks, some government work, the occasional private home. But integrity is important to us, *amigo,* in our final product and in the way we do business. Money is never our final consideration. We have to believe in the integrity of the project, or we don't do it. If that makes us less wealthy than many counterparts in the industry—" he shrugged "—then we are less wealthy. But our consciences are clear. *Una buena conciencia es una buena almohada,* eh? A good conscience is the best pillow. You can sleep soundly that way. We believe that, *amigo.*"

Diego focused his attention on eating, as did Lucas. Because he knew Diego so well, Lucas knew that this silence meant he was thinking, mulling something over. He definitely had more to say, but attempting to rush him would not hasten the words.

As Diego smeared honey on a sopapilla—a kind of flat pastry best eaten slightly warm—his eyes refocused on Lucas. Lucas knew then that Diego was again ready to speak. He could not, however, have anticipated Diego's next words.

"How is Rachel?" Diego's voice was quiet.

Lucas hesitated in spreading jam on his own sopapilla and eyed his friend. "She's...well," he offered. "We separated quite some time ago." Lucas had become accustomed to this truth, yet he felt shame in admitting it to Diego. It smacked of failure, or at least it did when presented to a man like Diego.

"I know you are separated, my friend. I am very aware of that. What I am wondering is why you say she is well?" He regarded Lucas levelly, his eyes hooded, his opinion disguised.

Lucas shrugged uncomfortably. "I've seen her recently. Several times lately, and she seems well. Well enough, anyway. As lovely as ever."

"*Sí,* she is beautiful, that one. On the inside, too." Diego poured another glass of iced tea from the pitcher on the table and began preparing another sopapilla. "She lives in one of our communities, you know, one of the inner-city revitalization areas designed to bring families back to the city. She and Michaela. Did I mention that these are very inexpensive compared to other homes and that there is an upper ceiling on the income level of people allowed to live there?''

Lucas's only response was a sharply indrawn breath.

''*Sí, amigo,* you perhaps understand what I am telling you. You've had it very comfortably with money, no? No worries for you. Rachel has not had it so easy. She struggles with many things, raising her little girl by herself. Many people would wonder what kind of scum the child's father is. I wonder that myself.''

Squeezing more lemon juice into his tea, Diego's smile was slightly mocking. ''I've surprised you this time, no? I haven't seen you in many years, *amigo,* but I continue to know Rachel. She, too, is my friend. She is *familia.*''

That simple statement explained so much, carried so much weight.

Lucas's eyes widened. Diego seemed especially intense, making the comment.

''Why so surprised, Lucas? You surely know that I couldn't hold Rachel in any higher regard than I do.'' He paused, his eyes not wavering from Lucas's face, daring him to challenge or deny the truth of his words. ''You know that. Did you know that she is very well known in the Hispanic community? She is well regarded. She is a good woman and has worked hard, not just for herself and Michaela, but for her people, too.''

He swallowed a mouthful of iced tea, then went on. ''Traditionally, Mexican people can be suspicious of modern medicine. I don't mean they neglect getting treatment, but maybe they are skeptical sometimes. Certain techniques, they can be seen as interfering with God's will, that kind of thing. So our people don't always think to see a doctor when they should. There are people who only do it because Doña Raquel is suggesting something, because Doña Raquel can help them trust the doctors and the procedures.''

''*Doña* Raquel? I heard someone call her that at the hospital.''

''*Naturalmente.* Raquel is Rachel in Spanish. But *doña,* that is a sign of respect.''

Lucas pondered this—Rachel hadn't mentioned that it was a respectful title—only that it was a title.

''I think,'' Diego continued, his eyes narrowing as he sought to remember the history, "it came from Spain, as a title, you know, for the noble people. But now, in Mexico, it is used to show that someone is honored. Rachel is. When Michaela became sick, when we knew she needed a bone marrow donor, Rachel organized a bone marrow drive. She put special attention toward the Hispanic community, hoping Michaela's match would be there. It wasn't. But many, many people came, hoping they would be the one to help the *niña* of Doña Raquel. The result, even though it didn't help Michaela, was to greatly increase the number of Hispanics in the donor registry, so that they can help themselves a little quicker when it's necessary. Rachel could help the people understand it was a way of supporting their community, a way of rallying behind one another. She understands the way tradition works among Hispanics. Of course, many of us noticed that you did not participate, even when your daughter's life was at stake."

Lucas felt the accusation pierce through him. "I didn't know about Michaela. I only found out she existed—" he calculated the days "—a couple of weeks ago. Rachel…left before I ever knew there would be a baby."

Diego emitted what Lucas knew was a Spanish curse, understanding its meaning despite the language barrier. "How could you not know?"

"She disappeared. She left. She didn't tell me. I didn't know. I never saw her again until she showed up at my office several weeks ago. But for five years, we've been leading separate lives."

"You have been doing that, *sí*." Lucas saw the glittering in Diego's eyes, and was reminded forcefully that he had seen the same look in Rick's eyes not too long ago.

"Rachel asked me then to be tested as a donor. I did and I matched. The transplant is in progress. They've actually done the main portion."

"I know."

Diego smiled, seeing Lucas's expression. "*Sí*, Lucas, I told you this is my family. Little goes on with Rachel that I do not know about. Would you imagine that I, myself, have not been tested as a match? Of course I was. I just wondered what you would tell me."

Diego became silent then, returning momentarily to his lunch.

So I'm being tested, Lucas realized, *in a way that has nothing to do with being a bone marrow donor.* He could sense that Diego was drawing some conclusions, very likely about *him.* No point in rushing anything. Lucas waited for Diego to continue.

"About Fuentes de la Juventud, it is not just me, you know, *amigo,*" Diego resumed. "I have partners, cousins, who also would have to approve such a decision. As for myself—" he shrugged "—of course, I have my doubts about you. But I also remember you from many years ago, I remember your talent and the potential you had. But the others—" he shrugged again "—they will say, *'Dime con quién andas y te diré quién eres.'* You know, in English—" Lucas could feel Diego translating the expression "—you would say something like 'A man is known by the company he keeps.'" He smiled sheepishly. "I don't always translate so well, and some of the expressions say it better in Spanish, I think. The Spanish comes to me first. I have to think of the English."

He paused, apparently thinking of another expression. "A better one is, *'Quién mal anda, mal acaba,'* which would be—" again he thought for a moment "'—If you spend time with bad men, you will become one of them.'" Satisfied with his translations, he sat back in his chair.

"And that, my friend, is the real problem. You see, *amigo,* your father—" there was that shrug again "—he is known, *comprende,* and not because he is a good man. You have been with him a long time and you have done nothing to improve your own reputation. You have not separated yourself from him, *comprende?* You have been his instrument. People see this, they see what you did to Rachel. The reputation it creates is not so good. It doesn't suggest that you are a man of integrity."

Lucas felt himself blush, stunned and horrified that he could. He recalled easily what Rick had said about other people witnessing what he had done and having an opinion about it. Diego seemed to feel the same way. "Maybe it's better late than never," Lucas suggested.

Diego inclined his head. "Perhaps."

Suddenly Lucas remembered something else Rick had said to him. "Diego, what does *casa chica* mean? And *pela*-something?"

Diego smiled, the corners of his eyes crinkling. "Where did you hear these words, *amigo?*"

Lucas suspected they weren't nice Spanish words. Rick had hurled them at him in anger, after all. But he wanted to know, nevertheless. "It was something Rick said to me."

"Ah, *sí.*" Diego nodded his head, his laugh crinkles deepened. "Rick would have reason to. *Bueno,* let's see, I think you mean *pelado?*"

"Yeah, that sounds right." Lucas tried to replay the conversation in his mind.

"*Pelado,* it means plucked chicken really. But we use it to talk about men who, inside, are weak, but try to show that they are strong by being...obvious, rough, crude, immoral. They are puffed up about themselves, *comprende?* They treat women very badly, without respect, thinking they are showing their strength. Sometimes they are violent, given to revenge over nothing. Mexican men like to be thought of as macho, maybe that is not so different from men in other cultures. But with our machismo, there is a certain attitude. *Pelados* think they show their machismo, their masculinity, by their behavior. They try to strut, *comprende,* with their pride. But because they are weak inside, no one believes their displays. To be called such a one is nothing to be proud of."

"No, I had figured that much out."

Rick certainly doesn't see me in a flattering light, Lucas had to admit. *But, then, why would he? He's Rachel brother, after all.*

"What was the other?"

"*Casa chica.* He said something about turning Rachel's home into one."

"Ah, yes, and you did, too. A little house of love."

"Well, that doesn't sound so bad," Lucas said, relieved.

Diego smiled thinly. "Except that it is what a man arranges for his mistress. Normally the wife never sees it, never knows about it. Certainly a man does not set up his mistress in his wife's home. Surely Anglo culture doesn't encourage that?"

Lucas was vaguely aware that he was shaking his head in denial. He didn't know what to say.

He'd never thought of it that way. He couldn't say that anything that had occurred with Rachel was actually encouraged by white culture. The results hadn't been intentional. Not that it excused him, he knew.

"But you did do this, *sí?* Once Rachel left, you put the other woman there. Rachel couldn't have come back to you if she'd wanted to—there was no place for her to go. And she owned the place, too, didn't she? Is she, since you're still married, is she also still paying for your mistress's home?"

Lucas knew that the color was draining from his face. Diego clearly knew there had been no divorce. What would Diego think if he told him that Alana had chosen the condo, that Lucas had given Rachel no choice but to live there? Then again, maybe Diego knew that, too.

"You show no class, *amigo.* No honor. And Rachel deserves better than this."

A sudden surge of suspicion—and anger—shot through Lucas. "How well do you know Rachel, Diego?"

Unconcerned, Diego shrugged and responded, "I told you she is *familia.* I know her very well. But never well enough. I care for her deeply. I think you should not insist on more answer than that." His voice had turned hard. "Rachel is a changed woman, Lucas. She was always calm, gentle—but she had fire, too. Now too often she seems…subdued. Not unhappy exactly, but not happy, either, not in the full sense of the word. It reminds me of what you see with nuns."

"Nuns?" Lucas regretted that his voice squeaked, but Diego's comparison bewildered him.

"*Sí.*" Diego had a faraway look in his eyes, almost seemed to be talking to himself. "I suppose nurses have it, too, but I think of it with nuns. I am Catholic, *comprende?*" He shrugged, smiled slightly. "She is serene, solemn. Dedicated to something that brings her joy, but the happiness seems—I don't know how to explain it—as if it is distant, not touchable. As if she has given up something else that might have also been joyful in order to devote herself to what she has chosen. For Rachel, that would be her daughter and her work. Both make her happy—I don't question that. It is that Rachel is too solemn, too often. The fire doesn't show itself like it used to.''

Lucas thought he had seen the fire lately, in the form of anger. Rachel—at least the Rachel he had known—tended to be calm and serene, not easily ruffled. She tended toward passion and laughter. Anger was very out of character for her. He knew what Diego meant. Rick had mentioned it, too. Rachel had always felt things deeply and thrived on it. She now seemed…untouchable at that deeper level. Or as if she wanted to be untouchable. Truly untouchable, Lucas reflected.

Wounded. That was the word he'd chosen. It seemed more accurate than ever.

''I suppose the question is really whether the change is temporary or if she has lost part of herself that she can never get back.'' Diego hadn't realized he'd spoken aloud. He cleared his throat, changing the subject. ''I will speak to my partners, *amigo.* I will think on the matter. I can promise you nothing. Your reputation is such that we may not be willing to take the risk. But I will consider it. As for you—'' he pointed at Lucas ''—you also have much thinking to do, no? Sometimes a man must take a chance, he must risk something, to do what he believes is right. You have been careless, *amigo.* You have not thought of anyone but yourself. To help your daughter, that is a good step. But you have many others to take. Think, Lucas, and do the right thing.''

With that, Diego stood, dropped money on the table, and left the clubhouse. Lucas sat transfixed. The conversation with Diego had covered many topics, even if Lucas had started it by asking for a job. Not that he had intended to do that, but it had broken the ice, so to speak. He was incredibly relieved that he was finally pursuing a career move—just admitting he needed to make one was helping. But Diego was right. He did have some loose ends to take care of. He suspected they would be more complicated than his job preference.

All in all, Lucas decided as he pocketed the keys to his Lexus, it was turning into a productive day. A satisfying day. He was making decisions and found that it felt surprisingly good. He wondered why he had always avoided decision making before, preferring instead to just let things happen. Today he knew the glow of taking charge of his life.

Of course, Diego hadn't promised him anything beyond ''thinking about'' Lucas's business proposition. Still, Lucas felt inexplicably hopeful about his chances.

The thing was that simply admitting he wanted out of Neuman Industries, letting someone else know, had taken a significant load off his shoulders. Lucas knew a big, dumb grin was spreading over his face just thinking about it.

His step felt lighter. His mood, too. Making a good decision could do that to a man. It was a new experience for Lucas.

Which brought him to the next decision he had made today. It had been remarkably easy, really. It was just a matter of doing it.

He'd spoken to Charles Toliver, company attorney for Neuman Industries, who had pulled out a couple sheets of paper. Lucas had signed them where Charles indicated and, just like that, Lucas was no longer listed as the owner of a certain condo in Scottsdale.

Neuman Industries had already been named as the secondary owner—had actually been paying for it—so signing over his individual interest in the property had not been at all complicated.

Lucas had wanted to tell Alana about the change of ownership right away, give her the key he still carried. He was washing his hands of this particular thing immediately. However, Alana had not been in the office. No one had been sure where she was, so Lucas decided to stop at the condo and either give Alana the key and paperwork or leave them for her. He could let himself in with his key one last time if it came to that.

Yes, his step was lighter than it had been in years.

He practically skipped up the stairs to the front door, ringing the bell excitedly.

When no one answered, a wave of disappointment washed over Lucas. He really had wanted to do this face-to-face. Still, all that really mattered was that he got it done.

He slipped his key in the lock and opened the door. He stepped inside, noting the cool white-and-gray interior.

No, he thought, *not cool—it's cold. Why did I ever let Alana convince me it was perfect?*

He knew why. He wasn't proud of it. But the simple truth was that it had been easier to let someone else make the decision, to follow what they stated to be the truth. Because it was easier than thinking for himself.

He walked from the tiled entry toward the living room, which was straight in front of him. He glanced around, wondering when he had last been inside the place. He had never really lived here. Of course, he and Rachel had lived here for about a year, but he'd been gone as much as he'd been here. Unpacking and repacking a suitcase. That was about the extent of it. Then, once Rachel had left, Alana had arrived. Lucas hadn't wanted to live there, with or without Alana, so he'd left. It could never have felt like home to him. Yet, he had never bothered to legally disown the place.

This place still didn't feel like a home to him, though. It didn't feel like anyone really lived here. More like they just stayed here.

A rustling behind him made him turn around.

"Hello, Lucas," came the purring voice that now grated on his ears rather than arousing him. "Change your mind after all? Do I have something you want?"

Alana, obviously emerging from her bedroom down the hall, was enfolded in something sheer and frothy and black. Lucas knew it was intended to tantalize but found he could only wonder why she was dressed like that at three o'clock in the afternoon. Her perfume wafted in his direction, smothering him from all sides as she drifted past him, continuing toward the kitchen.

Lucas followed her, eager to finish the business of relinquishing his claim on the condo. "No, Alana, not at all," he called after her. "But I do have something to give you."

"A gift?" She half turned back toward him, letting her wrap fall open so that her bare flesh was revealed.

"Not exactly."

Alana's movements were sure and precise. Lucas was slow to realize she had placed a bottle of champagne and two glasses on the counter.

"So, Lucas—" her eyes gleamed "—where shall we start?"

Soft thuds behind him caused Lucas to turn around again, bringing into his line of view the unmistakable sight of his tousled father clad only in a bathrobe.

"Alana, baby, what are you doing?" His voice was slurred, from what, Lucas chose not to consider. "Come back to bed, sweetheart."

Alana gasped softly. Only then did Arnold Neuman notice his son leaning against the kitchen counter.

Arnold seem flustered for a brief second before bellowing out, "Why are you here, Lucas? As you can see, Alana and I are busy. We don't need your hclp."

"I wouldn't offer my help, although it seems to me you need somebody's. I actually had a little business with Alana, Dad. As you know, she wasn't in the office."

"Her *business* is with me at the moment, son."

"Share your *business* with her all you want, Dad. I certainly don't want it."

Lucas turned away from his father, disgust roiling in his stomach. Looking at Alana hardly offered any relief. He needed to do what he'd come for—and get out. He could feel bile rising in his throat. He didn't know how long he could suppress it.

"Here," he said, slamming the documents down on the counter. "My name's off as owner. It's Neuman Industries' property now." He looked at Alana, who had let herself be pulled into his father's grasp. "If you want your name on the papers, Alana, you'll have to negotiate with them. I'm out of the picture. Here's my key. I have no use for it."

Dropping it on top of the papers, Lucas briefly registered satisfaction at Alana's dumbfounded expression. She'd apparently been certain Lucas's arrival had meant something different and she had been wildly rising to the challenge of entertaining both him and his father at the same time. An involuntary shudder rippled through him—he couldn't think of anything more repugnant than passing time that way.

Lucas strode briskly toward the door, his father bustling after him, Alana standing limply in the kitchen, fingering the paperwork Lucas had left there.

"Don't go all superior on me, son. You turned to Alana, too, when you needed a woman. Why shouldn't I?"

Lucas didn't dignify that with a response. The image of sharing a woman with his father made Lucas nauseous. Rachel's comments on his father's behavior came to him with a new clarity. His stomach lurched again. Sweat was breaking out on his forehead. He felt weak.

"Ah, come now," his father sputtered when Lucas didn't respond. "You know how it is. I have needs, Lucas. Your mother and I haven't had that kind of relationship, hell, since you were born. She *knows* I have other women. It's okay with her. I've explained that to you man-to-man." He brushed back his thinning, too-long hair. "So don't try some self-righteous, holier-than-thou routine with me. I'm not buying it. You did the same thing."

Lucas wanted to leave, but something his father had said gave him pause. "What do you mean, I did the same thing?"

"You turned to Alana for diversion."

"Not until after Rachel had left."

"Yeah, right, son. All those trips. All those hotels. All those exotic locations. I'm not a fool and neither are you. I know you, I know Alana. Figuring out what you were doing together—hell, boy, that sure ain't rocket science. Or brain surgery. Although—" he chuckled, anticipating his own wit "—it could be called playing doctor, I guess."

Knowing his father wouldn't believe him, Lucas tried again, anyway. "I wasn't with Alana until Rachel was gone. I didn't cheat on Rachel. Ever." Lucas had never said that before. He hadn't realized the explanation, the distinction, wasn't clear to everyone. And yet, here was more proof of what people had been thinking.

People had assumed the obvious.

Only, it hadn't been obvious to Lucas, not at the time.

"Like I said, yeah, right." Arnold's beady black eyes peered out of his puffy face, sizing up his son. "Well, this time, I didn't come to Alana until your mother told me to leave. So my story is nearly the same as yours. Just like I said."

His father had his full attention now. He kept talking, even without encouragement from Lucas.

"Told me to get out, she did. So I left. Of course I came to Alana. She knows how to take care of a man. I'm feeling much better, too. What a difference Alana makes." He chuckled, again impressed with his wit. "Your mother will come to her senses in a few days and then I'll go home. But in the meantime—" He grinned slyly, winking at Lucas, Lucas staring back at his father's face.

It occurred to him then that he had inherited his father's eyes. That Michaela had inherited those eyes, as well. But Michaela's eyes, despite her illness, were clear and pure. His father's were dead and flat. They held no life. Lucas felt the sudden urge to know how his eyes looked—what did they say about the state of his soul? What would he see there? What did others see?

How close am I to becoming my father? The thought was new to him, and did nothing to appease his lurching stomach. Lucas could stand it no longer. He had to get out of there.

He escaped the condo, but not before his churning stomach decided it was going to punish him. He was going to be sick, no doubt about it. He nearly slipped on the stairs in his haste to get back to his car. A hedge of bougainvillea bordering the parking lot had to serve as camouflage for his problem.

He felt a pang of regret for the magnificent lunch he'd eaten with Diego, knowing he wouldn't want a chimichanga for a while.

Diego. God, has it only been a few hours since we had lunch together? Lucas tried to laugh but found it came out more like a moan. He wondered if Diego would consider this due punishment for the lessons he had to learn, or if he'd just consider it a waste of a good lunch.

Chapter 11

God, what a hellish encounter. How did such a great day go so wrong?

Leaving behind the condo as he drove away, the images Lucas had so recently viewed wouldn't leave his head. Of course, now he vividly understood that Rachel's claims regarding his father had not been exaggerated. They'd had the ring of authenticity about them, certainly, when she'd told him. Now he knew. There was no more room for doubt or questioning. He could no longer avoid the truth about his father.

And yes, this is my father, for God's sake. For better or for worse. Of course I didn't want to side with Rachel when she tried to tell me what was happening. But how many times did I tell her she was overreacting?

Over and over, he knew.

At least I never called her a liar. It wasn't much to cling to, to prove to himself that he'd been decent to Rachel on this subject, but it was all Lucas had.

So now he faced the truth about his father, about what kind of man he was. Rachel had called him a lecherous pig. Rick had called him a snake. Even Diego had been highly unflattering in his description of Arnold Neuman, suggesting he was a ''bad man.'' Lucas tried to raise a defense for his father, but found it impossible.

He had driven automatically, mechanically, and was surprised to find himself at his parents' estate in Paradise Valley. *Or maybe,* he considered, *maybe it's just Mother's place now.*

He parked the Lexus and went in search of his mother.

''Hello, Lucas,'' she called from the garden where she was trimming roses. Sophie Neuman loved flowers. She'd always contributed to the gardens in a hands-on way, winning the respect of the gardeners not only because she cared but also because she knew what she was talking about. She said the flowers brought a bit of beauty into her life. Lucas thought maybe she had needed that more than he had ever realized.

''I decided I wanted some fresh flowers at dinnertime. Will you be staying?''

''Sure, Mother,'' he said, kissing her cheek as manners, and habit, dictated. Truthfully, Lucas felt anything but hungry. ''I'll go in and wash up.''

Sometime later, surprising himself by doing justice to some sort of exotic chicken preparation, Lucas found himself sitting in the sunroom with his mother. Another magnificent Arizona sunset had just finished its act. Sophie had her cappuccino, her preferred after-dinner drink. Lucas had chosen brandy.

''I saw Dad today.'' Lucas couldn't be sure why he introduced the topic, other than that he couldn't get it off his mind. And he needed to know if what his father had said was true, if his mother had thrown him out. But etiquette stood in the way—Lucas had no idea how to actually ask his mother such a thing.

''Was he with her?'' she asked lightly, her eyes turned toward the water fountain in the garden. At night it was lit up, its spray rippling in iridescent waves. Another of Sophie's favorite things.

''Who?'' Lucas caught the undertone of distaste in her voice, but wasn't sure what she was asking.

His mother laughed. ''Alana.''

''Well, yes, actually, he was...with her.'' Lucas was too surprised to lie—and he couldn't see the point, anyway.

''I figured that's where he'd go. He's been looking for a

reason to stay with her. The difficulty this time will be when he tries to come home."

"Don't you want him to?"

"No, dear, definitely not." She was calm and cool, as usual, but Lucas could tell she was serious. She inhaled deeply. "Lucas, I want to know my granddaughter. I want to be a grandmother. That will not be possible with your father in the picture."

"He's told you this?"

Sophie's laughter tinkled again. "No, not exactly. But Rachel was right to want to protect her daughter, Lucas. We, your father and I, haven't treated Rachel very well. It's not surprising she would assume the same treatment would be directed toward her daughter. It shames me to admit it, but she's right. Arnold will never behave toward Rachel...in a healthy way. He would never care for the child, other than to use her as a weapon against Rachel."

"But, Mother, you talked that way, too." There was no purpose in hiding from the truth at this point, Lucas decided.

"Yes," Sophie agreed, surprising Lucas, "and I'm not proud of it. I was...supporting your father. Fulfilling my role, you know." She paused, gazing at her fountain, drawing strength and serenity from it. "Much like Rachel, I have tolerated a lot from Arnold. But, where Rachel created the room to be free of him, I didn't. I couldn't. Or so I thought. Having a grandchild has changed things. I've missed out on enough because it was what Arnold wanted."

"Missed out? What do you mean? You have what many women would want."

"I've never had a loving marriage, Lucas. I did my duty. I married and I produced an heir. I haven't been with your father since then. He disgusts me that way. He's never been faithful to me." At Lucas's raised eyebrows, she laughed lightly.

Lucas was surprised—not that she knew but that she would admit it to him so easily. Apparently, Sophie had also decided it was the time for truth.

She confirmed it again. "Oh, yes, Lucas, I knew. I also made sure there would not be children by any other woman. That's the only thing I demanded of him. Now I will require his absence. He will not deprive me of my granddaughter."

Lucas studied his brandy, startled to realize he hadn't even tasted it yet. He knew it would be exceptionally good—his father wouldn't stock anything less.

"Lucas, I know what your father is. So do you." She stood up and walked over to the switch that controlled the lighting on the fountain, flipping it off.

Returning to Lucas, she put a finger beneath his chin, tipping his face up. "You have some thinking to do, Lucas. My greatest happiness has come from you, my son. I wanted you to have everything and be everything you wanted to be. I wanted better for you than I had. You married for love. Rachel was not who I would have chosen for you, but I could see you were happy with her. Happiness is something my marriage never brought me. I was horrified when I realized that your marriage had turned into what I had. I also regret, more than I can tell you, my role in seeing that your marriage fell apart. I know I contributed. I should have stood up to your father. None of what he expected of you with Alana or for the company was really required—or right. None of it. His demands were, quite simply, wrong. I'd never thought about it until I heard Rachel at the hospital. She was right."

She took a deep breath. "It hurt me the other night, Lucas, when you told me what you think of me. It made me take a long look at myself. I didn't like what I saw. I've done what I was taught I was supposed to do, yes, but I never meant to lose myself when I did it. I've only just realized that that's what happened. But those were decisions I made. I can't blame them on anyone else. I can only try to do better from now on."

Her green eyes were soft, misty with tears. "I had no idea that having a grandchild would be so...important to me, Lucas. I'd never really considered how it would make me feel. When I found out about her, at first, I just kept thinking of her...as a possession, I guess. Something we needed to obtain. Then when I was standing in that hospital, and it was sinking in that she was there, that she was sick, and that I might never see her. Then I knew." She cleared her throat, her voice suddenly thick. "What does she have, Lucas?"

"Leukemia."

"Oh," she answered, "I see. And she is receiving the best treatment, the best care?"

"Without a doubt, Mother. I told you, Rachel has been a good mom to her. That she is a nurse hasn't hurt. We just have to wait and see. And hope. And pray." Lucas wondered if his mother did that sort of thing.

"Of course," she agreed immediately.

She let her hand drop away from his chin, but her eyes never left his face. "I love you, Lucas. I've probably not told you that often enough. I was trained not to. But I want you to know it. I want you to love your child the way I love you, and I want you to do better for your child, as a parent, than I did for you. I made mistakes, Lucas, plenty of them. Don't make the same mistakes I've made. I'm happy to see what your daughter means to you—and that you can admit it, act like it. Now what are you going to do about your wife?" She patted him on the head, as only a mother can do, regardless of her child's age. "Think about it, Lucas."

She left then, leaving Lucas in the dark.

This is hopeless, Rachel decided, sitting in her office. Alone.

She tossed the deck of cards down on the table, letting them scatter where they fell. She'd been playing solitaire—*winning* at solitaire, since she preferred to adapt the rules in her favor as she went—for nearly two hours now. She had soft music playing on her little radio, trying to avoid some of the ghastly late-night call-in talk shows. It was 12:15 a.m., she noticed. And she couldn't sleep.

Insomnia. Her frequent companion, right along with tension, worry, fear and hope. And fatigue. What a bunch they were.

But this time Rachel was also caught in trying to retrain her body to accept nighttime hours as the time for sleeping. She'd worked the night shift for so long that switching to a more normal schedule was not agreeing with her.

And a tendency toward insomnia didn't help the situation.

Rachel accepted that the insomnia was an outlet for her body, that it allowed her to cope with all the emotions she lived with but wouldn't show. That skill—the ability to mask what she was feeling—had been valuable when she and Michaela began battling leukemia. Since the diagnosis, Rachel had existed in a suspended emotional state, one that allowed her to always be braced for bad news. As a result, she just…didn't feel, whenever it was possible. Just the way she'd managed to deal with Lucas. And leaving Lucas.

But the emotions would not always agree to be buried. They protested when she shut her eyes.

How can I be so tired yet so completely unable to sleep?

Lying down on her bed, she tried to relax. After another twenty minutes, Rachel sat up, admitting defeat. Sleep would not be coming anytime soon.

With a sigh she got up. At her bathroom sink, she splashed cold water over her face, patting it dry on the towel. She picked up her toothbrush, trying to decide if she should get dressed just as she would when beginning any other day. Or whether she should get ready for bed a second time, trying to fool her body into sleep.

Unable to make up her mind, she brushed her teeth. That could be a first-thing-in-the-morning or a last-thing-at-night activity, so it didn't commit her either way. Picking up a brush, running it through her hair, she decided to call it a new day. She slipped on a pair of jeans, obviously unprofessional attire, but her favorites nevertheless.

"And I'm not working right now—this is my own time," she told the darkness, attempting to reassure herself. "I'm supposed to be sleeping, anyway, so if I want to wear my jeans, I will."

Rachel slipped out of her nightgown, rejecting the notion of wearing a bra and quickly grabbed a white lab coat from her wardrobe. She buttoned it up the front, more demurely than she normally would, given that she wore nothing underneath it this time.

Quickly, she prepared herself a cup of tea. Steaming mug in hand, face scrubbed clean, she stepped toward her office door.

Suddenly she realized that she had decided to go sit with Michaela and also that she was not wearing any makeup. She never entered the outside world without the protective mask it offered. Hesitating momentarily, she spoke aloud. "*Dios mio* Rachel, it's two in the morning. No one will care that you're not in full makeup." She drank as much tea as she wanted then headed down the corridor, toward her daughter's room.

Standing beside Michaela, watching her sleep, Rachel swallowed a lump in her throat.

''La niñita más linda del mundo,'' she whispered, believing it, knowing it was true, despite how ill Michaela looked. And it was awful, seeing her like this. It shook Rachel—no matter how she tried, she couldn't help it.

Of course, Rachel Neuman, the nurse, had seen many patients at this stage of their treatment. She knew they all looked like this, more or less. Frail, abnormally pale, hairless. Nearly lifeless.

Yes, it was the normal state, but seeing it on her own little girl was something she didn't care for.

Rachel gave herself a mental shake. *Michaela looks normal…normal, Rachel, normal for the circumstances.* She emphasized the word to herself, drilled it into her soul.

Sighing, Rachel sat down, pulling the enormous lounge chair close enough to Michaela's bed so that she could reach over the siderail to hold her daughter's hand.

It had been six days since the major cell infusion that counted as the bone marrow transplant—considered ''day zero'' in the countdown. Now they were into the count up, that portion of treatment that involved watching all sorts of numbers—blood counts especially. They were the proof that the new bone marrow was doing its job.

Once Michaela had stabilized, Rachel would resume her shift. After that, Michaela would still be staying in the hospital for several weeks. Typically, the stay was at least six weeks after day zero. Even then, returning home demanded controlled circumstances and precautions. That was when Rachel would have to take leave, several weeks at least.

She awaited this eagerly, anxiously. That would mean real progress in Michaela's health.

Rachel sighed again. Waiting was difficult. But there was no choice.

And then—there's Lucas. Another sigh.

An unofficial semitruce had emerged between Rachel and Lucas since the hospital encounter with his parents. Rachel felt awkward about that day, really awkward. Still, she couldn't have done anything else.

You could have been more tactful, a voice whispered in her head.

Almost immediately a louder voice answered: *Tact has no effect on Arnold Neuman. It would have been a waste of time.*

In a sense, Rachel had tried to be tactful with Arnold for years. She had removed herself from his presence as much as she could. To no avail.

No, she had said exactly what needed to be said, and she would do it again if it meant protecting Michaela. Still, uneasiness bubbled inside when she considered some of what she'd said to Lucas. Things that needed to be said, things that probably should have been said years ago—but they came from deep inside Rachel and she didn't like to throw them in people's faces. Even if it was about time Lucas heard it.

Frustration and rage and the need to defend Michaela—those had been a combination she couldn't conquer.

I'll control myself from now on, she vowed. Losing control was too embarrassing. She had to live with herself afterward.

Rachel could only guess what was going through Lucas's mind about that day. They hadn't revisited the conversation since then, but there had been no further hospital visits from his parents. Rachel was satisfied with that.

He is making an effort at the fatherhood thing, Rachel had to acknowledge. *He brings something to the parent role that I can't necessarily be.*

He'd shaved his head. He'd been hesitant about it. He'd asked her opinion. Michaela had laughed—or, at least, had come as close to laughing as she could these days.

"Now you still look like me, *Papá,* even with no hair."

Lucas had been thrilled that Michaela had understood the gesture. Rachel had been touched by the anxious thought that had prompted him.

"I can't exactly undo it now if she doesn't like it," he'd said.

He was making an effort, definitely. Rachel knew he cared deeply for Michaela and he was really trying to be a father to her. *Under circumstances that can't be the easiest way to get to know one's daughter,* she had to admit.

Strangely, Rachel knew she could trust Lucas in his interactions with Michaela. He was new to the task. If he made mistakes, they would be genuine mistakes and not something nefarious. His feelings for Michaela were sincere.

Rachel closed her eyes, admitting privately that the problem was between Lucas and her. That's where the trust breakdown existed. She had to be careful. Steer clear of wishful thinking. And other similar pitfalls.

The fact was she still loved him. There was no point questioning it any longer. She'd been around him enough lately, conscious of her own reactions to his presence. No, she could no longer deny that her love for him still thrived within her. That meant he could still hurt her as no one else ever could. Or had.

In the darkness she knew—she didn't want to be hurt like that again.

Chapter 12

Think, Lucas. How many times have I heard that lately?

Lights of the city twinkled in the valley below, but Lucas was focused on the darkness of his mother's sunroom.

Lucas downed his brandy in one gulp, refilling his glass and setting it on the table beside him. He leaned forward, his elbows on his knees, his head in his hands.

My God, haven't I done enough thinking lately? Isn't my brain about ready to explode with all the thinking I've done?

He reached over to pick up his brandy, took a gulp, not pausing to appreciate its fine quality.

And everything is so tied together. I pull on one strand, try to think about that, and it tightens things up somewhere else. So, I've got my parents to think about. Or, maybe I should say Mother and Dad. They're not a combined unit anymore. They're separate entities—maybe they always were. Then there's Michaela. Rachel. My career. Well, hell, that just about covers everything that's important in my life.

He raised his glass to his lips, slamming down the remainder, despite the way his throat was beginning to burn, knowing he would feel the effects soon. He poured another glass, raising it to his lips, as well.

Maybe getting drunk isn't the answer. It won't solve anything.

Defiantly he took a mouthful. Then another. He didn't want to listen to that voice.

Clear thinking, that's what I need. But, hell, it's beginning to feel like all I've done lately is think. And what's it getting me? Have I figured anything out yet?

Okay, he might be making some progress on the career front. He had a good feeling about Diego. If nothing else, his personal leave from Neuman Industries could easily turn into a resignation.

Yes, he sat up straight. *That's it. I'll resign.*

The thought brought a smile to his face. But, Lucas recognized, it was very close to being a drunken smile. And getting drunk was the kind of thing his father would do. He slammed his glass down on the side table, carelessly sloshing the expensive brandy, nearly shattering the delicate crystal. He was making another decision.

He needed coffee, that's what he needed. He went back to the main part of the house.

His puttering around in the kitchen would not be appreciated by the cook several hours from now, Lucas knew, but he started a pot of coffee, anyway. He used the same kind of machine at home, so at least he knew how to operate the thing. Finding all the necessary bits and pieces, however, required a few minutes of slamming through cupboards. This mission addressed, he sat down to wait, drumming his fingers on the kitchen table.

This lasted only a few minutes. He jumped up and began pacing the kitchen floor, perhaps trying to ward off any effects of the brandy, perhaps trying to use up some of the frantic energy racing through his brain.

Finally he sat down with a cup of coffee. A warm glow began to take shape inside him, as he began, he hoped, to calmly analyze what needed analyzing.

Okay, then, he'd already examined his career and made a decision. He was making progress in that category, but he'd started on that first. He'd called Diego before Rachel had reentered his life, so her reappearance hadn't motivated him on that score. He'd told Diego he wasn't happy at Neuman Industries.

Now he knew he never had been. Once the initial thrill of employment had worn off—no, he'd never been happy.

Right. Seeing his career in its true light and making adjustments so that he would like what he saw—that was definitely progress. He could feel good about that much at least.

What about Dad?

A good question. A difficult question. His unhappiness at work was connected to his feelings about his father. His mother was right. He knew what his father was. Maybe Lucas wasn't very clear about what his mother was anymore, but she was in some kind of flux herself, so that was okay. Lucas did, however, recognize his father for what he was. He'd probably known for a while, but had preferred not to think about it. So he was thinking about it now. And seeing the truth, admitting the truth.

Finally, the filter through which Lucas had always viewed his father fell away. He could no longer hide behind the childish notion that his father was perfect. His father, in reality, wasn't a good man. He treated other people poorly. Arnold Neuman used other people—whether or not the other parties realized it. And he was bigoted for sure.

He had no respect—or true liking—for women. Despite viewing himself as a ladies' man, he felt only disrespect toward women and saw them as having no other purpose than to elevate his status as a male—through whatever available means he saw. A *pelado,* Lucas realized.

Honor and integrity were not personal characteristics of his father. They weren't professional characteristics, either, Lucas admitted ruefully. Fuentes de la Juventud was known as a company with a conscience—but Neuman Industries certainly wasn't. Those reputations led directly back to the men heading the organizations.

I've stood beside my father. What does that say about my personal integrity? The question hurt.

If Lucas had had any doubts about it, he knew then, unequivocally, that it was time to step away from his father. It had been for a long time. He had given his father far too much credit, far too much benefit of the doubt. And he had gone along with his father's opinions for far too long—his father's flawed opinions, which had also played a role in the mess Lucas had made of his marriage.

Stop right there.

Lucas wasn't ready to think about Rachel yet. He jumped up and fixed another cup of coffee.

His mother. Yes, she'd admitted to making mistakes and to wanting to make some changes. Namely, she wanted nothing to do with his father. That was probably a good idea, Lucas thought. If she was away from him, away from his influence, she might be able to discover herself again. She might still think she had to play a role—some habits were hard to break—but at least she'd have the chance to create her own role. As she had said, she just wanted to do better from now on. Lucas could relate to that.

Briefly he lumped them together again, saw them as his parents. He could see, if he forced himself, that he had tried to deliver what his parents expected. Rachel was right about that. But he was a grown man now, and he could make his own decisions. He *could.*

His mother also wanted to be a grandmother. She was excited, truly excited, about this possibility. Diego's words about nuns came back to him—about them being happy in a certain, limited way that their life choice allowed them. Lucas thought this fit his mother, as well. She rarely, if ever, showed emotion. Lucas had become accustomed to thinking of her as cold. Tonight he had seen more feeling from her than ever before.

He considered her words—he couldn't undo the past. Unfortunately. But, just as she had said, he could do better from now on. And wasn't that exactly what he had already decided recently?

He had a daughter whom he was getting to know, whom he already loved. He treasured her, felt right about the world when he thought of her. He enjoyed being with her, even under the strain of the current situation. She was part of him as nothing else ever had been. He understood what his mother meant about wanting the best for one's child. He felt it. Even as a novice father, he knew the feeling very well.

Michaela felt something for him, too, which thrilled him. When she called him *Papá,* when she would hug him, delivering love with the absolute honesty of a child—Lucas didn't have the words to describe how that made him feel. It filled him, it fulfilled him. It was like nothing he had ever expected to feel, nothing he'd known existed. And he'd almost missed it. So he'd faced that, too, faced the fact that responsibility had its good side. Michaela was his responsibility, a joyful responsibility. The word no longer made him flinch.

What made him flinch was…his wife. He knew he didn't want a divorce. He knew, when he let his mind wander, that he liked the idea of being a family with Rachel. He could feel how wonderful that would be. He could remember, so easily now, what it had been like to be married to her. Life had just been better with her. Much the way it was better with Michaela.

Thinking of how Rachel melted under his touch, Lucas knew it couldn't get better than that. Except that it could—if she would only go with the feelings she wouldn't acknowledge. Go with them the way she had before. When they'd been happy together. Before all the hurt had happened.

He missed Rachel. He had missed her all this time. He liked being around her again, despite the circumstances. If he was honest with himself, he knew he wanted to be in her life as her husband.

Could he convince her of that? Or had he completely blown his chance?

He had not been a good husband, he could see that now. It didn't matter why. He could blame his parents, but ultimately it was his fault. He had taken the marriage for granted. Hell, he'd taken Rachel for granted. He'd been so caught up in what he thought he was supposed to get from the marriage, ideas his parents had fed him, that he'd never considered what she should get. He'd never thought about what he should be *giving*.

He'd never thought about what they should have had *together*. What the two of them should have been sharing. He'd just let things happen. At least, that's what he thought he was doing at the time. He'd complained about Rachel not supporting him—but, dammit, she was right. He hadn't supported *her* when she'd needed it.

During that crucial time in their marriage, he had declined to take responsibility for his life, for his own actions. He'd followed the path of least resistance. Usually the one his father recommended.

That's why he'd brought Alana into his marriage, made her the third party in a relationship that should have only had two. He'd brought in a successor while Rachel was still there, just as she'd said. Then he'd made sure that Rachel had no place to return to if she'd wanted to. Diego had said that.

His parents had encouraged the relationship with Alana and, Lucas now admitted shamefully, it had indeed been easier to do what his parents wanted. To let Rachel absorb the fallout. She had argued about it at first, all his trips, all the time he spent with Alana—about how the two of them, Lucas and Rachel, didn't have a life together anymore.

He'd had no time to listen to her concerns. She'd said he was gone too much. He'd said he was doing what he had to do to build his career. She'd asked him to slow down, to include her in his life. He'd said she needed to grow up, to get a clue about the world he lived in now. She'd said he needed to live in his marriage more often. He'd said she was nagging him. She'd never mentioned it again. Ever.

He thought of his return from Las Vegas.

Why the hell didn't I drop to my knees and swear that nothing like that would ever happen again—and mean it? Why didn't I tell her that I had been stupid and blind but that I wouldn't do that anymore? Why didn't I tell her I was sorry?

He had been sorry. He'd also been very confused, by what he'd done—or nearly done—to say nothing of why he'd been in that position. Because of the state of their marriage, and his state of mind, he'd been unable to tell Rachel that. Unable to ask her to help him. Unable to say he wanted to fix things, to make them the way they used to be—or even better. He should have told her.

If he had...how might things have been different?

Finally, Lucas began to grasp what he had really lost that night. He could finally comprehend what Rachel had meant when she said that night was the end—an end following a year of careless, casual, irresponsible behavior on his part.

For the first time, Lucas felt remorse and regret, not only for his behavior during his last year with Rachel, but also during all the years since then. He'd let Rachel down. He'd let himself down, too. And, although he hadn't known it, he'd let Michaela down, as well.

What he'd brought home from Las Vegas—the evidence, the attitude, the hand without its wedding band—had been too much for Rachel.

He couldn't change it now. He could only try to do better.

And he fully intended to do better. Because he still loved Rachel. He had never stopped. Even though he had allowed her to walk out of his life.

He'd been given the chance to walk back into hers.

He would do better from now on.

Lucas checked the microwave clock. It was 3:45 a.m. He'd consumed two pots of coffee, eating no food as he went, which probably accounted for his energized state.

Or maybe making decisions, sorting out your life, does this to a guy. Lucas wasn't sure about that.

He knew his mother had had a room prepared for him, but he wasn't going to use it. There was *no way* he could possibly sleep. Not tonight. Or, rather, this morning.

At four o'clock, he decided he would leave to go to the hospital. He wanted to see Michaela. He wanted to see Rachel.

But he had one small item to take care of first.

Well, maybe two, he amended. *Two pots of coffee tended to go through a guy.*

First, he opened the kitchen "junk drawer," something his mother had always insisted they needed, although it was completely out of character for her to advocate such a state of messiness.

Or, at least, he had always assumed it was out of character. Now Lucas wondered. Maybe that was a glimpse of who she really was. He'd have to keep an open mind.

Shuffling things around, he finally found what he was looking for. He ripped a sheet of paper off the tablet that he had located, then popped the cap off the cherry-red marking pen.

"I love you, too, Mother." He wrote the words, then folded the sheet of paper in two. He dashed upstairs, where her bedroom suite was. The door was closed, as it always was. But it wouldn't be locked.

Carefully he opened the door and crept into the room. His mother was a light sleeper. He didn't want to wake her. He went over to her vanity, propping his note against the mirror. He knew she would spot it immediately. He turned to leave then, but something made him go back over to her bedside instead.

She looks younger, he thought, noticing that the tracks of tears were visible on her cheeks. *More relaxed than I can remember ever seeing her. I hope the tears helped.*

As he left the room, pulling the door shut beside him, he wondered. Had she cried often, throughout her marriage, in the privacy of her own suite of rooms? Would she be happier now? *Una buena conciencia es una buena almohada.* Isn't that how Diego said it? A clear conscience is a good pillow. Or something like that. Maybe that's what his mother had finally found. He hoped so. His mother had paid her dues.

Dawn was creeping up in the east, radiant pink streaks slashing through the pale blue of the new morning. Last night's moon was still visible high above him. Lucas was going to the hospital. He had a daughter to see, a family to spend time with. Maybe a marriage to mend.

He smiled, a genuine, full-fledged smile.

Stepping off the elevator, Lucas briefly considered that a few weeks of regular visiting had eased his hospital-induced panic. He was comfortable here now. He had managed to establish a reluctant working relationship with the nursing staff, so when he arrived at 5:00 a.m. to see his daughter, his presence was only briefly acknowledged as he went to her room. Mutual good-mornings passed between them as he went his way.

Lucas grabbed a face mask, put it on and went into Michaela's room.

"She looks awful," he whispered, his gaze riveted to her face, silently admitting that her pallor looked deathly. He'd been assured this was normal progress, but it felt—and looked—horrible. He took a deep breath. He reached over to pull back the lounge chair, preparing to sit down.

Only then did he see the figure in the chair, her hand tangled through the bed's side rail. He caught his breath. It was Rachel. Sound asleep, hair draped around her shoulders, sitting with her knees pulled up to her chin, her other arm wrapped loosely around her legs.

Lucas watched her, feeling warm inside.

His woman. The woman he wanted to spend the rest of his

life with. His heart lurched. Desire and love rolled together, tied themselves together, the way they always had with Lucas.

All they needed was for Rachel to admit her own feelings, the ones that were fighting to surface. Everything would be fine if she would just follow what he knew she was feeling.

Watching her sleep, he felt his body begin to stir. She looked so…inviting. So familiar. So right. Soft and warm in her sleep, vulnerable in this private moment. Fragile in a way he didn't associate with Rachel. Not angry, at the moment, as she seemed to be so often lately.

Lucas wondered vaguely if everyone looked softer in sleep.

God, I want her.

He loved her. He wanted her. With him it was nearly the same thing.

That had been one of his mistakes. He hadn't understood the connection until now.

Her eyes opened. Lucas felt, rather than heard, her soft gasp when she recognized him standing over her.

"Good morning, Rachel."

"*Buenos días,*" she mumbled sleepily. "I guess I fell asleep." She peered at Michaela, giving her hand a quick squeeze before extricating her own hand from the bars of the side rail. She lifted her arms over her head, stretching, pulling her lab coat tightly across the breasts which were bare beneath the fabric.

Lucas noticed. His body noticed. He had to think of something else. "I think you're still asleep."

"Hmm?" She stared back at him uncomprehendingly.

"Come on," he said, reaching for her hands and pulling her from the lounge chair. "Let's get you back to bed."

She mumbled something again, but put her arm around Lucas's waist for support, her hair tumbling forward in a vanilla-scented cloud. Yes, spicy vanilla and…*her* scent. Recognition—and desire—gushed through him. Lucas slipped his arm around her waist, thankful that she was too asleep to notice his response to her. He took a slow breath, inhaling deeply.

Yes, my body thinks bed would be a great idea.

Gently he led Rachel from Michaela's room toward her office. Lucas had never seen Rachel's sleeping quarters—that, after all, was private. But he found it this morning with no difficulty. He helped Rachel lie down, quickly deciding not to remove or even loosen any of her clothing.

He pulled the sheet up to her chin, remembering that she always slept better covered, even in the heat of the summer. The only time she preferred nothing was after making love.

It's probably not the best time to think of that, Lucas lectured himself. But the memory lingered.

Rachel stretched a little, settling one hand next to her face in a loose fist, the other one stretched out across the sheets.

As if she's looking for someone next to her, Lucas thought. At one time, that someone had been him.

Her lips parted and she sighed.

Lucas leaned over and kissed her. It was a chaste kiss, as far as kisses went, but he felt the sizzle go all the way to his toes. His throbbing body hardened even further, although he wouldn't have believed it possible.

Rachel had kissed him back. Softly, gently—and utterly unaware of it. But completely naturally. Without reluctance. Without pulling away.

Lucas stood and smiled down at her. Then, rearranging his own clothes to be less constricting and more concealing, he left her office. With a big smile on his face. And a glow in his heart.

Rachel slept, deeply, soundly. Better than she had in a very long time.

Chapter 13

Several weeks after the BMT, Michaela was showing real progress. Of course, medically, her life was still controlled, but she was reemerging, a new butterfly anxious to leave her cocoon—perhaps a little faster than she should.

She wanted to *do* absolutely everything. Her energy supply, however, was quickly depleted. She needed frequent naps, which she hated, insisting she wasn't a baby. Typically, though, she was practically asleep even as the protests left her mouth.

Such was the case today. Lucas and Rachel had gathered in Michaela's room, specifically to watch yet another in the string of hospital-provided children's videos. Michaela rarely saw the end of these films, tending to drift off to sleep midway through. This had happened today—Rachel and Lucas watching Michaela fall asleep and then watching the heartwarming, sometimes swashbuckling, finale of the animated feature in question. Michaela always had questions on the parts she missed, and her parents had learned rather quickly that they should expect to deliver a detailed summary in order to satisfy her need to know.

Eventually, blank blue dominated the screen.

''You've shaved it again,'' Rachel commented, absently regarding her husband's shiny head with a lazy grin.

Patting his newly bald pate, Lucas smiled. ''Yeah. It was starting to grow back already and I thought it would be better if I was hairless as long as Michaela is, you know? I thought I should stay bald, too.'' He chuckled to himself. ''I was surprised how fast it came back. I was getting pretty fuzzy again.''

''Well, you always did get your five-o'clock shadow pretty early in the day.'' The words had been spoken innocently and involuntarily. However, they pointed to a familiarity between the two of them that sent two red flags of embarrassed color rushing to Rachel's cheeks.

''Yeah,'' Lucas agreed, glancing at Rachel, wondering if she knew how intimate her words sounded to him, how his body relished them. ''I guess it's nearly the same thing.''

Rachel stood, needing to distance herself from this conversation and also to wake herself up. Her body clock continued to protest her change in hours if she sat still very long. She was always in danger of falling asleep at an inappropriate time. Falling asleep with Lucas would definitely be best avoided.

She walked over to the window, gazing out at the busy streets of Phoenix, stretching.

''She is doing better, isn't she.'' Lucas's remark was more a statement than a question, but Rachel knew he still sought confirmation. As Michaela's parent, she needed that confirmation, too.

''Yes.''

''I mean, I realize she'll be pale, that the hair—'' he swallowed hard, acknowledging that the hair loss was somehow symbolically significant to him ''—the hair will take time to grow back. But—'' he glanced at Rachel, not raising his head completely but still giving Rachel enough of a look that she recognized the anguish darkening his gray eyes ''—she is improving, right? This is…normal.''

''Absolutely normal,'' Rachel confirmed. ''It varies a little from one person to another, of course. Michaela seems to be starting to feel better even though her appearance hasn't caught up yet. The way she wants to jump in and be busy—'' her voice grew husky and she stopped, taking a deep breath, trying to regain some composure, before she continued ''—that's normal for Michaela. I mean, that's how she acts. She's always busy and eager to get into things. Curious. So, for me to see that coming back, for her personality to be showing up—'' her voice broke ''—even though she can't maintain it very long, that is a good change. *Sí, sí,*'' she whispered nearly to herself, ''that is good.''

Lucas left Michaela's bedside, making his way to the window where Rachel was standing. Moments like this were difficult for Lucas, wanting as he did to hold Rachel, to take her in his arms and share the emotion with her. Yet, he had promised himself that he wouldn't force physical intimacy on her. He didn't mean sex, either, although that was on his mind, too. He wanted more than that with Rachel, much more, and he knew that meant taking it nice and slow. Rushing her was not an option. That, in turn, meant keeping his impulses under control.

Not sure what else to do, he shoved his hands in his jeans pockets and rocked back on his heels. Then, leaning toward her, careful to avoid any suggestion of touching her, he whispered, ''You can relax with me, you know. I told you I'm here to share this. I am sharing this. Take a deep breath, Rachel, and let go a little.''

Rachel followed Lucas's instructions and gave him a sheepish smile. ''I guess I don't know how.'' She smiled, a little brighter this time. ''I'm trying, Lucas.''

''I know.'' And he did know, more than she could understand. In spite of his good intentions, Lucas reached toward Rachel then, tracing the corner of her smile with his thumb.

Her smile faltered a little—but she didn't pull away. Instead, embarrassed color zipped back into her cheeks and she gave an awkward laugh. ''Thanks, Lucas.''

He smiled, too, a warm glow building inside him.

A companionable silence reigned for a few minutes, both of them alone with their thoughts. Which brought to Lucas's mind some things he hadn't mentioned to Rachel yet.

''Did you know I went golfing with Diego the other day?''

''No, I had no idea.''

''Yeah, it was sort of an impulse. But, even more of an impulse—I asked him for a job.''

''What?'' Rachel was shocked. Lucas spending time with

Diego? Lucas leaving his father's company? Lucas being *independent* of his father? Unthinkable in the Lucas she had known.

If only he'd done that years ago— She stopped the thought right there. That kind of memory-lane trip would serve no purpose.

"Surprised you, did I? Me, too."

Well, Rachel thought, *that helps a little. At least he realizes it, too.*

Lucas started to run his hand through his hair, hesitating when he felt the bareness up there on his head. "It's time for the change. Sometimes I think I should have never started with Dad. I thought I could learn there, that it'd be a good way to start. And I felt like I owed him something for helping me get through school. He thought so, too. As I'm sure you recall."

Lucas shook his head, feeling dismal. "I don't think I owed him my entire life, though. I'm not even sure I learned anything I want to know, anything good or worthwhile."

"Good parents don't lay guilt on their kids about paying them back. That's not what parenthood is about." Briefly, she rested her hand on his elbow. "Any return your father deserved on his investment in you was paid back a long time ago—if you owed him anything in the first place. And you've learned plenty. You wouldn't see the value in what Diego has to offer, if you hadn't seen the other side clearly, too."

She let her hand fall back to her side, somewhat surprised to notice she'd touched Lucas. But she'd said something that needed to be said.

"I'm not sure how long I can stay working there." He had inclined his head when she touched him. He looked toward her now, from under thick black eyebrows. "I'm on leave now, technically. But I've decided to resign."

"I think that's good, Lucas. No, I think it's great." She was stunned, to the core. But she did think this was a good move for him.

"Amazing, isn't it? That I finally get it?" He raised an eyebrow at her. "It surprises me, too. But it feels right, as well. Makes me mad I didn't know how to take a stand before now."

At this, Rachel visibly started. It was an echo of her own

thoughts, an echo of what she had wanted so long ago. Had Lucas changed?

Of course he has, she told herself. *He couldn't have done this before.*

"And what did Diego have to say about this?"

"He's thinking about it. I guess there are cousins and such involved?" Rachel nodded her head, and he continued. "Cousins who have to give approval. But even if it's not Fuentes de la Juventud, I'm absolutely sure I won't be going back to Neuman Industries. I'll have to start looking elsewhere."

Rachel nodded again, thinking about Lucas's chances with Diego. She couldn't guess what would happen there.

And she had no concept of Lucas not tied to his father.

"You should know, too," Lucas was saying, "Mother and Dad have split up."

"You're kidding!" Rachel was well and truly stunned. "Why? How? When? I guess it was sudden?"

"Well," Lucas drawled, bemused by Rachel's reaction to this news, "the ironic thing is...it's because of Michaela."

Rachel's stomach dropped, and the color drained from her face. Never in her wildest dreams had she imagined that their prejudice ran so deep that the mere existence of a mixed-race granddaughter would destroy their marriage.

"Oh, Rachel, I'm sorry." Lucas was contrite. "I didn't word that very well. What I mean is that my mother is deadly serious about being a grandmother. She wants to know Michaela. And she wants to protect Michaela from my father. It seems that the discussion we all had at the hospital got her thinking about the negative presence that is my father. That you're right in believing he would be horrible to Michaela. My mother decided she'd gone along with him on enough things for enough years. So, basically, she's kicked him out. And says he won't be allowed back in."

"Dios mio," Rachel murmured, *"en cada villa, su maravilla."*

Laughing softly, remembering that "Will wonders never cease" had always been a favorite expression of Rachel's, Lucas said, "I couldn't agree more."

Motioning with her hands, making a parting-of-the-Red-Sea

movement, Rachel said, "So then, you've both stepped away from Arnold."

"I guess you could say that, yes."

"So, eventually we will need to talk about grandmother's rights."

"Yes, Mother will want that. Genuinely."

Rachel nodded. It was a turning point, both in how Lucas and Rachel related to one another and in how they were going to be parents. More and more, they seemed to be working that part out.

Much was left to discuss, much still needed sorting out. But they were feeling easier with each other, as if grounds for talking might eventually emerge. Just as a platform for a chaste kiss upon departure had emerged that very day. Neither of them said anything, but both enjoyed it thoroughly.

From then on a routine emerged without much effort. Rachel and Lucas managed to make it comfortable for all three of them. They'd never really gotten around to discussing an arrangement. Their agreement that Michaela's needs were paramount had governed everything. They'd simply gone from there.

Most days, Lucas arrived in Michaela's room shortly after Rachel. Rachel usually left then, believing it was important that Lucas have private time with his daughter. Around noon, before Michaela's lunch, Rachel would return, and both parents would walk with Michaela. Rachel then stayed with her during lunch until it was her own bedtime. Much to Michaela's disgust, she usually needed some sleep both during her father's morning visits and her mother's afternoon visits.

Rachel wasn't sure what Lucas did during the afternoon, but she knew he often returned to see Michaela in the evening. She saw him from time to time while she was working.

"*Buenos días, mija,*" Rachel said, arriving in time to see Michaela sitting at a table by the window, busily stringing beads. "How are you this morning?"

"Fine, *Mamá.* I ate all I'm going to for breakfast. I don't like all that hot cereal stuff, but I ate the toast and the fruit and I drank the juice."

Rachel smiled to herself. Michaela had always been direct—trust her to casually declare herself "fine." And she'd never cared much for hot cereal. These were touches of Michaela's normal self, and Rachel treasured them. "What are you making?"

"This will be a necklace for *Naná,*" Michaela explained, not pausing, not looking up, referring to Rachel's mother. "She likes lots of colors, so I'm using the best ones." She bit her lip in concentration, the tip of her tongue creeping out of her mouth as she successfully strung another bead. "*Papá* gave me this kit. Isn't it cool?" Success achieved with the most recent bead, Michaela paused and pointed at the items spread out across the table. "It's got stuff for friendship bracelets. See? I'll do that when I finish this."

Rachel gave Michaela a hug and sat down in the chair opposite her. Michaela continued intently stringing beads while she watched, savoring every second of her daughter's reemergence.

A click alerted them both to the opening of the door. Lucas entered.

"Buenos días, Papá," Michaela chirped.

"Buenos días, Michaela, Rachel."

Rachel smiled her welcome, eyeing with some trepidation the bag Lucas carried.

"You've brought something else?" Rachel had innocently mentioned to Lucas that Michaela would need quiet activities to keep her busy once her energy and attention span began to return. Lucas had taken the suggestion to heart, bringing with him books, puzzles, games and what Rachel called Lego for girls, referring to the pastel-colored building blocks. To his credit, Lucas also made a point of participating in whatever activities he brought, ensuring that Michaela knew what everything was for and exactly how to use it.

Rachel, too, had contributed her fair share of special items from home, including Michaela's favorite stuffed animals. Between the two of them, Rachel and Lucas had managed to create a home-away-from-home atmosphere for Michaela, with one corner of her room serving as a cache for everything.

Sheepishly, yet proudly, Lucas nodded and dramatically pulled a box from the bag. "Ta-da," he intoned.

''Chinese checkers!'' Michaela squealed.

''She knows the game?'' Lucas's face fell a little. He'd been counting on teaching his daughter about this particular game. He had found her to be just as bright as Rachel had said, even a little precocious, and had taken it upon himself to find things she didn't already know about. He wasn't having a lot of success, however. He'd been so sure about Chinese checkers.

''Oh, yes,'' Rachel said nodding. ''She adores Chinese checkers. And—'' she leaned toward him conspiratorially ''—I must warn you, she's very good.''

Lucas chuckled at this. ''Why does that not surprise me?''

''Papá,'' Michaela was continuing, ''you open it, okay?'' Already she was gathering her beadwork. ''*Mamá,* help me put this away. I'll finish it another time.''

Rachel obeyed her daughter's request, carefully stacking the jewelry kit amongst Michaela's other possessions. Then she returned to her seat.

Michaela had already arranged the playing board and claimed her favorite blue marbles. Rachel and Lucas were left to fend for themselves.

An hour later Michaela had won four games while her parents had only taken one each. Lucas had quickly realized that, once again, Rachel had not exaggerated Michaela's ability.

Also obvious, however, was that Michaela had expended her morning's energy. She was nearly asleep already. Rachel helped her back to her bed, and tucked her in, while Lucas cleaned up the site of the Chinese checker massacre.

And so another aspect of their hospital routine was established. Together, Rachel and Lucas played cards, checkers, Chinese checkers, or whatever other game Michaela selected, every morning. All three of them. Like a family.

''Rachel.''

She looked questioningly at Lucas, having detected an odd note in his voice.

His eyes were trained on Michaela, who was tucked in her bed, quickly falling asleep. So far this morning, the three of them had engaged in several rousing rounds of Go Fish, followed by what was by far Michaela's longest walk around the hospital ward—without stops for resting. It was nearly six weeks since day zero and her progress was evident.

Michaela continued to push her limits of endurance, and today had been no exception. Now she was tired.

At the same time, the ''truce by default'' that had established itself between Rachel and Lucas, over a month ago now, had become broader and even less formally defined. The truth of it was, Rachel and Lucas were getting along. They were both nervous, their concerns for Michaela being one cause. The other cause was less clear, but it had something to do with spending time with each other. And being comfortable together.

''Rachel,'' Lucas said again, more urgently this time, his gaze still riveted on their daughter. ''Does she have eyelashes?''

Rachel blinked, looked at Lucas, then switched her attention to Michaela. Rachel had noticed several days ago that Michaela's skin tone had crossed the line into the healthy range, although she was still pale. Now Rachel inspected her more closely. And there, curling gently against the curve of Michaela's cheek, were the infant-like wisps of Michaela's black eyelashes. Once again.

''Yes, Lucas,'' Rachel whispered, caught between reverence and exuberance. ''She does.''

Their gazes locked then, as they stood on opposite sides of the bed.

''La niñita más linda del mundo.'' Lucas quoted the Spanish. He, too, believed it, and spoke for both himself and Rachel.

They smiled together, suddenly unable to suppress the bursts of laughter—sounds that were remarkably close to giggles—that seemed to worm their way out into the room. As a stress breaker, laughter went a long way.

''Excuse me, Rachel,'' a voice interrupted as Rhonda, the nursing assistant, popped her head into the room. ''Oh, good, you're both here. Paul wanted to see you, both of you, as soon as you have a minute. He's in his office.''

She was gone that quickly. So, too, was the smile from Rachel's face. For her, being summoned by Paul Graham was something to be dreaded. She had heard so much bad news from him.

''We should go, then.'' Rachel was turning toward the door.

She was cold already, beginning to tremble inside, imaginary ice shards shooting through her, splitting her into thousands of tiny, frozen pieces. She hoped her legs would carry her, that she wouldn't disgrace herself by fainting in the reception area. But she wasn't confident about it.

Lucas, although new to the scenario, was quick to catch on. "Rachel," he grabbed her hand, "I'm here this time. I'm sharing this. Okay?"

She nodded wordlessly, swallowing hard. But she didn't let go of his hand. She held it tight, fingers threaded through his, all the way to Paul's office. Even when she sat down in front of Paul's desk, she held on to Lucas's hand.

She'd always taken the news alone. She just couldn't bear to hear more of the same, yet, of course, she would if she had to. But this time, she had a partner. She needed—and welcomed—his support. She wouldn't analyze it deeper than that.

"So Rhonda found you both," Paul Graham began, noting the tension between Rachel and Lucas immediately. "Is something wrong?"

Rachel didn't answer. Her wide, blank eyes told Paul what he needed to know. He'd seen that carefully schooled expression on her face many times. He realized then what she was thinking, would have correctly interpreted the situation, even if Lucas hadn't spoken.

"We thought you might want to see us about a problem."

"No," Paul was vigorously shaking his head. "Damn, I'm sorry. I should have realized before. I should have been more specific when I requested to see you. No, I do have news, but it's good news."

He smiled. So did Lucas. Rachel couldn't manage that, not yet.

And she still didn't let go of his hand, which Lucas didn't mind at all.

"It's been almost six weeks now, and Michaela is coming along very well. I think by the end of the week she will be ready to go home."

Rachel's heart began to hammer, so hard she was sure the others could hear it. She felt dizzy, warding off the faint feeling she had, desperate to avoid that kind of reaction again in front of Paul—or in front of Lucas. She had hoped, really hoped, for this for so long. Yet, she'd also been afraid to hope. She'd been afraid to let herself think about it. She *hadn't* let herself think about it.

She'd had no idea that relief could be so intense.

Lucas felt it, too. He couldn't breathe. *In fact, it's just like it was when Rachel announced I had a daughter,* he thought. *Just like that—again.*

He was grateful he was sitting down, knowing his legs felt weak. He could feel Rachel trembling, and tightened his grip on her hand. Instinctively he knew this trembling was different from the trembling he'd first felt when they had left Michaela's room.

"I'll mention that you need to prepare her home environment," Paul resumed. "It's my duty as Michaela's doctor to deliver the information, although I know you know the speech as well as I do, Rachel. Nevertheless, you know you will need to disinfect and sanitize the place, that you'll have to limit visitors and so on. In your case," his voice sharpened, "we need to enforce restrictions on *you,* starting now. You are on leave, Rachel. You cannot do everything by yourself, so please don't try."

"I know." She chewed her lip, unconsciously stroking Lucas's hand with her thumb. "I'm on leave now?" That part of his statement had only just penetrated her brain.

"Yes. I know you, Rachel. Which brings me to you, Mr. Neuman—" Paul readjusted his emphasis "—I'm hoping you will take it as your mission to see that Rachel…stays in line. It won't be an easy task, but if she knows I'm assigning it to you, she might cooperate and be reasonable." Paul smiled.

Each was silent for a minute.

"So, then," Rachel began, "I'm on leave now? Right now? I don't have to work tonight?" Realization was slow to dawn on her.

"That's right, Rachel. Go get whatever you want to start taking home—get out of here and get things ready for your daughter."

Paul saw Rachel swallow, saw her rapid blinking. This time, he realized, it wasn't up to him to offer support. A different man sat in the position.

Observing Lucas and Rachel together, Paul knew that whatever their problems, lack of love had not been the issue. It radiated from both of them—no matter how hard they tried to hide it. He wondered if they were as transparent to other people as they were to him. Then again, he considered Rachel to be the daughter he'd never had. And Michaela, his granddaughter by extension.

He hoped these two could work it out. Whatever "it" might be.

"You two need a few minutes alone."

Receiving no response from either of them, Paul slipped from the room, giving them the privacy they deserved. Good news required privacy sometimes, just as much as bad news.

Rachel stood as if in a dream. She found Lucas already standing, still clasping her hand in his.

But she felt numb.

How can I feel numb? Doesn't numb mean that I can't feel?

Turning to face Lucas, she vaguely felt his arms close around her, she blankly registered that her body was being folded against his.

"Oh, honey, it's okay. Rachel, it's okay. It's better than okay," he whispered, murmuring over and over, using soothing words that didn't make sense to Rachel. He stroked her back, pulling her hair free from the barrette that trapped it behind her head. He rocked her against him, knowing the instant her hot tears broke over the dam that had held them back for so long.

"Rachel, honey, it's okay. I'm here. It's okay. It's good news. It's great, Rachel. Michaela can go home. She doesn't have to stay here anymore."

Rachel had no idea how long she stayed in the circle of Lucas's arms or how long she cried. She only knew that she was where she belonged, and that everything was going to be all right.

Eventually she became aware that she was doing two things that were off-limits to her: crying and making physical contact with Lucas. She backed away from him, scrubbing angrily at the tear streaks left on her face.

"No, honey." Lucas grabbed her hand again. "Don't pull away. We need each other. There's nothing wrong with that." He found her other hand. "Rachel, let's go to lunch. Let's celebrate. This is worth it, don't you think?"

It sure is, he thought. *Michaela going home means a big improvement in her health. I can have a real relationship with Michaela, not a hospital relationship. And Michaela going home means Rachel and I have things to work out. We won't be limited to a hospital relationship, either. We'll be able to be together. As much as possible. Oh, yeah, this is worth celebrating.*

"Come on, Rachel. We can act like overjoyed parents. We have reason to." He smiled at her, the special smile he'd always reserved for her. "I'll get us a table, someplace special."

"Okay," she sniffed, trying out her smile. "I need to go clean up a little. I'm sorry—" her smile changed to something shy "—about that little flood."

"Oh, no, Rachel. You had that coming. You deserved that. And you never—" he let go of one hand, tipping her chin so that she looked into his eyes "—you never have to apologize to me for what you're feeling. Never. Okay?" He didn't wait for an answer. "Now, go. Get yourself ready." He pushed her, jokingly, gently, toward the door. "I'll make that call."

About fifteen minutes later Rachel met Lucas at the reception desk carrying a suitcase.

"I thought I'd get a jump on things that need to go home," she explained, sheepishly. "I hope that's okay."

"Of course it's okay, Rachel. Whatever you want."

He took the suitcase from her, shifting it to his right hand. His left arm curled around her waist, pulling her to his side. He held his breath.

Rachel held her breath. Then she slipped her arm around his waist and melted against him, finding her place, fitting there, just as she always had.

Chapter 14

Durants was an old, well-established restaurant in central Phoenix. Rachel had never been there, but she had certainly heard of it. Unfortunately, she wouldn't remember much about this visit. The excellent food, the exquisite champagne and the exceptionally discreet atmosphere—all these were completely lost on her.

Her daughter was coming home.

And the man she loved, her husband, was *courting* her. Or at least it seemed that way.

Rachel decided not to dissect it right now. Instead, she was going to float along in the lovely, glowing little world she'd been transported to as soon as the meaning of Paul's words had sunk in.

Not just good news, she averred, *the best news I've heard in a long time. News I'd despaired of ever hearing.*

Which is probably why she'd assumed the worst when she'd been told to go talk to Paul. It had always been the worst. Until today.

And she was marking the occasion with her husband, something she'd never even considered doing. She still loved him; she'd admitted that a long time ago. Today she simply wasn't going to worry about it. She wasn't going to fight it. He probably knew, anyway.

"I guess we should discuss what kind of schedule you want to live by, now that she'll be home," Rachel ventured.

"Yeah, we could. Or we could just see what feels comfortable. It may take some time before Michaela gets into a routine. The process of moving home may wear her out." He sipped his champagne. "But we don't have to decide the specifics today, Rachel."

She agreed and gave herself over to the day. She ate what he ordered for her and toasted her daughter's health, *their* daughter's health, numerous times. She smiled. She laughed. She shared this time with Lucas.

And she felt a little bit of her internal armor give way.

"Come on, Rachel, we can share a slice of cheesecake," Lucas coaxed. He, too, felt the magic of the day. "It'll finish off the meal."

She smiled at him, feeling shadows flicker across her face. She wondered if he knew what she was thinking—that she'd never been out to celebrate something with Lucas before. That he'd never ordered for her in a fancy restaurant, shared champagne or cheesecake with her. He had done so for others, she knew. But not for her. This was her first time. Shaking the shadows away, she demanded that she not dwell on it. Today was hers.

Lucas had seen the shadows, had realized that Rachel had forced out her sad thoughts, hadn't allowed them to stay. He couldn't be entirely sure what she had been thinking about, but he had a very good idea. Now was not the time to go into detail, about anything. He'd already decided that. But he could hint. He could set the foundation. She needed to know that he understood her thoughts.

"It'll be okay, Rachel." He squeezed her hand as it rested on the table. "Rachel, I can't undo things that happened before. But I can do better from now on. I *will* do better from now on." He squeezed her hand again, suddenly desperate to make her understand *his* thoughts, knowing it was a first, important step. "Give it a chance, Rachel. Sharing dessert is a small place to begin."

Rachel stared at their clasped hands. She swung her gaze

back to Lucas's face, unable to speak. *So he did know where my thoughts had gone.*

"Please, Rachel." His clear, dark eyes pleaded, too. He'd never wanted anything so badly. He decided she needed to hear that, too. "I want you back, Rachel. I want to be together. I know it's not easy or simple. I know we have things to discuss. But I think you should know how I feel."

She sighed, a decision made. "I'll share the cheesecake, Lucas. We'll take today. We'll have to see about...anything else."

Lucas released the breath he'd been holding. He smiled. He flagged down the waitress and ordered cheesecake. With cherries.

Rachel was thinking, dreamily. Softly.

There is something incredibly erotic, sensual, about your man feeding you from his own fork—especially cheesecake. When he puts that creamy sweetness in your mouth. And you let him.

Rachel refused to analyze her thought or the fact that she actually was eating from Lucas's fork. She felt herself glowing, riding a magic wave, and not about to disembark at this point. No way would she disturb the slow-motion movements or the soft watercolor images surrounding her.

That very same magic found her, later, agreeing to dance with Lucas in her town house. He'd gone over to her CD holder and put on some music. Only when she heard the first strains of the Mavericks did she realize what he'd really done.

They had danced for hours when they'd first married. They'd danced in their kitchen—it was big enough if they avoided the table, and it had a tiled floor. The Mavericks, a western band, always had plenty of dance songs on their albums, including slow ones that let a couple get close. She'd left everything behind when she moved out, but she'd bought her own Mavericks CD. And that's what Lucas had chosen today.

And Rachel chose to share it with him, moving into his arms naturally, molding her body against him just the way she had before. Feeling the way she'd always felt when he'd held her. Glowing from somewhere deep inside. Radiant. In love. Loved, too.

And for today that was okay.

Because Lucas was trembling nearly as much as she was. His rapid, erratic heartbeat matched hers. Their breath was mingling, creating the one scent that only the two of them could create.

Laying her head against his shoulder, Rachel recognized her own surrender. So, too, did Lucas.

He stroked her hair, differently than he had in Dr. Graham's office. The feel of her hair, the feel of *her*—it was exactly how it was meant to be. He didn't even realize it when his lips began to move, caressing her cheekbone just where her eyelashes would flutter. Trailing along toward her ear, down her neck, until he was burying his head in her glorious hair—the very hair that he had stroked, combed his fingers through, so many times in his dreams.

"Oh, Rachel, I've missed you so much." Need was rushing through him; desire would not be denied this time.

"Me, too, Lucas."

The dance continued, but it no longer had anything to do with the music playing on the stereo and everything to do with love.

"So perfect. It's just so perfect with you, Rachel. The way I remember."

She stiffened at his whispered words.

"It's true, Rachel. You know it is. Let me show you."

Rachel met his gaze, knowing he wanted her to accept his words. And she loved him so much, she could listen. In this moment.

Maybe she'd never believe him again, but in this moment it was working for her. For now, she could give herself over to his words. And let herself feel what she could only ever feel for him.

It was his breath against her skin that was her undoing. She had dreamed of that, had woken up in the night so many times thinking she felt it. Only to find herself alone.

His breath against her skin. It stirred her hair—and also something inside her that she had carefully tucked away many years ago. Something she had left for dead.

This is seduction, pure and simple, Rachel decided.

Not that he was talking her into anything. She knew what she was doing, what she needed. He was giving her an opportunity, yes, but he wasn't talking her into anything. She knew that.

And so did Lucas. He knew it very well, knew exactly what she needed, exactly how she would respond.

Yes, seduction, Rachel confirmed, *but maybe not so pure.*

Fleetingly, she considered that Lucas knew what he was doing because he had had so many opportunities to learn, and not just with her. She wondered about the other women he had done this to, whether he was comparing notes.

Then she decided this was not the moment to dwell on it. She knew she would eventually, because she had some insecurities of her own. But right now…right now, Lucas was running his fingers through her hair. He was kissing her. She was kissing him.

They had found their way to her bedroom, their clothes had fallen by the wayside. His skin, his warmth, became her world, closing around her, pushing away everything else. It was his mouth that was consuming hers, his hands that were bringing her body to life. His body that she stroked, his body that she needed so much.

He teased her, caressed her, tasted her, coaxed her, brought her to the edge time and time again—only to retreat, leaving her wanting more. Leaving her weak.

And then he gave her what she wanted, what she needed, letting her warmth surround him this time, letting her shatter around him even as he fell apart in her arms.

This moment was theirs. And it was enough.

Wow. It wasn't a very profound thought. But it did sum up ıow Lucas felt when he stirred sometime later. He stretched, azy, satiated, reaching for Rachel, only to find an empty space where she should have been. He heard the water running in the bathroom, realized that Rachel was taking a shower.

He stretched again and felt an enormous stupid grin spread across his face. If she was in the shower, he could stop…and emember…Rachel.

Wow. Yes, it deserved a wow. *And much, much more.*

One thing hadn't changed: how it felt to be with Rachel. How it had always been with Rachel. The souls touching and all that. He remembered; it was better than he remembered.

He was cautiously, optimistically, beginning to suspect that happiness might be his again. Knowing Rachel as well as he did—or at least, as well as he *had* known her—Lucas knew that making love meant she still felt something for him. She had gone to bed with him because going to bed with him had felt right to her. And that meant she still cared. That meant he could hope.

His grin turned into a full-fledged smile. If they were going to put the past behind them and have a chance at a life together, Lucas reasoned, knowing that their sex life would still be as fulfilling as it ever had been—well, that was a very positive development.

At the same time, Lucas thought, *today changes everything. It's a step in the direction we need to be heading. Together.*

Lucas attempted to see the bedside clock, checking for the time. He couldn't quite see it, though, and he wasn't willing to go to the effort it would have required. He dropped his head back onto the pillow. He was pretty sure he and Rachel had actually dozed off together. He hadn't known when Rachel left the bed, but it would have been rare for him to fall asleep with her still awake. If they fell asleep after lovemaking, it was always together—he caught his train of thoughts.

That was before, stupid. It's been a long time since then.

Lucas knew he shouldn't take for granted that anything that happened now would be exactly like it used to be. Still, being with Rachel was the most natural, perfect thing.

He leaned over again, this time finding the clock—5:00 p.m. That meant the afternoon was coming to an end.

And that I should get dressed.

Hearing the water still running in the bathroom, Lucas decided to explore Rachel's house. He wanted to see what kind of place she had created for herself and Michaela.

I am not prying, he told himself, *just getting familiar with the place.*

He liked her home. That was his first general impression. Nothing cold and impersonal here, not like the condo he'd bought.

Everything was based on a color that Lucas saw as oatmeal—sort of an off-white with other nubby, neutral colors flecked through it. The primary accent colors throughout were forest green and cranberry. The coordinated color scheme worked well with the open floor plan, he decided. It was warm and comfortable.

"Just like Rachel," he whispered to himself.

He smiled at the large basket he saw sitting on an end table in the living room. It was decoratively laden with yarn-and-popsicle-stick god's eyes. One of Michaela's many art projects over the past few weeks. Everyone who had come in contact with her had walked away with a god's eye. Or two or three. Lucas himself had several that he had taped to his refrigerator. One he'd hung from the rearview mirror in his car.

Thinking of Michaela, he remembered that her room was the only exception to this basic color scheme. Her room was bright and cheery, highlighted with equally bright primary shades of red, yellow and blue. A room Michaela hadn't seen for a while, Lucas realized with a pang.

But that was about to change.

Lucas wandered into the kitchen, contemplating fixing a light meal before they returned to the hospital. However, a thorough search of the kitchen revealed virtually no food. While Lucas was confident in his ability to boil water and therefore prepare rigatoni, he saw absolutely nothing that might be used to give the pasta some flavor.

She really hasn't been living here. The obvious fact came home to him. She had said as much, of course, but only now did he see the remark for the very accurate statement it was. The bare kitchen provided a stark contrast to the homey feeling everywhere else.

The water upstairs stopped. Rachel had finished her shower.

Deciding to wait for her, see what she wanted to do, Lucas opened the sliding glass door that led to the patio area and stepped outside. It was warm, but on the shady side of the building, so it was bearable. He unfolded a chaise lounge that was leaning against the wall and stretched out, watching the wispy white clouds drift by overhead.

She's found a good home, Lucas thought. *She's made a good home.*

Of course, the Scottsdale condo he currently lived in, the one he'd moved to nearly five years ago, would put this to shame in terms of luxury. But his place wasn't half the home this was. Not even close.

Despite the long-term absences of the occupants of Rachel's town house, it still felt like a home.

"Are you ready?"

Lucas jumped at Rachel's voice. He hadn't heard her slide open the door.

"Sure, if you are."

He followed her back into the house, noticing that her hair was still slightly wet. She had pulled it up in some sort of twist, then stuck in what he saw as Asian hair picks. Mother-of-pearl, he decided. They looked beautiful set against her magnificent chocolate hair. She smelled fresh, vanilla-y. Like herself. Unbelievably, he felt his body tighten with desire. Again. As if he was seventeen.

Curling his arms around her waist from behind, he pulled her against him. He was already rock hard, ready for her. He took a deep breath, inhaling that scent that was hers alone, burying his face in her hair, thinking about removing those hair picks he had just been admiring. He was again nuzzling her neck, her earlobe. He felt a tremor shoot through her. He had known he was ready to be with her again. Now he knew she was ready, too.

"Lucas," she said in a voice that sounded odd to him, "I've got to get back to the hospital." He was momentarily disconcerted by her change of subject, and slackened his hold on her just enough that she was able to pull away from him.

"I've called *Mamá*," she was saying, "and told her about Michaela. She's already organizing the cleaning shifts we'll take. We decided it would be best if the carpet was cleaned as soon as possible. Then we can do the rest of the cleaning. Rick will do the carpet. He gets into that sort of thing." She smiled faintly. "So I decided to take some fresh clothes back to the hospital. I'll just plan to stay there until the carpet dries, and then we can move back in." She motioned toward a small suitcase she had brought downstairs. "So we can take that with us when we go."

It occurred to Lucas then that she was avoiding his eyes. She was keeping her head averted. ''Regrets already, Rachel?''

She didn't look at him, but Lucas could see the blush that rushed to her cheeks.

''Honey, what we shared, that was incredible. It was great. It's right between us. It always was. You know that. There's no need for regrets.''

''Yes, Lucas.'' She licked her lips. ''It...was great. Great sex. You're right. I have no regrets.''

''Well, then, that's okay.'' He reached for her. He was kissing her again, his breath on her skin again. She was responding, kissing him back, giving in to the shimmer that was stealing over her.

''I want you again, Rachel. Badly. Right now.''

She stiffened in his arms, making Lucas wish he'd kept his thoughts to himself. Things had been progressing just fine without words.

''I can't, Lucas,'' she whispered. ''I...I'm not sure I'm ready for this. I need some time. Please.'' She took a deep breath, sensing that he was getting the message this time, wondering exactly what her message was. Dios mio, *but I am confused.*

Sighing heavily, he stepped back.

She was heading toward the door now, but turned to face him again. ''Look, Lucas. What we shared, for me that was special. I know it doesn't mean anything,'' she said, the words bubbling out of her mouth, ''but, still, for me, it was a golden moment, something apart from my real life—''

''It didn't mean anything?'' He was getting loud, struggling to control it. ''Why do you say that?''

Rachel didn't answer but gave him a look he didn't understand. Annoyance? Because he'd interrupted her? Or because she was having regrets? Or because she didn't believe him?

''The thing is, I'm not used to that sort of thing. It's not like I bring men home—''

''Rachel, I know that.''

''*Dios mio,* you are just not understanding me, are you? No, I have no regrets. It was wonderful. It was special. I'll never forget it. But I can't *do* this, Lucas. Don't you see? It matters to me. It goes too deep for me. I—''

"Rachel, is it possible that you actually think it doesn't matter to me?"

"Maybe." She shrugged.

My God, she has a low opinion of me, Lucas suddenly realized.

"You have different expectations than I do. You can handle this sort of thing." She fluttered her hand in the air, trying to punctuate her explanation.

Lucas stared at her uncomprehendingly.

She took a deep breath, wondering if she could possibly explain something she didn't entirely understand herself. "Look, Lucas, I've told you before that I live one day at a time. But I do it with responsibility, very heavy responsibility. If I didn't have that part, it might be easier—or even possible—for me to be with a man in a way that doesn't touch me inside. Casually, you know. But that isn't how it is for me. It does touch me. It overwhelms me." She met his gaze, her golden eyes turbulent. *Can't you see that love is involved for me?* She pleaded silently.

In fact, Lucas didn't understand. He'd decided things between them were going damn near perfectly. He couldn't understand why she would say that what they'd shared didn't matter to him. True, he saw sex as a natural progression, one they'd been heading toward from the minute their paths had crossed again. If he'd made that progression more quickly than Rachel, been able to adjust to that progression more easily, well…then he was a little ahead of her on that path.

But she'd been ready today. She'd made the choice this time. Now she seemed scared again.

He took her hand. "Rachel, sit down a minute."

Hesitantly she did.

"Was it too soon?"

She took so long to respond, Lucas had nearly decided she hadn't heard him. When she did respond, it was a quick shake of her head. "No."

Through it all, Rachel believed she *did* have a commitment to Lucas. Just that it wasn't necessarily mutual. She was far too aware of the mismatch between her ways and Lucas's. The only thing she'd known to do was avoid physical contact with him. Now that that door had been opened, it would not be easily closed again.

"Please, Rachel," Lucas intoned, "help me understand."

She looked at him, tears glistening in her eyes. "I just think that...what it means to me is different from what it means to you. And that matters to me. I'm the one it hurts."

He still wasn't sure he understood her exactly. Being with her couldn't possibly be more important to him. Despite her denial, he thought the difficulty was a timing thing. That they were operating at different speeds. He would need to slow down. Give her more time. He didn't have much choice. "It's okay, Rachel."

"*Bueno. Gracias,* Lucas."

She stood, resuming her trek toward the door. Lucas understood that he was expected to follow. With a sigh that was part frustration, part exasperation, part something he didn't have a label for, he adjusted his pants, picked up her suitcase and followed her.

Chapter 15

"*Gracias, Mamá. Hasta luego.*" Rachel hung up the phone glad to hear that the cleaning of her town house was going according to plan. Rick—with Diego as his assistant—had cleaned the carpet, and Rachel had now been instructed by her mother that it would be okay to return and finish the other necessary work. She wasn't altogether sure whom her mother had assigned to the cleaning crew, but Rachel had no doubt that the house would be ready for Michaela's return in three days.

Three days! Rachel threw back her head and laughed out loud. It was all just too unbelievable.

Today, in anticipation of cleaning, Rachel was wearing denim shorts and a red T-shirt. She had covered her hair with a red bandanna, preferring that to the constriction of a barrette. She just needed to tell Michaela where she was going and that she would probably stay the night at the town house. Somehow she thought she could get more done if she wasn't worried about a return-to-the-hospital deadline, especially because she was likely to be sweaty and smelly by the time she was finished.

"*Hola, hermana.*"

Rachel looked up from her packing, knowing that the fabulous smile of Diego Fuentes would accompany the greeting. He'd always called her "sister" even though that was not their true relationship.

"*Hola,* Diego. *¿Cómo está?*"

His answer was a quick hug and a kiss on the cheek.

"I've been to see Michaela," he explained, a twinkle in his eye, "but I thought I would stop and speak to her mother, also."

Rachel took in Diego's appearance, noting that he was letting his black hair grow again. He'd cut it short a few years back, having decided to look more like a conservative businessman, as he explained it. But the short cut really wasn't his style. She could see that soon it would be shoulder length again, and he'd be pulling it straight back into a short ponytail. Personally, she thought he wore it well, a look that was clearly a throwback to an earlier time. A time of warriors, she thought. "I'm glad you did, Diego. It's been too long."

"*Sí, sí.*" He flashed his wonderful smile at her again. "I guess we have a big day coming, no? She is so much more her normal self now. She has been so brave. As has her mother."

Rachel moved to stand beside Diego at the window. Slipping his arm around her shoulders, he squeezed briefly, letting go before she could panic. Over the years Diego had come to know exactly how long she could tolerate physical contact. He always made a point of pushing her limit, believing that if he didn't it would be all too easy for Rachel to slip away to a place where no one would reach her. He tried to keep her in touch, insofar as he could.

Rachel enjoyed the momentary warmth of Diego's hug, secure in the easy camaraderie they'd shared since childhood. "It is unbelievable," she agreed.

"And how is the mother of the child doing?"

"She is thrilled, excited, anxious…"

"Scared?"

She glanced at him quickly, acknowledging his astuteness. He knew her so well.

"Yes," she admitted. "A little bit scared. Afraid to believe. Unwilling not to."

Diego went to sit on the couch, allowing her some breathing room. "Perhaps that should become your motto, Rachel."

"What do you mean?"

Diego sat back, brought one leg up to cross the ankle over his knee. "I think, *hermana,* that believing—trusting—is difficult for you. Life has taught you to be wary. You have been...only existing for some time, no? Afraid, *sí.* But perhaps also...waiting. Sometimes it takes more than hope. Sometimes you must take a risk. Sometimes you must take action."

Rachel did not have a response. She heard the truth in what Diego said.

"*Hermana,*" he continued, "what you have been waiting for is within your reach. For Michaela, certainly. But also for yourself, as a woman. If you can believe, *corazón.* If you can trust it."

She opened her mouth to speak, but no words came.

Diego stood and walked back to the window. He tipped her chin so she could not avoid looking at him.

"Think, *hermana,* of what it would take to make you complete again. What do you need? What do you want?"

He bent to kiss her cheek again, wondering if Rachel had any idea what it was costing him to speak to her so. "I would like to see you happy again, *corazón.* We all would. You deserve it. Take the chance."

Diego was a good man, Rachel knew that. She wished she had been able to turn her feelings for him into something more something a man like him deserved. It would have simplified her life unbelievably. She did love him deeply, but it would always be as a brother. She respected him and his opinions She knew that he truly did want her to be happy and that he understood what it would take.

"*Hasta luego,* Rachel."

Rachel did not immediately move away from the window She knew what she needed—what she wanted—to be complete again. She simply had no idea if she could manage it.

A few minutes later, composed, she left her office.

"*Buenos días, mija,*" Rachel chimed as she entered Michaela's room.

Michaela's color was normal now, apricot, just like her mother's, just like it had been before. Her gray eyes no longer looked hollow and lost in her face, the way they had over the past few months, when she had felt so miserable and had tried so hard to disguise it. Maybe most important, she had a headful of soft, downy black hair.

She's got more than peach fuzz, Rachel decided. *A little more and it will actually look like a short hairstyle.* She smiled again.

"Buenos días, Mamá," Michaela answered with a smile, her arms outstretched for a hug. Today Michaela had apparently decided to play Barbie dolls. Malibu Barbie and Teresa were sitting on the table, legs crossed, presumably contemplating their ridiculously extensive wardrobes.

"Having a good morning?"

"Sí, Mamá." She eyed Rachel closely. "You're dressed different today."

"That is true." Rachel laughed. "I'm dressed for cleaning. That's what I came to tell you, *mija.* I'm going home to help *Naná* clean, to get everything ready for you to come home. *¿Claro?*"

Michaela squealed at this, dashing toward Rachel for another hug. "Of course that's okay, *Mamá.* I want to go back home so bad. I can't wait."

"I know, *mija,* I know."

"So, clean it good, *Mamá,* and clean it fast."

"Okay." Rachel was still laughing, adoring these instructions that sounded so very much like her daughter should sound. "I will. I'll probably stay there tonight, okay? So I won't see you until morning."

Michaela pursed her lips, crinkling her forehead in thought. "Well, okay. I guess you have to. *Claro, Mamá.*"

"Gracias, mija. Hasta mañana." Rachel hugged her daughter again, kissing her on that fuzzy little head.

It was time to get down to business.

When Rachel arrived at her home, she found it empty. No one was there to clean with her, but evidence of someone else's hard work was everywhere.

Someone had already purchased and put away a fair supply of groceries. Rachel had no idea who that might have been. She checked her cupboards and fridge, making mental notes of what she now had to choose from.

"Ah," she said aloud, "my money's on Rick and Diego being the grocery shoppers."

This conclusion was based on her findings in the freezer. She discovered four different flavors of ice cream, as well as some frozen sugary product that came on sticks. Rachel, Rick and Diego had always believed that ice cream could cure anything and it would be like those two to fill her freezer with such things. She smiled.

Rachel wandered through the house, taking inventory of what had already been done. From what she could tell, all basic cleaning had been completed. It appeared that floor mopping and window coverings were all that were left.

Dios mio, Rachel wondered, *was* Mamá *here when she called me this morning? How did they get so much done?*

Rachel couldn't quite figure out how this had happened without her knowledge. She'd believed she was very much on top of the cleaning progress. Apparently not.

The doorbell interrupted Rachel's meandering.

"Hey, Tanisha." Rachel felt glad to see her neighbor. Rachel had missed her. Tanisha's daughter, Vanessa, was only one year older than Michaela, and the two of them were tight friends. They had all spent a lot of time together before Michaela's illness. Rachel realized now that she hadn't seen Tanisha since before Michaela's BMT. She couldn't remember the last time she'd actually seen Vanessa, although Vanessa routinely sent messages to Michaela at the hospital. Michaela needed help reading them, but she adored getting mail.

Still, Rachel hadn't seen Tanisha in quite some time. "How's it going?"

Then, noticing a box sitting on the ground behind Tanisha, she amended her question. "Or maybe I should ask, what have you got?"

Tanisha laughed. "I've brought you your bedspreads, Rach. I had them dry-cleaned. I thought about washing them, but when I got them over to my house, I realized there was no way they would fit in my machine. So off to the dry-cleaner I went."

"Thanks, Tanisha." Rachel meant it, and she knew Tanisha knew she meant it. Money was not in abundance around this area, and the dry-cleaning bill for two bedspreads would have been significant. But Tanisha considered it a gift, and there would be no point in arguing the issue.

Stepping outside, Rachel helped Tanisha bring in the box. They unloaded it and spent the next hour talking and replacing bed coverings.

After Tanisha's departure, Rachel approached the tasks she knew she needed to complete. First on the list was floor mopping: the kitchen, the utility room, and all two and a half bathrooms.

That task completed, Rachel carried her bucket of dirty water and the mop outside and set to cleaning up her equipment. Then she noticed the miniblinds sitting on the table. A quick examination of them told her that they were desperately dusty and needed cleaning. She knew that Rick and Diego had taken down all the window coverings before they had done the carpet, with the idea that it would preserve the cleanliness of the carpet if *clean* window coverings were rehung after the carpet had been taken care of, rather than trying to remove dirty window coverings over clean carpet. Rachel figured her drapes and curtains must be at the dry-cleaners.

The miniblinds had obviously either been forgotten or time had become a factor and they hadn't been touched after they'd been removed from the house. Shrugging, realizing that it didn't really matter either way, Rachel gathered up her cleaning supplies, bringing them out to the patio. She might as well do this where she had plenty of room and where she could use the hose to its full advantage.

Back in the kitchen, Rachel savored the very thought of the sandwich she was preparing—genuine deli-cut turkey, fresh lettuce and tomato, not prepared by a hospital cafeteria. When she was about two bites from finishing, the doorbell rang again. Stuffing the last bit in her mouth, she went to answer the door, finding her father, brother and Diego standing on the step, amid drapes and curtains and copious amounts of protective plastic wrapping. She invited them in and spent the next several hours helping them return her window coverings to their proper places. She was glad she'd been there to oversee the process—none of these helpers seemed to remember which set of coverings had come from which window. Rachel wasn't sure she would have liked the effect their decorating efforts would have produced, as much as she loved the men themselves.

Following their visit, she went back out to the patio, checking the dryness of her miniblinds.

"Hi, Rachel."

She jumped. She hadn't heard Lucas's approach.

"Sorry. I didn't mean to sneak up on you. I rang the bell, but you didn't answer. I was sure you were here, so I started looking around a little. I discovered this little path and just sort of kept following it. Someone, your neighbor Tunisia—"

"Tanisha," Rachel corrected automatically.

"Yes, well, she opened the gate for me. Seemed to know who I was. I didn't realize I'd end up here, that it would bring me directly to you, but I guess it's okay that it did."

He smiled at her, and she felt her pulse quicken. She had that floating sensation in her stomach—butterflies—and knew that Lucas's arrival had sent her rushing back into that special spectrum he created for her.

"You know—" he was looking around the courtyard of the complex, nodding his head approvingly "—you've found a very nice little village to live in, Rachel."

"Yes, I think so, too." She found her voice.

He reached over and undid the latch on her patio gate, entering her little garden area. "Can I help you with those?" He'd spotted the miniblinds.

"Yes, actually. I could use the help. I washed them this morning. *Papá,* Rick and Diego were just here, putting up curtains for me. I should have checked these then so they could have helped me, but I didn't think of it. So I'm left still needing to get them back inside." She was babbling, and she hated it, but she couldn't stop, either.

Lucas smiled and began loading his arms with miniblinds. Very quickly, Rachel was glad of his help. The miniblinds were cumbersome and most of the work was at ceiling level. He was taller than she was and could reach much more easily. And two sets of hands proved very useful.

Until they tried to hang the blinds in her bedroom. These blinds were big. Floor-length. Ten feet across. They went beneath the drapes, next to the glass.

The cords were tangled. They got them untangled. They

hoisted the blinds up, ready to put them in place. One side slipped, leaving them skewed, out of balance and completely unmanageable. They sorted that out. They got them in place, evenly balanced this time, were ready to slide them into the little brackets—and one of the brackets broke. The blinds fell to the floor with a highly rhythmic clatter. And a thud.

Had she been alone, Rachel knew she'd have been issuing some very colorful language, her most expressive mix of Spanish and English.

As it was, she and Lucas just started laughing. Kept laughing. Couldn't stop laughing. Pretty soon they had tears from laughing. They tried to talk but couldn't for the laughing. They sat on the floor, side by side with the jumbled miniblinds, and laughed.

Until eventually they were in each other's arms, and both of them knew where they were headed.

And neither of them was laughing anymore.

This time it was no gentle reunion. No dreamy, soft-edged romance. This time it was hunger. Two starving people desperate for each other.

Scrambling to get closer, each one's mouth seeking the other's, fusing, not wanting to break away.

His shirt, suddenly unnecessary, was pulled away, discarded. Rachel was finding the taste, scent and feel of his smooth golden skin, the crisp blackness of his chest hair—something he hadn't had when he'd been twenty—and the flat, hard coins of his nipples. Her hands, her mouth, traveling everywhere. Her man. Absolutely.

Her hair freed from its bandanna, Lucas's hands combing through it, burying his face, breathing in Rachel. Her red T-shirt, her denim shorts, her satin bra and panties—all of them left her body. Scattered wherever they landed. Her body beginning to quiver, ready for his touch, unable to stop the cries of need. Need fulfilled when his thumbs began to stroke her distended nipples, and then fulfilled again when his mouth took over the job.

"Oh, Rachel, I can't wait. I can't...go slow."

"I don't want you to."

He slid home then, Rachel meeting each thrust with a rhythm of her own, pulling him deeper, closer—needing, wanting, loving every bit of him. And Lucas giving her everything he had to give.

Afterward, they collapsed together on the floor, still entwined, still connected, side by side with the tangled miniblinds and the forgotten clothes.

"Rachel, honey, wake up." Lucas's voice and breath on her skin caused Rachel to stir. Somewhere in her brain, she knew she must have slept because she was now waking up.

"Rachel," he whispered again into her neck. "I need you again."

At that, Rachel became aware of Lucas, warm and throbbing against her thigh—and of herself, utterly boneless and melting and ready for him.

Just like it had always been when they had awakened together.

"Yes, Lucas, now." Her words were whispered, but their urgency was conveyed.

Needing no further encouragement, Lucas shifted to slip inside her, and they were together again in a slow, delicious powerful ritual, reaching the final sweeping strokes together as well.

"Did I rush you?" Lucas asked, stroking her hair.

"No." She smiled. "Not at all."

"Are you hungry?" He was kissing her mouth again, tasting her.

"For something besides you, you mean?" she asked in between kisses.

He laughed then, jokingly, tenderly, nibbling at her ear. "Yeah, for something that might sustain us in a different way."

Still lying on the floor, Rachel turned to check her bedside clock, surprised to see that it was nearly seven o'clock. She'd already decided to stay at the town house tonight, of course. Now she knew she wouldn't be alone.

Reaching for her panties, she said. "I suppose we should have dinner."

"Rachel." Lucas caught her hand. "We're alone, right?"

She nodded.

"You're not expecting anyone else tonight, are you—not even the cleaning crew on a return mission?" His smile said he remembered the numerous times during their marriage when marathon lovemaking sessions had been interrupted by the inopportune arrival of her *familia.*

And how Rachel and Lucas had smoldered until those visits ended, when they could turn to each other again.

Rachel smiled, tracing his mouth with her fingertip. She remembered, too.

"No, Lucas. I'm not expecting anyone."

"Then let's not dress."

"What?" She was laughing, relishing the feel of his chest hair—that new sensation—against her as he lay propped over her.

"Let's not dress. No one will know. All the drapes are back in place. And we won't really be needing clothes, will we?"

"No. I guess not."

He stood up then, extending his hand to help her.

And suddenly she was embarrassed. Heat rushed to her face—all-over salmon, she was sure. Quickly she ducked her head until her face was at least partially concealed by her cascading hair.

Not that they'd never before indulged in nudity in their home. They had. They'd made love wherever, whenever they'd wanted...before. But that was then. That was...before.

"Rachel, what's wrong?" Lucas tried to tip her face up to him, meeting resistance. "Tell me."

She shook her head.

"Rachel, look at me."

She raised her head slightly, still hiding behind her veil of hair, glad it was long enough to partially disguise her breasts as well as her face. Unconsciously she crossed her arms in front of her body, folding them across her stomach.

"Rachel, honey, come on. What is it?"

Her mouth opened, but words were slow to come. "You may not...want to see me, you know, running around naked."

"Why not?"

On the one hand, Rachel was thinking "because I don't look nearly as good as the women you're used to." She hated thinking that way, but there it was.

On the other hand, she could tell him the other half of what worried her. It was probably more important, anyway.

"I don't look...like I used to."

Lucas wasn't following her train of thought. He shook his head. "What do you mean?"

"Just what I said, Lucas." She slipped away from him, welcoming the distance. "I'm not young...and firm...the way I was the last time you...saw me like this."

Rachel was quite aware that they'd made love a scant day or so ago, but she'd hardly been parading around without clothes that time.

"Rachel." Lucas smiled. "I don't look like a kid anymore, either."

She thought immediately of his chest hair. "Yes, Lucas, but you look like a man now. You look better. You're still hard—"

"Well, not so hard at this minute," he said through a devilish grin.

She smiled in exasperation. "Not that kind of hard, dope. You're...I don't know, lean, fit. Filled out the way a man should be. I—" she faltered "—I'm not...firm and perky anymore. I'm not twenty and...I've had a baby. I have stretch marks, Lucas. There were some difficulties with Michaela's delivery and I had to have a C-section—"

Lucas blanched involuntarily, hit hard by this sudden blast of reality, of what Rachel—and Rick—had experienced. The very thing that he, Lucas, had not participated in. Renewed disgust with himself swamped him.

Rachel saw his expressions, and interpreted them as being directed at her body. "*Bueno,* Lucas," she began with some spirit, "so gravity has done its thing with my breasts. I have stretch marks and a five-inch scar. It's a bikini cut, so to speak, so it's not horrid. I'm not a total cow or...or a troll, Lucas, but I certainly don't look...*better.* Maybe it would be best if I cover up before I roam through the house with you."

Lucas caught her shoulders, lowered his mouth to kiss her, stroking her hair back away from her face with his fingers. He reached down to cup her breasts, letting them fill his hands, his mouth never leaving hers. Until he was ready to suckle her—then he went down on his knees, burying his face against her, his tongue stroking and caressing, his teeth tugging ever so gently. His hands found her waist, trailing gentle fingertips across what he believed were the stretch marks she referred to.

His mouth continued to travel downward, nuzzling and kissing the faint streaks in her flesh that were evidence she had carried his child. His fingers stroked her legs, from her calves to her thighs and back again, and again, until they found their ultimate destination. Giving her the most intimate of caresses with his mouth, Lucas allowed his fingers to stroke the fine line he noticed at the top of that dark triangle, realizing that it was this that had allowed his daughter access into the world.

Rachel's entire body was trembling, every nerve screaming. Her hands, which had been combing through Lucas's hair, were now riveted to his scalp in the unconscious effort to support herself against her knees buckling. She knew the little gasps, the husky moans, were coming from her mouth, but she was powerless to stop them. Just when she was sure she couldn't take anymore, Lucas stopped. He stood and cupped her face in his hands. She could feel him, rigid and burning with heat, pressed against her. With difficulty her eyes fluttered open, meeting his gaze.

"Rachel, you are more beautiful than ever. Really. Your changes—they're badges of honor, Rachel, for bearing your child. Because she was yours then, it was your strength that brought her here. It had very little to do with me. To know what you did, to know that my child began her life inside you—that is the most incredible, amazing thing to me. You are a woman, in every way. A real woman, Rachel."

Momentary images of the glamour queens Lucas had chosen flashed through Rachel's mind—they were women, too, she thought, women without stretch marks, scars or sagging firmness.

The images vanished, though, as Lucas scooped her into his arms and carried her downstairs. He set her down on the couch, resuming his worshipful attention to her body with his hands, his mouth, his breath in her hair. And, finally, with his body, too. He entered her slowly, so slowly, continued slowly, steadily, even when Rachel begged for more.

"Let it happen, honey. Just let it happen."

And she began to quiver from the inside out, from the outside in—her special whimpers escaping her again, her hands raking Lucas's back, pulling him into her, closer. Still, he maintained his slow, steady pace, even as he felt her quivering turn into the slow, steady convulsion that made her cry out—and that brought him to a slow, hot, shuddering climax, too.

Sometime later Rachel awoke to the smell of grilled cheese sandwiches, which Lucas was bringing toward her with great fanfare, on a platter, offering the very simple food as a gourmet meal. Just as they had done earlier in their lives, when a student's budget had curtailed their experience of fancy dining.

Rachel had no idea how appealing she looked, sitting on the floor, using the coffee table as a dining table. Her silky chocolate hair shimmered with her every move, mahogany glinting in the light of the candles Lucas had lit. Her skin glowed apricot, somewhat darker in places where Lucas had marked her. She only knew she felt perfectly happy, perfectly fulfilled, perfectly beautiful.

Her thoughts were for the man who had brought her to this point. The man she knew was wanting her again, watching him in fascination as his arousal became more distinct. Oblivious to the fact that it was her unending, adoring stare that was bringing on the change.

Leaning toward him, she placed her mouth over his, her tongue mating with his.

"You taste toasty," she murmured against his lips.

"Hmm. I should taste like you." He smiled, his eyes wide and black.

"Well," she said, licking her lips, pretending to decide. "Maybe. That could be it."

She continued her ministrations, gradually climbing onto his lap, straddling him as he sat. She didn't cease her efforts until after the ultimate tremor rocked him a little while later.

Rachel didn't move from that position, content to rest her head on his shoulder, his arms around her waist, his breath in her hair.

Sometime after the candles died down, Rachel sensed Lucas carrying her back to her room—sensed, too, that they would make love again before morning.

She was right.

Chapter 16

Her eyes were red. She knew it. She'd jumped from the bed when she'd realized tears were coming. Lucas must not see them. She'd headed for the shower, hoping that would drown out any noise she might make. Ultimately she hadn't really made much. She'd cried buckets, but couldn't be sure it had helped her. Not yet, anyway.

Tears that had been dammed up for years, tears that went with feelings that had been buried just as long, translated into gallons and gallons of water when they finally broke through the dam. Those tears had found that first minuscule escape route that day in Paul's office and apparently she had not yet exhausted the tear supply.

Except Rachel never cried. Absolutely never. And as she had viewed her red, swollen eyes in the bathroom mirror, she had decided that this was a good policy for her to follow. She did not weep elegantly, beautifully, femininely, and she didn't look too great afterward, either. In fact, she concluded, she looked absolutely ghastly in the aftermath. Yes, that was one more reason to avoid tears.

So she grabbed some clothes—whatever she could reach easily—and went downstairs into the kitchen. She fidgeted.

She started a pot of coffee. She didn't even like coffee. She always drank tea.

Then she picked up a Handiwipe and a bottle of spray cleaner and began scrubbing imaginary spots off the kitchen counter that had just been meticulously cleaned by her mother or one of her appointees.

Scrub, scrub, scrub.

Stupid, stupid, stupid.

How could I be so stupid? Rachel was furious with herself. *Why did I do this again? The other day—that was a miracle day—that was different.* Dios mio, *how could I let this happen? Where was my restraint?*

Scrub, scrub, scrub.

Stupid, stupid, stupid.

What do I do now?

It doesn't mean anything, she reminded herself. *Many people...do this all the time and never think anything of it. In Lucas's world, the kind of people he's used to don't expect declarations just because they have sex. They don't get all soppy thinking it means love.*

I can do that. Rachel straightened her shoulders. *I can pretend, anyway. Pretend that love wasn't involved for me. It was a physical release. That's all.*

And yet Rachel knew this wouldn't work for her, either. She just wasn't made that way. So her only real solution would be—

"*Buenos días,* Rachel." Lucas didn't have much Spanish, but all the time he'd spent with Michaela had taught him some basics. He figured he needed all the practice he could get.

Clutching her Handiwipe to her chest, not caring that she was soaking Lysol into her T-shirt, Rachel spun and gasped at his arrival.

"Oh, Lucas," she breathed. "I didn't realize you'd come downstairs."

Lucas stared at her, bewildered by her rather feral appearance—the unkempt hair, the carelessly chosen clothes, the makeup-free face and the wild, swollen red eyes. None of this was typical of Rachel. Not at all. He moved toward her, instantly concerned. "Rachel, what is it? Is Michaela okay?"

"What? Huh? Why do you ask?" She was baffled by the questions.

"You look..." Lucas searched for a diplomatic word "...upset. I thought maybe the hospital had called."

"Oh, yes, I see. No, no, she's fine. I haven't heard from the hospital or anything." She started scrubbing the counter again. "Why do you ask?" She was distressed and she was repeating herself.

"Rachel," he said calmly, reaching out to stroke her elbow, tact going out the window now that he knew something else was the reason for her state. "Rachel, you look awful. What is the matter?"

She pulled away from the contact. It was the last thing she needed right now. "'What's the matter?'" she asked of the ceiling. "What's the matter, he wants to know. How do I answer that?" She slammed her spray bottle down on the counter, threw her Handiwipe into the sink and began pacing the length of the kitchen. Anything to get away from him.

Throwing her arms into the air, pointing at him with a flourish worthy of an Italian opera star, she said, "*Dios mio,* Lucas. I don't even know where to start."

"You could start with me." His voice caressed her senses, brought heat to her core.

And she fought it down.

"Or I could start with you. Either way works for me." His joke fell flat.

Making a noise that sounded remarkably like a growl, Rachel raked her fingers through her hair with a violence that told Lucas exactly how her hair had achieved its current lion-mane look.

"I'm just teasing, Rachel."

"Oh, yes. Of course you are. I should have realized. We're only talking about sex. I mustn't take it so seriously."

She marched back to the sink, gathered up her cleaning supplies again, began seeking out spots of dirt. Or potential germs.

"Rachel, that isn't what I meant. What we've shared is wonderful, exceptional sex. I don't mean to sound like I don't appreciate that."

"Oh, okay. *Bueno.* You *appreciate* having sex with me. Yes, right. Wonderful, exceptional sex—and you appreciate that.

That's very nice.'' She drew a deep breath, unaware of the bitterness lacing her words. ''Except that, for me, Lucas—*Dios mio.* This just isn't how I do things. It matters to me.''

She was pacing, waving the spray bottle around, letting the cloth drip on the floor.

''It matters to me, too, Rachel.''

''Right, some kind of need thing that men have.'' Spraying and wiping, spraying and wiping. ''I don't mean it's exercise, Lucas.''

He frowned, looking for a way to respond. ''I didn't mean that, either. What we've been having, Rachel, it's like I remember. It matters a great deal to me.''

He tried to sound calm, to not let his own fear and confusion show in his voice. He'd tried to go slowly, tried to give her time. Somehow, for Rachel, it had apparently still gone too fast. ''We've rebuilt a friendship, haven't we? That's a start, isn't it?''

''*Sí, sí.*'' She nodded her head agitatedly.

''Has this still been too fast for you?'' His voice was gentle, trying desperately to understand what was upsetting her so.

Rachel took a shaky breath. ''No, Lucas, not too fast. It's been too...deep.'' The last word was a whisper.

''Rachel, I know things have been a little strange. Our recent experiences haven't been a typical life.'' He smiled, reaching toward her. ''But it's okay.''

She sidestepped his touch, knowing it would only scramble her and that she couldn't cope with it at the moment. ''How can it be okay?'' she asked, her voice breaking.

Suddenly she crumpled to the floor. She sat sobbing, her back against the cupboards, her knees pulled to her chest. Burying her face against her knees, letting her hair serve as a shield between herself and the outside world, her tears would not be denied. ''How can it ever be okay again?''

Alarmed, Lucas regarded the sobbing heap that was his wife. He knew they were in a strange position—he'd even tried to say that. There were still issues, there were still things to deal with. Of course there were.

But they'd made so much progress.

And yet, through all that, Lucas had never seen Rachel like this. This wasn't just floods of tears, as had been the case when they'd learned Michaela would be coming home. More was involved here. Sobs that wracked her entire body, deep shudders that seemed to be coming from her soul. He knew she was building distance between them, protecting herself.

Lucas squatted down on the floor beside her, involuntarily extending his arm so he could brush the hair away from her face.

She flinched at the attempted contact and scooted the eight inches necessary to provide a moat between her own ground and Lucas's. She continued to hold herself in a curled ball.

"Rachel," Lucas began, not sure what he would say, fear ricocheting within his own heart. "We'll be all right, Rachel. Trust me."

Lifting her head, Rachel tried to focus through her tears. "Trust you?" She sounded as if the idea was utterly foreign to her. Which, of course, it was. "How can I trust you, Lucas? You betrayed me."

She'd finally said it. The thing that was central to it all, the thing that had hung between them all this time.

"You betrayed me, Lucas. You betrayed our marriage and everything we had." Tears glistened on her eyelashes, dripped from her chin onto her shirt, mixing with the cleaning fluid dampness.

Rachel had never allowed herself to ponder this. She had never faced her pain and anger over Lucas's desertion. She had regrouped and reidentified herself, and then moved on. She had done what was necessary for survival. And survive, she had. But only just.

"Everywhere I looked, there was Alana. Every spare minute—or what might have been a spare minute—you were with her. I was slow to understand I was competing with her. And how could I possibly compete with her? Or with any of the other women you've been with since Alana? I'm not that type. The sophisticated, glamorous type. I'm just me."

Her voice broke. "No wonder I lost, Lucas." She looked him in the eye, her pain evident. "I loved you with everything in me. And it wasn't enough for you. If I love you now, how can I believe it will be enough this time? How do I know that your attraction to me at the moment isn't just because I'm convenient right now and that the minute someone else is convenient you'll be off with her? Or the minute someone else looks interesting? Or the minute you need that spot of glamour in your life? I don't know what prompts you to make those choices." She took a deep, shaky breath. "How do I trust you again? How?"

Lucas's heart began to pound. This was it, the topic they'd danced around for ages. The topic that had ended their marriage. Unless they could face this, all the rebuilding would be for nothing. Because it would have been built on a hollow foundation. "I don't know what to say, Rachel."

And he didn't.

"Being betrayed by my husband, well, it left scars, Lucas. It shook my confidence, my faith, my ability to believe there was anything good in the world. And then I had a child, *gracias a Dios,* and some of that was restored. But as for having a man in my life, even if you were someone new, someone I'd just met, I'd be having trust issues. I know, because I've been extremely unsuccessful at dating attempts." Her voice was hoarse following all the tears, tears that were very likely to reappear. "But it was *you,* Lucas, it was you who caused me so much pain, so much grief. It was you who embarrassed me. Who dragged my pride and my love through the mud. How can that be okay?"

He couldn't deny it. He'd gotten off easy, in a way, and he knew it. He had somehow avoided confronting this aspect of his relationship with Rachel.

God knew he'd done a lot of confronting in the past months. His job. His parents. His responsibility toward—and love for—Michaela. But, if he was honest, he'd somehow hoped he and Rachel would never need this discussion. That they would be able, somehow, to rebuild without clearing the air on this aspect of their relationship. He didn't know how to talk about it yet. He had hoped things would take care of themselves on this score. He'd kept waiting for things to return to normal.

"How do I know you're not just trying me on for the diversion? To see what it's like on the other side of the tracks? How do I know that our entire marriage wasn't based on that sort of curiosity?" Bitterness punctuated every syllable. "Am I the first woman you've been with who's had a child, Lucas? Is that it? Or is it to compare natural curves to those created by plastic surgeons? Have you forgotten what that's like? Or have you forgotten what it's like with a brunette who is not trying to be a blonde? Let me think, what was it you said before?" She considered a minute. "Oh, yes, perhaps you just wanted to compare—a then-versus-now thing."

Suddenly her face crumpled and she was again overwhelmed by tears. "*Dios,* I am so sorry. You don't owe me this explanation."

Lucas was floored by her comments. He'd no idea she might be harboring such insecurities. This, at least, was something he might be able to discuss.

"You see, Lucas," her voice interrupted his thoughts before he could speak. She faced him squarely with wide eyes that were decidedly tiger-like although still brimming with tears. "I know how your life has been. I don't make a deliberate effort to know, but it is hard to avoid. There are plenty of people, you know, who want to tell me things 'for my own good,' 'because I have a right to know,' 'to keep me posted.' I see the society pages in the newspaper and segments on the television news, so I can't help knowing that you're...a busy man. That you spend time with a variety of women. Gorgeous, elegant, sophisticated women."

"Arm candy." Lucas squirmed at this piece of truth, but figured she deserved what honesty he could manage.

"What?"

"Arm candy. Yes, I attend a lot of events, and yes, I always take a date. At first it was Alana. Then it was...then it didn't matter. It could be anyone." Lucas had never held much faith in the notion of cloning, but when he considered Alana and the troupe of artificial blondes who had followed her, he had to wonder. They were all incredibly the same.

Rachel winced at the remark, but said nothing.

"I discovered that there are always women willing and interested in being seen in the right places. Once the word is out that a guy's looking for that, it's easy to find dates. A woman wants publicity, she wants to be seen. I can provide that easily enough. I need a woman in the picture. We both get what we want, what we need."

"Of course."

Lucas mulled over these comments. He was being honest.

He could see how it had been. How empty and superficial his world had become. That he had been so disillusioned and unhappy when Rachel had walked back into his life wasn't really surprising. Yet he was no more confident about communicating this to Rachel now than he had been five years ago.

Anger began vying with pain, prompting another round of mortifying tears that Rachel really did not want to shed. She took a deep breath, running her hands through her hair. "Lucas, please try to understand. You and I are different in some important ways. You are the only man who...fits me. You, however, are not so particular. The equation is more flexible for you. For you, all cats are gray in the dark. That is not so for me. And I can't be one of many gray cats."

Thinking he perhaps understood what Rachel was getting at, Lucas offered, "Rachel, I've dated many women. Being still married to you, I probably shouldn't have. But I do not, I do *not,* go to bed with them just because we've been on a date."

Rachel thought it might be foolish to believe this, just because it was what she wanted to hear. But it was a nice thought.

"Really. I told you they're arm candy. It's the truth. I haven't been having relationships. Or one-night stands, either, for that matter." He thought for a minute. "I don't actually know when I was last with a woman, now that I think about it, other than with you. Recently."

Lucas's admission didn't exactly warm her heart, but she tried to take it in a positive spirit. Taking a deep breath, she continued. "So then, you weren't...seeing someone when...we started seeing each other." It was almost a question.

"No."

"You're sure?"

"Definitely." He'd been on his own for a long while, that was for sure.

Rachel stood up, reclaiming her spray bottle and cleaning cloth.

"Rachel." Lucas remained seated on the floor, unwilling to do anything that might make Rachel feel pursued. "Were you seeing anyone, Rachel?"

She shook her head, croaking a laugh at the absurdity of the question. "I've already said I couldn't."

"But did you try? I mean, it's been five years."

"Lucas," she said coldly, "as you might recall, in the past five years I've been raising my daughter, my daughter who has recently been ill. Generally speaking, men, and dating men in particular, have not been at the top of my priority list."

Momentarily Lucas felt contrite. It was true that the two of them had spent the past five years in very different activities. It was, however, critically important to Lucas to know. He started thinking. "Let's see. You've been at the hospital for that reason, but you worked there before that. So, if you were involved with anyone, it stands to reason it could have been someone from the hospital." He was pushing, and he knew it.

Rachel compressed her lips, saying nothing.

"Paul," he stated definitively.

"Paul?" she repeated dumbly. "Paul Graham?"

"Why not Paul Graham?" Lucas asked. "He's an attractive man, I would think. He's been a fixture in your life. It's obvious the two of you are close."

"*Dios mio,* Lucas, he is like a father to me!" Rachel's shock was genuine. "I would no more date Paul Graham than you would!"

Lucas believed her. But it wasn't an adequate answer. He had to know. "Did you try, Rachel?"

"Is that any of your business?" Her voice was soft.

"Well—" he realized he might be pushing a little too hard "—we're still married and…we probably need to work on the 'no secrets' thing."

"Okay, fine. Lucas, I can tell you I tried—and failed—at two relationships. These were men I spent a lot of time with—I wouldn't say we dated. One was a visiting doctor from Mexico. He was nearly as lonely as I was. The other was Diego. He is truly too much a brother to me for that to ever work, but he was there for me when I needed someone. That's it. Two good friendships that did not involve sex. Nothing as colorful or diverse as your pastimes, but there you have it." The bitterness was in her voice again.

Briefly Lucas reflected that perhaps this wasn't such a good topic of conversation after all. The thought of Rachel with another man—even though she hadn't actually "been" with either of them—made him feel physically sick. Thinking of Diego in that capacity was even worse than considering her with some unknown, faceless doctor from Mexico. Diego would have been able to take over his family, to raise his daughter, if things had gone in that direction.

And she's been forced to watch your parade of babes for years. Lucas began to understand Rachel's pain, the pain he had caused, at a level he had never before comprehended.

"Having said that, maybe now is the time to point out—" she paused, wondering if this had occurred to Lucas at all "—that we haven't exactly been taking precautions. I haven't been with anyone else, so I'm not a risk."

Strangely, knowing Rachel thought he could be a health risk hurt. "I understand about precautions," he said somewhat defensively.

Rachel watched as another thought—an obvious thought—entered his head, revealing itself to her only because she could still read his face. They hadn't exactly been preventing a baby, either.

For Lucas the thought of Rachel facing another unplanned pregnancy, this time with him in the picture, did peculiar things to his heart.

"You would know it was your child this time?"

"Yes." He understood why she needed to ask.

She grabbed up the spray bottle again, heading toward the refrigerator, spraying it and wiping it until it squeaked.

"I guess I've been so focused on trying to do better," Lucas began, "which I still think is the main thing," he interjected quickly, "but it's meant that I haven't thought much about resolving what went unresolved five years ago."

She nodded. She'd been avoiding the same thing. "It was betrayal, Lucas. I've never admitted how that made me feel before. I don't know how that gets…fixed."

Her soft statement, and the mix of resignation and pain that colored it, caused Lucas to stand again. He didn't know how to fix it, either. He couldn't make it go away. He couldn't change anything he'd done. He couldn't really make Rachel feel better. This had to come from within her.

"You know me well enough to know that I can't have sex without being involved emotionally. It appears to be one way that we are different." She shrugged her shoulders, trying to shrug off the hurt this knowledge brought her. "So, I bond motionally, not just physically. It touches my heart. And that neans that something inside me that has been dead and buried or five years has been ripped out of its hiding place.'' She hrugged again. ''Like I said, I don't know what to do about t. I don't know how to handle it.''

She walked away from him, heading toward the sliding glass loor. She began spraying copious amounts of Lysol, began to erd the liquid into her cleaning rag. She was really only creating streaks at this point, but she needed something to do.

Eventually, unable to pretend that her cloth could absorb any nore liquid, she returned to the counter. She knew, too, that he room really couldn't accommodate any more cleaning umes. She certainly couldn't pretend that anything else needed urther sanitizing.

She started to pace, then stopped in front of the refrigerator. eaning her back against the fridge, she discovered that it was till vaguely damp.

Lucas watched her, alarmed and worried by these admisions. He had so believed that they were heading in the right irection. He, also, was at a loss to know what steps to take.

And then it hit him. He finally understood what they were eally talking about. What was missing.

''I love you, Rachel.''

For all that Lucas expected Rachel to follow her feelings, to dmit them, he'd never given her a reason to do it. He'd never ffered what he now realized she needed. After all, the relaonship worked in two directions, or it didn't work.

Rachel closed her eyes and again crumpled toward the floor, esuming her previous position of protection.

This time Lucas was immediately on the floor beside her, cooping her toward him, holding her, rocking her, soothing er. This time he knew how close to making another mistake e had been.

''Rachel—'' he tipped her face so that he could see her eyes —I do love you. So much.''

''I love you, too, Lucas.''

Renewed tears were coursing down her cheeks, tears brightned his eyes, too.

''I was trying so hard not to.'' She tried to smile.

''Maybe that was my problem, too. I just knew how much

I wanted you.'' Lucas kissed her, over and over, raining deli cate little touches along her face and throat, reverently, hun grily.

''Rachel, one of my many mistakes was that I didn't under stand that loving you is what makes *making* love to you s special. Sex gives me a way to show what I feel. I'm not s good with the words, as you know.''

Rachel knew she was his focus right now. For now, and on day at a time, she had to remember that.

He stroked her magnificent, presently wild, hair back fror her face. ''You've been the missing piece all this time, Rache That you weren't in my life was the reason nothing felt right.'

He gazed at her, taking in her flushed face, wishing he coul help relieve the angry swelling from eyes that had been cryin too much. ''I love you, Rachel. Really.'' He kissed her fore head, tasting a sweetness that had everything to do with love

Rachel decided to take another quick shower, a cool one thi time that might improve the swollen state of her eyes. She wa glowing, she knew. And yet, she still held back, just that littl bit. How long would it be like that?

She stepped out of the bathroom toweling her hair dry. Luca was sitting on the bed, watching her. He adored her body, a much as he ever had.

''You know, I'm not sure you really need clothes yet.''

A smile played at the corners of Rachel's mouth. ''Really Why do you say that?''

''Because you're quite lovely without them. And if yo would leave them off, it saves me the trouble of removin them.''

''Are you thinking of removing them?''

Rachel watched deliberately as Lucas slid off the bed, mak ing his way toward her. ''I'm thinking it's much better if yo just don't dress yet. While I, on the other hand, am very ove dressed.''

His hands gently cupped her breasts then, his thumbs whis ing against her nipples in an uninterrupted rhythm. His mou took hers, ending the need for further discussion.

Her hands busied themselves with his clothing, unzippin

letting unneeded items fall to the floor. Her arms crept around his neck, her fingers weaving into his hair.

"Oh!" she gasped as her body brushed against his. He was ready for her, but she knew he wouldn't mind being stroked. He wouldn't mind it at all.

Sometime later they lay together, their naked bodies still entwined, his fingers stroking the chocolate silkiness of her hair. He'd decided to at least try to express some of his feelings.

"Rachel, I want you to know...well, first of all, I'm sorry for how my parents were. I knew, but at the same time, I didn't know, what they were doing to you. That's the first thing." He stopped, smiling quickly at her, hurrying on. "Secondly, looking back, I think I really didn't realize that marriage takes some effort. You know, you don't just say the vows and that's the end of it. I really think I expected that marriage just *was,* that you really didn't have to do anything to keep it that way."

He stroked her hair, adoring its feel, just as he always had. "I married you because I loved you. It was the one and only time I ever defied my parents. Once we were married, it was like I spent the rest of my time trying to make it up to them. It's obvious, now, that that would mess up a marriage, put tremendous strain on it. That I needed to realize where my loyalties belonged, as a husband. I didn't see it then."

He reached over toward the nightstand, easily locating the hairbrush she had always kept there. He did love to brush her hair.

"I also need to tell you...about Las Vegas."

He felt rather than heard her indrawn breath. "Will it do any good to discuss it?" She felt so raw, having finally let the dam burst. She was new at this, just as he was.

"Well, some of it anyway. I was mad, damn mad when I left Phoenix that day. I knew things weren't right with us, which is why I asked you to come with me. Not that I knew that consciously. I thought you had a hell of a nerve to turn me down. Of course, now I know you really did have reasons."

He concentrated on brushing a section of her hair, watching in fascination as goose bumps formed across her shoulders as he did so. "But Alana was...really supportive, I guess, of my anger. Sort of fanned the flames. But it wasn't her fault, it was mine. I really never saw what was happening with her, not until I suddenly found myself...in bed with her."

Rachel's head dropped forward, causing her hair to cascade around her, shielding her face from view.

"Rachel, nothing happened with her then. Well, okay, we were...entangled, but I did stop. I suddenly realized what I was doing and that it felt completely wrong. I wish I'd latched on to that feeling," he acknowledged. "Anyway, I spent the rest of the night wandering Las Vegas, psyched up to be daring, but not really willing to follow through. I don't know what was wrong with me, especially when I got home."

Lucas set the brush on the bed and eased Rachel's hair away from her face, tipping her chin so she would meet his eyes. "I should have told you the truth then. I should have said I was sorry. I didn't. But I'm saying it now."

Tears glistened on the tips of her eyelashes. She nodded at him.

"I didn't see the position I put you in where Alana was concerned. I didn't see the direction things were headed in, how things looked to other people. I just never saw it. I should have."

She blinked, tried to meet his eyes.

"I probably could have told you things better than I did, Lucas. I thought I tried. I mean, I wasn't silent about any of it. But I never seemed to say the magic thing that would make you take me seriously."

"I wasn't ready to hear it, Rachel. I had some growing up to do, I guess."

She smiled, leaning toward his mouth, kissing him tenderly.

"I should have told you about Michaela. Sooner, I mean. No matter what, it wasn't right that you didn't know she'd been born."

"Thanks for that, Rachel. Honestly, I'm not sure how I would have reacted to the news before now. It would have depended, I suppose, on when you told me. But I'm very glad I know now."

Rachel bit her lip, thinking. "I just wasn't equipped, at that age, to cope as well as I might have."

"Neither was I."

They both smiled then. They had hit solid common ground.

"So," Lucas suggested, "maybe we weren't too young to be in love or to be married, but we were too young to know how to take care of the marriage."

They dressed and went downstairs, deciding to finish the pot of coffee Rachel had prepared before. Rachel was nervous. She had to do this *right*. She had to be honest. There could not be misunderstandings.

And it was still so new to her that expressing it was difficult. She faced him.

"I'm still scared, Lucas. You rejected me before. You hurt me in a way that only you could. It's not easy to open myself up to that possibility again. It's like I'm putting a weapon in your hands and trusting you not to use it against me. That's not easy." She shook her head. She was scared inside, no doubt about it.

"This is so hard, Lucas. At one time I would have given anything, absolutely anything, for you to act this way. But it didn't happen. And I quit thinking about it, quit hoping for things to get better. I had to find peace somehow, so I did. *Dios mio,* Lucas, I just got my daughter back. Can you understand how that feels for me? I'm thrilled, but I'm also scared. And now you're back in my life, in Michaela's life, saying you love me. I've heard that before from you."

"Rachel, what else do you need to hear?"

"It's not a question of needing to hear anything. I need to live it, Lucas. I need to learn to believe in it. I've never been a mother and a wife before. I've only been one or the other. I have to learn to be that person. To believe in being that person."

Fear rumbled inside Lucas—he wanted to fix this. Now.

"I guess," he said slowly, choosing his words with care, "I thought, over the last few weeks, that we were getting to know each other again. To like each other again. To love each other again. Was I wrong?"

Rachel smiled. "Not wrong at all. But," she cautioned, "I still hurt inside. It's been six years since my marriage started to unravel, but the hurt is still there. I've had so much anxiety with Michaela. I have to learn to trust again." She shrugged. "Trusting is a huge risk for me."

"A good friend recently pointed out to me that sometimes a risk is necessary in order to achieve things."

"You know, Lucas," she said, standing up, her coffee cup only half-empty. She had that faraway look in her eyes again. "That's exactly why I'm trying. A good friend recently said the same thing to me."

Lucas sipped from his cup, pleased with her answer. "Rachel, I swear things have changed. You already know I'm job hunting. You already know I won't be socializing with my father anymore. You know I love my little girl and want to be in her life. You know I'm your friend. And I have learned a lot about how to treat a wife."

"That's the kind of thing I need to have it be real." She was standing at the sliding glass door now, trying to see through the haze of streaks she had created, her arms wrapped across herself for comfort. She smiled slightly. "'Fool me once, shame on you. Fool me twice, shame on me.' I'm not sure I could take it a second time, Lucas."

Lucas drained his coffee cup. This was an important crossroad. Even if she wasn't trusting words, he had a few things he needed to say. Somehow he knew she wanted to hear them. She wanted to believe him.

He crossed the room, turned her to face him, picked up her hand, holding it between the two of his. Even when she pulled back on it, he wouldn't let it go.

"Rachel, I love you. The only time in my life that I've ever been happy was when I was with you. Then and these last months, since I've met Michaela." He shifted, reaching for her other hand. "If we need to learn to be with each other, okay. I can accept that. But understand—I'm not doubting us. I believe in us."

It occurred to Lucas that a few other things needed to be said.

He reached out to tip her face toward him, forcing her to meet his gaze. "I've been so alone, Rachel, without you."

"Me, too, Lucas. Alone and so very lonely."

"I didn't sleep with Alana, Rachel, while we were still together. I was faithful that way, even though I know it didn't look like it. I felt divorced, once you left. Once I'd signed the papers. And it was awful. But I didn't cheat on you, Rachel."

"I believed that when you said it five years ago, Lucas." Quiet conviction resonated in her voice. "And it did help to know you weren't sleeping around while you were still living with me."

They were silent for a moment, Lucas unconsciously stroking Rachel's hand as he held it.

"Can you forgive me?"

Rachel finally understood the difference between forgiving and forgetting. "I have forgiven you, Lucas. I haven't forgotten. I don't know if I can. Or if I should." She didn't hold a grudge. She just carried scars.

"Can you believe that things are different now? Can you trust me?" His voice shook with wanting her to accept what he was offering.

"I don't know." This was the problem, Rachel knew it well.

"Do you trust me with Michaela?"

She stared back at him, nodding. "Yes."

"Well—" he needed to put a positive face on it "—that's also progress."

"I want to...to trust you." The admission sounded shy. She needed to change the subject. "I think we should be getting back to the hospital."

Lucas let her go, although every instinct wanted to pull her into his arms, soothe her, make her forget her misgivings. Make her trust him.

But he couldn't *make* her do anything. What she needed was a reason to believe. Again.

Chapter 17

In the end, Lucas faxed his resignation to Neuman Industries.

He'd had no doubt at all that it was what he wanted. He had needed to decide on the most efficient, satisfying manner of carrying it out. Finally, he had decided faxing it would feel immediate. Of course, he sent the original in the mail with his actual signature so it would be accepted legally.

The fax was sent; the deed was done. Lucas wasn't sure how his father was going to react. A few months ago Lucas would have predicted a nasty scene, and just the thought of that probably would have changed his mind. Now he wouldn't be put off by the possibility of upsetting his father. Ironically, though, he was no longer sure that his departure would bother Arnold Neuman. Not these days.

In the end it wouldn't really matter. Lucas had made his decision and it felt good. When he returned from putting the envelope in the mail, the telephone was ringing.

''Hello?''

''Lucas, this is Diego. Perhaps we can meet again? My cousins, they would like to talk with you. I know it is short notice, but we're on our way to Filiberto's on Thomas Road. Can you get there?''

Lucas hastily agreed and dressed himself, equally hastily and ery, very casually. Filiberto's wasn't fancy and didn't have a t of interior seating, but they did have excellent, authentic lexican food. Lucas smiled to himself, thinking he was on the ay to becoming acclimated to such cuisine again.

Filiberto's was just the sort of thing he had missed. And, it ad to be said, Filiberto's could offer up delicacies that would elt the sinuses. His grin spread across his face. If he knew iego—and he believed he did—Filiberto's was another test. ucas was ready for that challenge. Pocketing his keys, he was early out the door when something made him stop.

He went back to his bedroom, straight to his armoire. He pened the door to its interior cabinet, reaching unerringly for little box—one he hadn't thought of in a long while and yet ad never forgotten. He opened it, staring down at the mel- wed golden glow of the small object it held.

In a few short seconds, he was evaluating that same golden ow as it encircled his finger. It looked—right. It felt—right. hat wedding ring that had left his hand five years ago.

It should have never been removed.

It was perfect on his hand.

Rachel couldn't say what was actually more important.

She was feeling bombarded. Bombarded, but happy? Was at the right word? Yes, bombarded and happy. Overwhelmed d joyful.

Michaela was home. Her first day home in—how many onths had it been? Rachel wasn't sure anymore and she didn't el like counting them. All that mattered was that her little rl was home.

In her honor, a restrained, although sincere, fiesta was un- rway. Rachel had known there would be food and family d lots of smiles, but she hadn't really expected it to be like is. Again her mother had quietly, unbeknownst to Rachel, rformed miracles at the town house. She had had help, of urse, but the entire place was decorated, full of balloons, epe paper flowers, and Welcome Home banners. Not to men- n food.

Still, toning down the exuberance was necessary and everyone knew it. No one wanted Michaela exhausted within fiftee minutes of her return.

Rick and his wife, Teresa, had arrived at the hospital at eigh that morning, ready to load any of Michaela's and Rachel' remaining possessions in their pickup. Lucas had arrived ju as they were leaving, about eight-thirty. Rachel, to her surpris had felt tears in her throat as she had said goodbye to h colleagues. Of course she would be back eventually, but in fiv years she'd never taken more than a few days off at a tim other than to give birth to Michaela. Being gone indefinitel was going to be strange for her. A goodbye-and-good-luc party had been held the previous afternoon, and the very sam tears that were threatening now had spilled then. And Rach was thoroughly disgusted with herself for crying, especially i public.

Michaela had been highly annoyed that she needed to leav the hospital via a wheelchair, but Lucas had laughed an scooped her into his arms, loading her into the chair, managin to make enough of a game of it that Michaela had laughed an gone along with it.

That's when Rachel had noticed it.

The ring. The one he'd "misplaced," so long ago. She' caught Lucas's eye, or rather, she had looked at him only find him already looking at her, his dark gaze steady on her.

"It's where it belongs, Rachel," he'd said.

He'd known what she was thinking. Just as he always ha

She felt those damn tears trying to rear up again. She thoug immediately of her own rings, the ones she'd taken off befo she'd gone to see a lawyer. The ones that were sitting in black velvet drawstring pouch. At the back of her underwe drawer, exactly where they'd been for five years. She hadn even taken them out to look at them. Not once. The me thought had been too painful for her.

She wondered where his ring had been all these years.

"I had the little box they came in, Rachel. You, uh, yo didn't take it with you." Again, he'd seen her thoughts dan across her face. He kept his voice low, as gentle as he kne how to make it. "My ring's been in that box since the day signed the separation agreement. The night you returned it me, I put it back on, afterward. I thought—I think I actual ıought that if I just put it back on, everything would be healed. 'hat it would be okay. That that would somehow erase what 'd done. This time, Rachel, when I put it back on, it felt right. : *is* where it belongs, Rachel."

Rachel had turned away, feeling fragile to begin with, for easons that had nothing to do with Lucas, and now *this*. She idn't want to confirm her weakness in front of the whole vorld. Or even the staff and patients on this floor of PCH. She urried on, in the guise of leading Lucas to the elevators.

Lucas allowed it. *Space,* he kept repeating internally, des-erately hoping that was all she needed. He'd have done any-ıing for her, just to have her believing in him again. *She just eeds some space.*

Michaela was quickly seated in the Lexus, thrilled with the ehicle. Rachel had to acknowledge that it was more impres-ive, gadgetwise, luxurywise, than her little Ford. She could nderstand Michaela's fascination with it. She could also un-erstand that after months of being cooped up inside a hospital, Iichaela was going to be impressed with everything. Rachel niled.

About halfway home, Rachel decided there was something ifferent about Lucas. She couldn't decide what it was exactly, ut it was there. He was different. And he was smiling.

As soon as they arrived at her town house and Diego came ıshing out, greeting Lucas with the hearty handshake and ughter long-since abandoned between the two of them—well, achel knew something very odd indeed was going on. It had een a good many years since she'd seen that. She'd have to ursue it at some point, but for the time being, she was being vept up in the festivities, and any interrogation regarding this newed and apparently thriving camaraderie would have to ait.

So Rachel had returned the kiss from Diego and the hug om Tanisha and had gone inside. Lucas, who was carrying Iichaela, followed her.

Hugging and kissing continued all around, laughing and cry-g somehow mixed in, as well.

Eventually, and much too soon to suit her taste, Michaela as tired. Simply worn out. The fiesta quietly folded then, Lu-s taking Michaela upstairs to her room, Rachel seeing her guests to the door. Then she went up to Michaela's room, coming to stand beside Lucas as he watched their sleeping daughter.

Involuntarily their hands joined. They stood, Rachel and Lucas, united by the love they felt for their daughter. And by the awe they felt at her return. By mutual consent, they turned toward the door and headed back into the hallway.

"Well, Rachel, I think I should be going, too."

Inwardly Rachel was sorry to hear him say it. She wanted him to stay. She wanted...him. She loved him. Of course, she did.

But it wasn't enough. She wasn't ready. *Was she?*

Lucas turned toward her, once they had descended the stairs. "I'd take it easy, relax if I were you, Rachel. Get some rest. You never know what kind of schedule she's going to be on trying to adapt to outside-the-hospital life again. She may wake up at eleven, wanting to stay up all night."

"*Sí,*" Rachel said laughing, "that is possible. Just the way it was when she was a baby."

It was momentary, instantaneous—the hurt that flashed across Lucas's face, in his charcoal eyes. But Rachel saw it even before he turned his head.

"I would imagine so."

"I—" Rachel cleared her throat "—I didn't mean anything by that, Lucas."

"I know. It's just one of those things that I missed out on and...well, I'm still discovering just how many of those things there really are."

They were at the front door. "Well, goodbye, then, Lucas. I know we need to figure out how to—" she waved her hand in the air, needing the body language to express herself "—*live,* now that she's home."

"It'll be fine. Let's see how she's doing and take it from there."

"Yes."

He leaned toward her, his mouth brushing hers lightly. "Good night, Rachel. I'll call in the morning before I come over."

"Okay."

Rachel closed the door. She listened for his car to start, hear pull out of the driveway. Then she burst into tears. Hurt, ıgry tears that Lucas had made no attempt at anything ıore...*involved.* And because she had wanted him to.

The next three weeks passed in a similar manner. Lucas ıme to her place every day. He spent time with Michaela, ›metimes taking her for a ride in his car. Other times the three ' them played games just as they had in the hospital. And lichaela was determined to teach Spanish to her father. He as trying, but to call it succeeding would be a stretch. Still, lichaela was undaunted.

They enjoyed one another's company, as twosomes and as threesome. Lucas would stay for dinner. Lucas would bring nner with him. They went for walks. They flew kites. They ent to the zoo. They went to the movies. They watched sun-ts.

Michaela had a long way to go before her life didn't include edical realities, if, in fact, it was ever to be completely free ' them. But this was a start, a step on the right path, and they ere all thrilled with it.

Lucas stayed with Rachel, sitting on the couch, watching levision or listening to music, and talking long after Michaela ıd gone to bed. They talked the way they always had. They ughed. And they talked some more.

Most nights, they made love—sweetly, gently or urgently, sperately—and everything in between. But Lucas never ayed the night.

They never talked about the breakdown of their marriage. ıey never talked about how they were going to resolve any-ing.

They just lived.

And it was wonderful. But it wasn't enough for Rachel. She eded so much more from this man. And she began to un-rstand just how scared she was. In fact, she was terrified. ıt this was the only man for her. She had no choice but to ke the risk. She wanted him back in her life—especially since was already there.

"Here, *mija,* take this napkin." Rachel smiled, knowing it ıs hopeless already.

Rachel and Michaela had been joined on their patio by her

neighbor Tanisha, and her daughter, Vanessa. Rachel ha bought a watermelon, and the two little girls were out to dem onstrate that they really could wear more watermelon than the ate.

''I think hosing them off is really the easiest solution, Ra chel.'' Tanisha was laughing, her ebony eyes flashing. ''Oka it might be the only solution.''

''You could be right,'' Rachel acknowledged with a sig sitting back in her chair, admitting good-natured defeat.

''Hey, Rachel!'' Lucas's voice carried toward them. ''Ca you let me in?''

He was standing at the side gate, the one that entered on the common green and that required a key.

''Just a minute,'' Rachel called, getting up to admit him.

''Oh, *Papá,*'' Michaela squealed, waving him over to he ''Look! We've got watermelon! It's so good! Come hav some!'' Juice, meanwhile, trickled down her chin and was b ginning to stick her fingers together.

''Maybe next time, sweetheart,'' Lucas said, his dark ey sparkling as he took in the happy messiness. ''Actually, Rache I was hoping you would come for a drive with me.''

''Huh?'' Taken aback, and with her mouth full of wate melon, Rachel wasn't pleased with her ineloquent response.

''Yes.'' Lucas laughed. ''I have something I'd like to sho you, talk over with you, if you could come with me.''

''Oh, *Papá,* can I come?''

''Not this time. This time is for *Mamá.* If she wants to.''

''Go ahead,'' Tanisha said, immediately picking up on t unique nature of Lucas's request and Rachel's awkward r sponse. ''We both know these two have to have a bath at th point. We might as well conserve water and bathe them t gether. I'll close up your place and bring Michaela home wi me. You know my place is sanitized, so she's safe. Especial since it's been over a month now.''

Rachel licked the juice off her fingers and walked over the hose. She let the water run over her fingers, trying to e tablish some composure. She couldn't begin to imagine wh Lucas had in mind.

''I'm not exactly dressed up,'' she felt compelled to sa

taking in his cotton canvas slacks and navy polo shirt. Casual, but hardly as casual as she was. It was nearly November, fall by the calendar, but temperatures were still warm and Rachel wore shorts.

"No need to be dressed up. As you are is fine." He smiled, but it didn't quite reach his eyes. Rachel couldn't decipher the message there, a fact that did nothing to calm her.

"I'll just get my purse." She kissed Michaela on the head, smiling briefly because this time it was actually *hair* she kissed. "You be good, *mija.*"

Rachel dropped into the Lexus's passenger seat, buckled her seat belt and tried to relax. It was a highly futile endeavor. As was trying to make conversation. She was baffled by Lucas's behavior, and couldn't think of a way to disguise her feeling. Lucas himself didn't seem inclined to say anything.

So they rode in silence.

Eventually Lucas pulled into Encanto Park, driving as if he had a specific destination in mind. He did.

He parked by the lake, gesturing that they should get out of the car. Without thinking, Rachel headed toward the water, watching the children, the ducks and the lovers who were scattered throughout the park. She found a shady spot, the perfect vantage point.

"It's beautiful, isn't it?" Lucas's quiet words startled her. She hadn't realized he had followed her, but of course he had.

"I've always loved Encanto Park," she murmured. "Even when I was a little girl. It just has always felt...I don't know, I guess I'm in tune with the enchantment of the place."

Lucas smiled, remembering Diego's explanation—had it been two months ago? Anyway, Diego's explanation made sense of Rachel's remark.

"It has just always felt good to me. Always." The late-afternoon breeze lifted her hair, the sun creating mahogany highlights. She closed her eyes against the presunset intensity of the light. "Michaela would love this."

Lucas glanced at her sharply, looking for...something. But she just looked beautiful and dreamy and completely oblivious to how Lucas felt about that. He cleared his throat. "I like it here, too." He stepped up behind her, encircling her waist with his arms, pulling her to him. Just breathing her scent. Vanilla, spice and Rachel. He would never get enough of it.

Rachel didn't fight the caresses, the light touch. She could feel the telltale rigidness pressing into her back. She turned to face him, her mouth eagerly seeking his, clinging to his. Her lips parted at the touch of his tongue, inviting more. He gave it. The kiss deepened. And went on and on. Dreamily. Sensuously. Sparkling in the sunlight that was slipping toward sunset.

Eventually Lucas broke off the kiss. He didn't let her go, though. "I didn't actually bring you here for this. Not that I'm complaining." He smiled, his eyes clear and dark, sharing with her their private joke over his favored expression. One he hadn't used in a long time.

"Neither am I." Rachel's voice was hushed. "I think it's this place. There's magic here."

"Mmm. Could be." Lucas stepped back, dropping his arm reaching to hold her hand. "Come sit with me, Rachel. We need to talk."

Rachel's heart lurched, but she knew he was right. The time had come.

They headed toward a bench that was situated near the water's edge. While Rachel sat on the bench, Lucas sat on the ground in front of it, his knees drawn up, his elbows resting on his knees. He seemed withdrawn suddenly, his gaze locked on some distant spot—maybe on the other side of the lake. It was a few more minutes before Lucas broke the silence.

"You know, Rachel, I quit smoking the day you came to my office."

She glanced at him, her eyebrows puckered into a frown.

He laughed, understanding that he'd offered a bizarre conversation starter. "Sorry," he said, "that probably seemed like a really random comment. You'd have to know that I started smoking because, well, Dad has always smoked cigars. They were always available at our meetings, our conferences, around the office. So finally one day I tried it. I wasn't particularly impressed, but Alana was. She told me it made me look successful. You can't imagine how badly I needed to hear that. Or how shallow my view of success had become, if I thought a cigar would prove it. They became a habit quickly, though."

He shrugged. "I remembered you saying that you thought

cigars were nothing but pacifiers for adults. But I would have defended smoking, especially against your opinion. Like everything else in my life, even though the attraction had begun to fade, it was easier to continue as I was than to change anything. Then you walked into my office, and I saw your face when you saw me with a cigar. I knew you saw a pacifier, even if I thought I saw a successful executive. I lost my taste for it that day.''

He smiled wistfully, his eyes trained on the pedal boat that was making its way across the lake, its occupants' laughter clear over the water, as they stomped on the foot pedals that operated the little craft.

''I've been thinking lately, Rachel.'' He began clearly yet thoughtfully. ''You need to know.''

Rachel shifted on the bench, automatically bringing her legs up, curling them beneath her. She was ready to listen. She just wasn't sure what she'd be hearing. She couldn't see Lucas's face. Or his eyes.

''When you left, Rachel, I was stunned. I knew that things—'' The words came haltingly. He'd been rehearsing, though. He took a deep breath, began again. ''I knew that things weren't right between us. Of course, I didn't examine that too deeply, but I knew. I told you before. That's why I asked you to come to Las Vegas.'' He glanced over his shoulder, waiting for her nod of confirmation.

''Yes, well,'' he continued, ''even though I knew it was bad, I didn't see that night as...well, the way you did. As a point of no return. I guess I really believed we'd just go on like we had, with you angry about it—or at least not happy about it—but living with it. I didn't see how serious I'd made it. That I'd crossed a line.'' He shook his head, remembering. ''Yet, when I looked at Alana that night and realized what I was doing—'' he shook his head again ''—something in me made me stop. Still, that was the only action I took to change things. Beyond that, it never occurred to me that you'd *do* something about it. That's me, though. It was easier to just let things go and see where we ended up. Until you walked in my office that day, carrying legal documents for me to sign. Until then I didn't understand it was the end.''

He stopped to comb his fingers through his hair, his hands coming to rest on his head.

Rachel held her breath, only releasing it when he continued.

"I'm not even sure how Alana ended up living in the condo, Rachel. You left, she descended on the place, I escaped. I went numb. Just totally numb once you left. Shock, I guess. Anyway, Alana was there, saying whatever I needed to hear. That's more or less how she operates."

He reached out to break off a blade of grass, needing something in his hands, something to fidget with. "Alana kept me very busy. In the public eye. Mostly it was just the same social appearances thing it had been for years. The key for her was how it looked. And we looked like a successful executive couple." He heard Rachel's sharply indrawn breath, but continued. "And eventually I started noticing that something was missing from my life. I wasn't quite sure what, but I did notice that no matter how surrounded by people I was, or how Alana was constantly with me, I was alone. Really, truly, completely alone. I was on autopilot. But I kept busy, as if that would take my mind off the sad state of my life. I guess it worked to some extent. Alana claimed the town house. I'd moved out as soon as I noticed she had actually moved in, and it was easier to just let it go than—" He bit off his words.

"Easier than telling her to leave," Rachel supplied for him.

"Yes. Exactly." He rested his elbows on his knees again, dropping the mangled blade of grass, linking his fingers together church-steeple fashion. "But I didn't want to live in that town house, anyway. And I only snapped out of it to a certain extent. I didn't realize until very recently why my life felt empty. And—" he smiled wistfully "—I have finally realized, Rachel, that the easiest way isn't necessarily the right way. I finally understand what that means."

He glanced back at her, noting she looked a little pale, but that she was listening. "Which is why we're having this conversation. It isn't easy. It's damn hard. But you deserve to know what I've been doing, what I've been thinking. To hear it from me and not someone else. Maybe I've finally grown up enough to see it and to talk about it." He shrugged.

"Maybe I've finally grown up, too, Lucas. I couldn't ever say things right before, either."

"Or maybe I've learned to listen."

She inclined her head. "And I'm listening to you this time." She laughed lightly.

He smiled, too. Then he returned to what he was needing to say.

"After Alana, well, I was still hoping to meet someone who made me feel less alone. And I dated a lot. But there was nothing there. Just nothing. Even though they were inevitably glamorous, beautiful women who were accustomed to a man's attention and seemed to enjoy what I offered."

Rachel caught a sob in her throat. "Lucas, maybe I don't need to hear all this."

"You need to hear it, Rachel. I need to say it."

After several long minutes Rachel responded. "Then just...don't look at me. Let me just hear you."

"Okay." He turned and sat down on the ground again, not quite touching her. "So, these women seemed content with what I was offering, which wasn't very much. As soon as they realized that all I expected from them was a public companion who would smile at the cameras, the dating ended. They would decline my invitations or I would move on."

He paused, wanting to say this exactly right, or at least as best he could. "I've thought a lot about trust lately, Rachel. And about appearances. That it is important, what people see you doing. That includes the good as well as the bad. Rachel, I need you to understand. I've made many mistakes. Many mistakes when I was married to you, many mistakes since then."

Tears trickled down Rachel's face, Lucas knew it without looking. He could hear her sniffles and the shuddering breaths she was trying to conceal. Still, she had asked him not to look at her, and he would honor her request.

"Listen to me very carefully. Please." He stopped, emphasizing what he had to say with silence. "Rachel, whatever else I've done wrong, Alana was my *only mistake.* Do you understand me, Rachel? She was a major mistake, but she was the only mistake. I didn't know, consciously, why I never went to bed with anyone else. I just knew I didn't want to. Alana—" he licked his dry lips, hoped his words were registering

"—was a mistake. But I never made that mistake again. I swear."

Rachel took a noisy, gulping breath. A sob.

Lucas got to his knees then, in front of Rachel, taking her face in his hands. "I love you, Rachel. And I'm so sorry."

Nodding, crying, Rachel entered Lucas's embrace, pulling him to her. He sat beside her, held her, stroking her face, breathing in the scent he needed. Loving her.

Eventually Rachel took another noisy deep breath, signaling the end of her bout with tears. "You were with many beautiful women, Lucas."

"But I was with them *in public only,* Rachel. There was nothing else with any of them. Nothing. I couldn't feel anything for any of them. I was *dead* inside. Nothing seemed to touch me. I just couldn't *feel*...anything...do you understand what I mean?"

"Lucas, that's how I've lived the last five years. Nobody could understand it better than me. Maybe the difference is that I knew it all this time. You've only just discovered it."

"I didn't realize what you would be thinking about my lifestyle, about these women," he admitted shamefacedly. "It was so obvious to me what those encounters were like. But until Rick and Diego pointed it out to me—beat me over the head with the news—I'd never realized how my life was interpreted by other people. Then my dad confirmed it. I'm sorry for that, Rachel. I don't know how you could even think of taking me back, believing that I'd slept with every social butterfly in the state."

"Let me go on record—" Rachel met his tentative smile with one of her own "—as saying that I have had issues with that very matter."

"Yes," he said, inclining his head. "And now that I understand what you were thinking, I don't blame you. Like I said, I got to thinking about trust. And, well, I know it requires trust to believe me now. But realizing what you'd thought I was doing, I see why things didn't fall into place for you the way they did for me. I gave you a pretty big obstacle to get over."

He turned toward her then. "Rachel, I've never told another woman I loved her. Only you."

Somehow Rachel met his clear, dark eyes. She saw the truth

there, knew that he meant every word. She knew it would take some time before she could think dispassionately about their painful past. But she believed him. He'd learned the hard way, too.

Lucas understood her, as well. The topaz glow in her eyes said it all. Gently he cupped her face in his hands, leaned forward until his lips touched hers. "Only you, Rachel."

Slowly he let his hands drop. He sat back in the seat. "There's more."

Rachel steeled herself, wondering, yet afraid to wonder, what else he wanted to add.

"My parents have become…interesting. They will never hurt you again, Rachel. I know how it was for you—I realize it, finally—and I'll always have to live with knowing I allowed that. But my father is completely out of the picture now, and my mother is…different. Mother really wants to get to know Michaela. In a genuine way, Rachel. She is so thrilled about being a grandmother—I've never seen her so happy about anything before. And she wants nothing to do with my father. She's…well, she's just different."

Rachel said nothing, just nodded her head, digesting this news slowly. She, too, had seen something different about Sophie at the hospital that day. She'd responded to it, whatever it was, when she'd taken Sophie to see Michaela.

"My father, on the other hand—" Lucas cringed "—he's worse than you know." He proceeded to explain what he had learned about his father, what he had seen, why his mother had thrown him out. "Rachel, it hit me, you know? I was in training to become just like him. How close was I, Rachel?"

She held him to her then, stroking his hair. She'd heard the despair in his voice. "Not close at all, Lucas. You've always been a good man, deep inside. He has never been. You've been learning to be yourself all this time, Lucas. And you're doing a fine job."

Taking a shuddering breath, Lucas marveled at how good it felt to talk to Rachel. He'd always been able to talk to her in ways he wouldn't have attempted with anyone else. So much had been bottled up for so long, he wondered how long it would take to really catch up. The release was exhilarating.

"It's funny, you know. The way you described society

women, with emphasis on their absence of personality or ability to speak for themselves. That's exactly how I see them. I told my mother I saw her that way, and it was apparently a turning point for her."

He blew out a long breath, so happy to have Rachel in his life like this. "You know I've been on leave from Neuman Industries?" At her nod he continued. "I've officially resigned. I'm free now. I hadn't realized just how much my spirit was dying there. My dreams will have a chance to be reborn." He smiled.

Rachel smiled back but didn't comment. She sensed there was more.

"Yes, my dreams will have their chance now because I've been accepted at Fuentes de la Juventud."

"Diego's Fuentes de la Juventud?" Rachel asked, as if there were several companies by that name.

"Yes." Lucas smiled. "In fact, that's why I'm looking at Encanto Park. The company is restoring a lot of the buildings in the area."

"Well, at least that explains why Diego seems to like you again."

"Yeah, I think we've worked out a few things. Hell, I know we have or he'd have never brought me into the company." He tipped her head toward him. "I have to prove myself. But he's willing to give me a second chance. He believes in me, Rachel." He kissed her then, gently.

He stood up abruptly. "Come with me a minute. I have something to show you."

Rachel felt unease clench in her stomach, but she followed him across the street and down the way a bit. Lucas stopped in front of one particular house—an old one, clearly one of the older homes of Encanto Park. Yet, it was special. It had character.

"I know it's a fixer-upper—" Lucas sounded nervous "—but actually that's what I'm doing. I'd like you to just, you know, look through the place. And give me your ideas."

So Rachel began to roam through the grand old home. It wasn't huge, but it was big enough. Like so many of the early homes in Encanto Park, it was on one level, with evidence of Mexican architecture throughout. Arched doorways, arched window frames. Beautiful wood flooring that needed serious polishing to bring back its glory. Spanish tile in the kitchen and dining area. Four bedrooms, three bathrooms, a huge kitchen that badly needed renovation. In fact, everything in it needed fixing up. Just as Lucas had said.

"Well," Rachel finally said, "it has a lot of potential, Lucas. I mean, the windows are great, they give it a wonderful open feeling. It's got a great backyard. Wonderful trees. It does need work, cleaning up, fixing up. But it's nice."

She wasn't sure what he wanted her to say. Many people would consider it too old, no doubt, but Rachel didn't see it that way. She'd never believed brand-new meant better. Instead, in this house she saw a home that just needed someone to take care of it, to love it, before it easily looked the part.

"I want to buy it, Rachel. It's one I've been assigned to refurbish, redecorate. But I want to buy it. I want to raise a family here, Rachel."

Rachel didn't meet his eyes, but she knew what he was saying.

"I'd like you to live here, too, Rachel. But even if you don't want to—or can't—I wanted your ideas about the place that I would offer Michaela, whether you thought it seemed like the right kind of home for—" he faltered momentarily "—for us."

Rachel's throat tightened. Yes, she had understood what he was saying. Not only the part about wanting her to live here with him, but also that he wouldn't buy something without her input this time.

"I think it's wonderful, Lucas. And I'm sure you'll be able to create here. Get your spirit healthy." She smiled.

"Yes," he whispered. She had heard exactly what he was saying. "I won't make the same mistakes again, Rachel. Please believe me." He smiled.

She smiled back.

"Come outside, Rachel."

She did.

"Sit down." He was already sitting on an old porch swing, one that looked in need of repair. "I've checked it out already. It's solid."

She sat.

"Rachel." He blew out a long breath, running his hand

through his hair—actions that reflected inner turmoil. "Damn, I don't know where to start this time."

"Just jump right in, Lucas. I'll try to catch on and follow."

"Talking about feelings is new to me, Rachel. I don't even think about them very well, to say nothing of talking about them."

"I know. But I really like it so far." She grinned, feeling almost shy.

"Me, too." He grinned back at her. Another long breath. "I've been trying not to pressure you, Rachel. I wanted you to have the space, the time, you needed to decide things. At first I think I was convinced that since I was ready for things to work out—well, that they just would. I finally caught on that it wouldn't be that easy. I wanted us to really be friends again, not just lovers—not that I'm complaining."

She laughed softly. "I know."

Serious again, he said, "I guess, for me, it's time to talk about where we go from here."

"I don't know what to say, Lucas." Her eyes were sad.

"Okay. I told you I love you. And I do, Rachel. More than I can tell you." He turned toward her, reaching out and tracing the curve of her cheek with his hand. "I want to be with you again. In every way, all the time. I want us to share a life, not just look like we're sharing a life."

He couldn't know that he was echoing Rachel's own fears, fears that had kept her up at night even when Michaela was still in the hospital.

Lucas stood up and began pacing the length of the veranda. "I want you to know, Rachel, for me you are the only woman who fits. All cats are not gray in the dark for me. As for you, you are no gray cat, my dear, in the dark or otherwise." He smiled, this time his eyes reflected it, too. "You are the most vibrant, alive, colorful person I've ever known. And I need you."

He blew out another long stream of air, his hands stacked on his head. "You are the only one who makes me whole." He broke off, trying to find the right words. "Loving you and wanting you are the same thing for me, Rachel. When I'm with you, my soul joins with you. You always said that's what it was, Rachel, and you were right. That's what it is with us. I know I can't undo the things I've done, Rachel. God, I wish I could, because I know it causes you pain. And that hurts me, too."

He walked back toward her, squatting down in front of her, forcing her to look at him. "I love you, Rachel. I am yours in every way, if you'll have me. I know you may not be able to forget what happened. I can't, either. Maybe we shouldn't forget it. But can we move forward?"

She was silent a long time. "How can I know things will be different?"

"Because they already are different, Rachel. *We* are different." He stood up again, leaning back against the railing that bordered the patio. "I'm different, Rachel."

She looked at him, her eyebrows raised.

"I am, Rachel. Tell me—would I have ever talked about my spirit before? Honestly?"

"No," she said with a laugh. "I guess I have to grant you that much."

He waved his hand toward the house. "I brought you here to look at it before I signed any papers. I know that you understand why." She nodded. "I wanted to do it right. And I want *your* opinion."

"Well, actually, Lucas—" Rachel paused "—I love it."

"Yes!" Lucas yelled, looking heavenward, his fists clenched in triumph. "Yes! Yes! Yes! I just knew you'd like it. I felt it the minute I parked in the driveway, before I even went inside. I just *knew*. But—" he paused, sincerity shining from him "—I wasn't going to decide for you. I wanted you to decide for yourself. I wanted us to agree on a place."

"Lucas, I didn't say I'd live here. I just said I liked it."

She stood up and began wandering through the house again, unconsciously looking at the place with a different eye. This time she saw the raw material, she saw what it could become. With the right family living there.

Deep inside, she knew. She wanted to live here with Lucas and Michaela. Together they were the right family to live here.

Certain things still hurt her. Perhaps they always would, perhaps that would ease in time.

But she knew.

And what she knew was more important, was stronger, than what she feared.

"Lucas?" She called out to him loudly enough that he heard her. He arrived in the doorway almost immediately. Maybe he'd not been trailing too far behind.

She held up her left hand for him to see: that morning, she'd finally replaced her own rings. One was the engagement ring—a half-carat diamond that had carried with it such promise and such hope. The other was a plain gold band, a smaller version of the one Lucas had been wearing for weeks.

"I know." His smile was gentle. "I noticed the minute I got to your place today. Even with watermelon juice running all over them. I noticed right away." He caught her hand, kissed her fingers.

"A symbol of love, right, Lucas? Endless. Maybe a little bit wounded in some places, then healed there, too. Deeper as a result. You think?"

"Yes, I do think. Back to where we started, only better."

She was looking out the window, imagining a young girl's voice filling the quiet air.

"Rachel," Lucas's breath was in her hair. He was behind her, his arms stealing around her waist. "I know you're scared. I don't blame you. I've tried to back off, but I wanted to help you believe." He nuzzled her neck. "I know you've started over once before, without me. Can we make a fresh start, together, Rachel? Here?"

Something in her mind still whispered "No," but Rachel's heart had other ideas. This was Lucas the man, not the boy. He was different. She was different. It was right between them, more right than it had ever been, because both of them knew what it felt like to lose what they had. They'd both tried to live without it, and both had found their lives sadly lacking. Empty.

Nothing was ever really guaranteed, but it was right between them. No question.

Something inside Rachel lurched, and she realized it was that internal armor of hers, this time crumbling, not just cracking. Because she didn't need to protect herself that way anymore.

And she was melting, melting under the pressure of Lucas's mouth, his hands—molding herself to fit him, instinctively, without thought, without effort. Just feeling, sensing. Letting her body and her soul hum in time with his. Letting her heart take her where it would. Because her heart knew what it was talking about.

Yes, she loved this man. Holding him close, acknowledging it even as he led her toward the empty master bedroom. He fulfilled her in every way.

Yes, she did love this man. No great newsflash there. But maybe, just maybe, it was worth the risk.

"I love you, Lucas." Her whispered words were soft, gentle. She wasn't entirely sure he'd heard her. "*Te quiero,* Lucas, *te amo.*"

He'd thought he would never hear the words again. The precious words that only Rachel could say. "Oh, God, Rachel, I love you, too."

Epilogue

Rachel eyed herself in the mirror, carefully smoothing the red-and-white sundress down over her hips. Its bodice was fitted, but the skirt swung full and soft. She turned sideways, getting the profile angle. Would Lucas be able to tell? Maybe.

She sighed, a contented sound reflecting a joyful spirit.

Three years later, so much had happened. Best of all, they were a family now, a true family.

They'd bought the house in Encanto. They'd been renovating ever since, but enjoying it. The serious things, like modern plumbing, had been dealt with prior to moving in. Since then they'd just continued to work on it.

Lucas was employed at Fuentes de la Juventud, ready to become a partner, definitely finding a niche there. Of course his dream had always been designing, but he had discovered that renovating appealed to him on a deeper level. Reworking, redeveloping, a structure that had originally been designed with care, bringing it back to life without obliterating the original ideas, Lucas found that supremely satisfying. And he'd found, along the way, that he had a knack for recognizing worthy antique furniture pieces when he happened upon them.

That's what he was doing on this trip. Mario Gonzales, officer irector in San Antonio, had wanted Lucas's opinion on "a ırge wood dresser that appeared to be old." So Lucas had one. His plane would be returning to Phoenix, landing in bout an hour. Rachel was keeping an eye on the time. She vould be there to pick him up.

Next month he was going to Mexico City, unaccompanied, or the first time. Michaela and Rachel had been working with im diligently on his Spanish. The result was that his Spanish 'as passable, and he'd been to Mexico City before. But he'd ever had to fend for himself before with Spanish as his pri- ıary means of communication. He was a little nervous about ., but consoled himself with the knowledge that most of the eople he'd see were not strangers. They were *familia*—truly is this time. They wouldn't let him get into any real trouble, lthough they might let him scare himself a little.

Michaela had continued to be healthy. Her health was still ıonitored, and Rachel still felt her insides give every time lichaela bruised herself or seemed to be too tired, but there ad not been any real cause for alarm. She was as recovered s anyone could be when they had once battled leukemia.

She was in second grade now, continuing to astound her arents with how quickly she caught on to everything. Her best iends at school were Ashley and Monica, but Vanessa was ill her *best* best friend. She didn't live too far away, and the ›ur girls spent a lot of time together these days.

"*Mamá?*" Rachel knew her mother was in the backyard ith Michaela, planting flowers, which they hoped would sur- ive the late-summer heat and bloom in fall. "I'm leaving now. kay?"

Her mother waved at her, spade in hand, encouraging her to t going.

Rachel hesitated, watching the dark head of her daughter ent in fierce concentration as she transferred a tiny seedling to the hole she had made in the soil. Rachel watched the ick, wavy black hair that cascaded down Michaela's back, omehow always managing to escape the ponytail meant to ontain it. But Rachel didn't mind. Not at all.

She crossed the veranda quickly, just to place a kiss on that ead of gorgeous hair.

"*Hasta luego, mija,*" she whispered, before dashing out o
the house.

Yes, so much had happened in three years. Including thi
little surprise she had for Lucas. He'd missed so much wit
Michaela. Rachel knew he regretted that. She wondered how
he would be this time.

Rachel had continued as head nurse at PCH, although sh
now worked days. PCH had moved from the Samaritan Healt
Center grounds a little while back, relocating to its own prem
ises, and with that move had come some shuffling of personne
and schedules. Rachel found that working days suited her jus
fine. Lucas supported her work, just as she supported his. The
had a balanced plan for getting Michaela to and from schoo
for getting meals and so on. They were indeed a family.

Another change involved Neuman Industries. Once a prou
group of hardworking builders, it had gone out of busines
within eighteen months of Lucas leaving it, although that ha
not been the cause of its downfall. It had been Arnold Neuma
himself. He had been involved in more than one illegal biddin
situation. Of all the things Lucas had suspected at Neuma
Industries, his speculation hadn't run in the financial directio
The news hadn't surprised him, but he couldn't have guesse
it, either. He'd taken some comfort in realizing that he couldn
be so much like his father if he hadn't anticipated these illeg
dealings. Anyway, Arnold Neuman was now doing time fo
what was really a white-collar crime—an ironic thing, reall
given how concerned he'd always been with rising above h
blue-collar origins.

Sophie Neuman was making a new life for herself. She ha
become a doting grandmother. In Rachel's mind, a *real* grand
mother. She did very normal grandmotherly things with M
chaela. While she had the money to bestow lavish and oste
tatious gifts on Michaela, she didn't. Rachel knew that Soph
had established a trust fund for the little girl, something eve
seven-year-old didn't have, but Sophie also managed to brir
reality into her relationship with her. Sophie was just as like
as Gloria, Rachel's mother, to be digging in the backyard wi
Michaela.

Maybe more likely, Rachel mused, *given her love of ga
dening.*

That wasn't to say that Sophie had given up the trappings of society life. She was a wealthy woman, not having been dependent on her husband for that. She still moved in the society circle. But she studied issues, paid attention to what was going on in the world. She developed her own views these days and wasn't afraid to say so.

Free of her husband, she faced the prejudicial beliefs she had cultivated. In fact, when she had tackled those viewpoints head-on, she had found it difficult to comprehend that she'd allowed herself to be on that side of the fence. She still struggled with that knowledge. One time, and one time only, she had apologized to Rachel. Rachel had accepted, knowing Sophie was sincere, and it had never been a concern between them again.

Another bright spot in Sophie's life was her regular, weekly tennis match with a certain Dr. Paul Graham, which neither of them ever missed. They were an eye-catching pair, both tall and blond and fit, although they weren't actually calling themselves a couple. And nobody was suggesting anything like that. Not to their faces, anyway.

Rachel pulled into the Terminal 3 parking garage at Sky Harbor International Airport. She still had twenty minutes until Lucas's plane would land. Walking into the terminal, she passed a vendor selling flowers, and located just what she wanted—four long-stemmed, yellow roses.

Yellow for Texas, the state Lucas was returning from. Four, well, because she needed four. Cradling the roses in the crook of her arm, she found a seat near the gate and began to wait. *How could so few minutes seem to stretch so long?*

She stood as she saw him coming through the tunnel. Handing him the roses, she stepped into the circle of his embrace, accepting his kiss.

"There are four?" He was puzzled.

"There will be."

His charcoal eyes seared into black, smouldering. His smile was broad, extending to his eyes, as well. "There will be?"

She nodded, slipping her arms around his waist, completing the circle they made together. A full circle, at last. "Yes."

Smiling at him, she turned her face upward, ready to meet him in a kiss. *"Y todos vivieron muy felices."*

Lucas didn't need to ask what it meant. He knew. And they all lived happily ever after.

* * * * *

✂ **Your opinion is important to us!** Please take a few moments to share your thoughts with us about your experiences with Harlequin and Silhouette books. Your comments will be very useful in ensuring that we deliver books you love to read.

Please take a few minutes to complete the questionnaire, then send it to us at the address below.

Send your completed questionnaires to:
Harlequin/Silhouette Reader Survey, P.O. Box 9046, Buffalo, NY 14269-9046

1. As you may know, there are many different lines under the Harlequin and Silhouette brands. Each of the lines is listed below. Please check the box that most represents your reading habit for each line.

Line	Currently read this line	Do not read this line	Not sure if I read this line
Harlequin American Romance	❑	❑	❑
Harlequin Duets	❑	❑	❑
Harlequin Romance	❑	❑	❑
Harlequin Historicals	❑	❑	❑
Harlequin Superromance	❑	❑	❑
Harlequin Intrigue	❑	❑	❑
Harlequin Presents	❑	❑	❑
Harlequin Temptation	❑	❑	❑
Harlequin Blaze	❑	❑	❑
Silhouette Special Edition	❑	❑	❑
Silhouette Romance	❑	❑	❑
Silhouette Intimate Moments	❑	❑	❑
Silhouette Desire	❑	❑	❑

2. Which of the following best describes why you bought *this book?* One answer only, please.

- the picture on the cover ❑
- the author ❑
- part of a miniseries ❑
- saw an ad in a magazine/newsletter ❑
- I borrowed/was given this book ❑
- the title ❑
- the line is one I read often ❑
- saw an ad in another book ❑
- a friend told me about it ❑
- other: ______________ ❑

3. Where did you buy *this book?* One answer only, please.

- at Barnes & Noble ❑
- at Waldenbooks ❑
- at Borders ❑
- at another bookstore ❑
- at Wal-Mart ❑
- at Target ❑
- at Kmart ❑
- at another department store or mass merchandiser ❑
- at a grocery store ❑
- at a drugstore ❑
- on eHarlequin.com Web site ❑
- from another Web site ❑
- Harlequin/Silhouette Reader Service/through the mail ❑
- used books from anywhere ❑
- I borrowed/was given this book ❑

4. On average, how many Harlequin and Silhouette books do you buy at one time?

- I buy ______ books at one time ❑
- I rarely buy a book ❑

MRQ403SIM-1A

5. How many times per month do you shop for any *Harlequin and/or Silhouette* books? One answer only, please.

1 or more times a week ❑ a few times per year ❑
1 to 3 times per month ❑ less often than once a year ❑
1 to 2 times every 3 months ❑ never ❑

6. When you think of your ideal heroine, which *one* statement describes her the best? One answer only, please.

She's a woman who is strong-willed ❑ She's a desirable woman ❑
She's a woman who is needed by others ❑ She's a powerful woman ❑
She's a woman who is taken care of ❑ She's a passionate woman ❑
She's an adventurous woman ❑ She's a sensitive woman ❑

7. The following statements describe types or genres of books that you may be interested in reading. Pick *up to 2 types* of books that you are most interested in.

I like to read about truly romantic relationships ❑
I like to read stories that are sexy romances ❑
I like to read romantic comedies ❑
I like to read a romantic mystery/suspense ❑
I like to read about romantic adventures ❑
I like to read romance stories that involve family ❑
I like to read about a romance in times or places that I have never seen ❑
Other: ________________________________ ❑

The following questions help us to group your answers with those readers who are similar to you. Your answers will remain confidential.

8. Please record your year of birth below.

19 ____

9. What is your marital status?

single ❑ married ❑ common-law ❑ widowed ❑
divorced/separated ❑

10. Do you have children 18 years of age or younger currently living at home?

yes ❑ no ❑

11. Which of the following best describes your employment status?

employed full-time or part-time ❑ homemaker ❑ student ❑
retired ❑ unemployed ❑

12. Do you have access to the Internet from either home or work?

yes ❑ no ❑

13. Have you ever visited eHarlequin.com?

yes ❑ no ❑

14. What state do you live in?

____

15. Are you a member of Harlequin/Silhouette Reader Service?

yes ❑ Account # ____________ no ❑ MRQ403SIM-1B

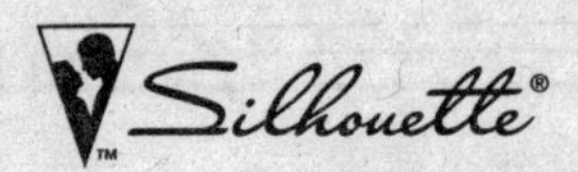

INTIMATE MOMENTS®

COMING NEXT MONTH

#1261 TRACE EVIDENCE—Carla Cassidy
Cherokee Corners
Someone had vandalized teacher Tamara Greystone's classroom, and it was up to crime scene investigator Clay James to find out who was behind it—and whether they'd be back. Mesmerized by Tamara's ethereal Cherokee beauty and desperate to keep her from harm, would the man of ice finally melt from the heat of their passion, or crack under the pressure of guarding his own heart?

#1262 THE TOP GUN'S RETURN—Kathleen Creighton
Starrs of the West
The government had told Jessie Starr Bauer that her husband was dead. And in many ways, the time spent as a POW *had* killed the Tristan Bauer Jessie had known. Eight years later, Jessie and Tristan reunited as strangers with only one common ground: the memory of a love worth fighting for.

#1263 SURE BET—Maggie Price
Line of Duty
In order to solve a series of murders, rookie officer Morgan McCall and police sergeant Alex Blade had to pose as newlyweds. Though they were reluctant to act on the obvious attraction flaring between them, danger led to desire, and soon their sham marriage felt all too real....

#1264 NOWHERE TO HIDE—RaeAnne Thayne
The Searchers
FBI agent Gage McKinnon's many years on the job had taught him to recognize a woman with secrets—and his new neighbor, Lisa Connors, was certainly that. Lisa couldn't help the attraction she felt for Gage but vowed to keep her distance. It was the only way to protect the ones she loved most....

#1265 DANGEROUS WATERS—Laurey Bright
When professional diver Rogan Broderick and beautiful history professor Camille Hartley each inherited half of a boat that held clues to a sunken treasure, they learned that Rogan's father had been murdered for his discovery. But could they find the treasure before the murderer did—and survive the passion that threatened to consume them?

#1266 SECRETS OF AN OLD FLAME—Jill Limber
A year ago, police officer Joe Galtero's felony investigation had led to a steamy affair with the chief suspect's daughter, Nikki Walker. But when she discovered he was using her to get to her father, she left him. Now she had returned to San Diego with a secret of her own—his child!

SIMCNM1103